CURE

KALI METIS

RUNNING
Wild
PRESS

CONTENTS

CURE

Published in North America and Europe by Running Wild Press.

Visit Running Wild Press at www.runningwildpress.com Educators, librarians, book clubs (as well as the eternally curious), go to ww.runningwildpress.com for teaching tools.

ISBN (pbk) 978-1-955062-31-2

ISBN (ebook) 978-1-955062-32-9

To all of those who have felt alone. You have a home. Welcome to our family.

PART I
A FAMILY HISTORY

CHAPTER ONE

She came to me for a cure. She didn't know she was walking into a war.

Nor that she'd be the key to a revolution.

CHAPTER TWO

Luna scooped icing into the piping bag. The customer had requested the flower petals to be in pale yellow and pastel pink with gold foil leaves. Her daughter turned eight on Wednesday and she wanted the decorations to be in her daughter's favorite colors. When Luna had first met with the woman, she found it odd that the woman was clearly a cinnamon spice cake with pumpkin icing but she requested a lemon cake with pink and yellow flowers. Once she clarified it was for her daughter, Luna understood why her instincts were wrong.

Luna gently massaged the icing bag, just enough so that the frosting would be a little more malleable. Her hands strong from hours of working on homemade gifts that were visually enticing little bits of magic, aromatically engaging, and undeniably appealing with flavors that made her customers crave each bite. A neighborhood favorite, *Bizcocheria* had been THE neighborhood bakery for years.

She looked up from the confection and smiled. Her assistant had been busy working on the standard baked goods that would be in the display cases until they sold out. The owner, Margarite, had been busy working on other items for special occasions, which allowed Luna to focus on the elaborate celebratory orders. Margarite represented the third generation to own the small and intimate bakery. Working here had been a dream for Luna. For Margarite being handed the family business had been the same as coming home.

Luna finished laying out the yellow flowers and she had begun to fill a fresh icing bag with pink icing when something distracted her. Some unnamable something screamed inside her head, which caused her to miss the bag and spill the freshly made bit of sweetness all over the table and create an abstract blob on the cake she had been decorating. Something was off.

Terribly off.

"Shit," Luna said in frustration. Just as she reached for a knife to scrape off the abstract art and begin again, the phone behind her rang. She didn't respond to the ringing, assuming the call was for another worker because typically no one called her during the workday. Her customers liked to talk to her in person; their passions for their special days reflected in their vivid descriptions of their elaborate cakes, cupcakes, and breads.

Luna's expertise had always been in custom creations due to her mystical ability to know someone's favorite flavors and decorations without them uttering a word.

"Hi, I'm Luna." She would touch the customer's hand. A sensation would travel into her fingertips and through her body. Her mind registered something *else*. Once registered, she'd smile as she told the visitor what only their touch could betray. "You must be a vanilla with a touch of lavender. Blue icing with a coconut dusting."

To date, she hadn't been wrong.

"It's for you," Margarite handed the phone to Luna. Since the baker's reputation well preceded her, she couldn't imagine why anyone would call. She thanked Margarite for the receiver though she kept her focus on the lemon cake with white icing and succulent flowers.

As she cradled the phone between her shoulder and her ear, she said "hello" with a must-be-a-wrong-number politeness.

She was greeted with an authoritarian male voice. "Is this Luna Auber? Daniel Auber's sister?"

"Yes." Luna hadn't seen her brother in a few months. She had tried to get in touch with him for their standard movie night. Once a month Luna, Daniel, and Javier, Luna's boyfriend, would eat homemade pizza and watch their favorite old movies. Typically, films from the '80s like *The Breakfast Club* or the '90s like *The Fifth Element, The Big Lebowski,* or *12 Monkeys.* For current films, they preferred the local movie theater which was the same theater they had crashed when they were in their teens. Same sticky floor, same popcorn coated halls, similar disinterested teenage workers.

For the past two months, Daniel had gone MIA. The only thing that kept Luna from calling the cops was Daniel's vague texts saying he was fine and that he'd get in touch with her "soon." Not unknown for occasionally odd behavior, Luna figured this was just standard Daniel stuff. She didn't want to come across as the overbearing, control freak sister. Although in this exact moment with a stranger on the other line, she wished she had opted for the control freak card instead of the cool sister card.

"This is the New Jersey Medical Examiner. I am sorry to inform you that we believe we have your brother's remains here. He seems to have passed sometime in the last seventy-two hours. I was asked to contact you to properly identify the body."

Luna stared at the half-done confection before her. Numbness crept over her; the words spoken through the phone wire had barely registered. "Are you sure that ..."

"If you could come by and confirm..."

Before her brain fully clicked back on, Luna said, "I'll be right there."

INTERLUDE 1 – I'M RELATED TO WHAT? - DANIEL

My fascination with our ancestry, dear sister Luna, started just out of curiosity. I mean, who are we? Where did we come from? I didn't really do it for the why of it all. Why did they leave us?

Okay, maybe I wanted to know that, at least a little bit.

No way did I think we were descendants of warriors. How cool is that! When my digging took me to a warrior from the Swedish Kings Army circa 10th century, I was floored. He must have done some serious damage. And check out his name - Ulf of Bjorn.

At first, I thought that was just a great name for a warrior and then I found out otherwise, which I'll go into later. He retired from protecting the king to be a farmer.

His specialty? Making cheeses and other dairy products. Sounds like your culinary skills are hereditary.

So, Ulf goes out during a massive storm. One of those that the rain came down in sheets. We get those in New Jersey too. I'm sure the flooding was pretty dramatic. Anyway, a neighbor, the daughter of the local blacksmith, found him wandering blindly near her home. He must have looked pretty messed up because she took him in.

Thank god for the oral tradition of recording history, otherwise we'd never have these details. She introduced herself as Freya and approached him with care and hesitancy. She asked him tons of questions, anything to try and find out who this guy was, you know? How weird must it have been to have this random guy show up outside her house during a raging storm. It's not like today when anyone could come to your door for just about anything. Plus, neighbors weren't right next door. The closest neighbor must have been at least a mile away, so this was a big deal.

She asked this guy stuff like where he lived and what's his name.

And guess what?

He didn't know. He couldn't remember anything. His answers were mindless grunts. He barely acknowledged she was there. His face was blank, his physical responses automatic. Without thought, he accepted a warm cup of tea.

Freaked out, she left him by the fire. She figured she better let her parents know what was going on. Her dad came over and checked the visitor out. He had a guess as to who the stranger was and volunteered to go out once the storm lifted.

With that hopeful bit, Freya returned to the stranger's side. The storm continued to perforate the night sky. Thunder cracked through the evening while lightning exposed the drenched skyline. She fell asleep next to him. Only once they were greeted by the morning light did it lift the storm clouds and bring answers.

CHAPTER THREE

Luna had never been to a morgue before. Hell, she'd never seen a dead body before. This was definitely not on her top 100 things to do in her lifetime. Especially not for this reason.

Sounds echoed in the nearly empty hallway. She followed the signs to a sterile room. She could smell the cleanser and emptiness that came with a thorough cleaning. The mortician, a mid-sized man with no distinctive features who seemed far too young to be in this business, greeted her upon entry. "You must be Ms. Auber."

She nodded. She curiously looked at the man. He could have been out of a sitcom, like one of those old shows her adopted parents watched on rerun like *Barney Miller* or *The Dick Van Dyke Show*. Hell, even his clothes were throwbacks. The thought made Luna laugh. The second she blurted out a chuckle, she realized the error and coughed back any more emoting. She needed to be here for Daniel, not compare this guy to their parents' favorite old TV characters.

With that, she swallowed more thoughts about him and the

cliched nature of the morgue. In the back of her mind, she wished she had stayed at the bakery. The drive over here wasn't so bad, but the actual building was more than she had anticipated with its art deco sculptures and cement fixtures...and it was a morgue.

Her preference was to make confections which translated into making people smile and if they didn't smile then she always found a way to help them see the lightness in the day. That's what she loved so much about her job; making people happy. It was much more soothing than identifying bodies. Especially the body of her brother.

The mortician guided her to a wall of metal cabinets. Each drawer shone in cleanliness. She wondered if they did this to avoid the distinct odors of death by replacing them with the odors and feelings of sterility, sanitation, and barrenness. Just the thought sent chills down her neck.

"Before we go any further," he said, "I will need to see some identification."

She quizzically looked at him. He knew her upon sight but needed identification? Really?

He noted her look and responded, "I don't anticipate tons of people to come here to identify bodies. That said, we do have policies and procedures that I need to follow."

She stared at him for a moment, her mind took a little longer than normal to process what he had said. She fumbled through her Targete' Special (aka Target-on-sale) purse and provided her driver's license. With that, he nodded in acknowledgement and pulled on a drawer. Out came a body covered in a white sheet. Just like in the movies. She held her hand over her nose in anticipation of something; what she didn't know.

"The body doesn't have a clear odor until after the 72-hour mark. I'd guess he passed closer to 46 hours ago so we were able

12

to reduce the decomposition in time to avoid marked visible changes."

The mortician lifted the cover to reveal the pale, non-emotive face of her brother. His eyes closed, thank goodness. She didn't want to imagine what it would have been like if they weren't but she couldn't stop her mind from bringing forward images of bulging eyes. Eyes wide in fear, in pain, in horror. She closed her own eyes to help force those images away and then opened them to see his still body before her.

She had always heard that the dead looked peaceful. She definitely would not have described the appearance as peaceful. He looked like an empty shell, like his spirit, his soul, those things that made him Daniel Auber, had left. She wondered where his essence had gone and if it was where he wanted to be.

"Yes, that's him. Daniel Auber." She reached out as if to touch him and then thought better of it. She missed him, but him in his entirety. His laugh, his chatter, his silliness, his comfort. Even his dorky comments, his nerdball ways. The boy he had been and the man he grew up to be. What laid before her wasn't her brother...wasn't her Daniel.

The mortician covered the body back up and closed the cabinet. The sound echoed through the chamber. He motioned for her to follow him as he began heading out of the mortuary and into the hallway towards a series of offices. Their footsteps echoed through the empty hallway; the only rhythm to the entire place.

"I'll just need you to sign some paperwork." He turned left down the hall and into an office with a smoked glass door. Inside the office, close to the entry was a desk. On the darkly stained oak desk awaited a stack of folders, a desktop computer, and a clipboard. He made his way behind the desk and picked up the clipboard. If this was any other time, she'd ask what all of the papers were for and what were the purposes of the other offices in this building. But at this time asking questions that had nothing to do with her brother's passing felt disrespectful.

Luna felt like there should be more to say, more to do for her brother than simply sign a bunch of paperwork.

"Do you know the cause of death? Did he leave anything?" These felt like the right questions to ask. She honestly didn't know. This wasn't in her cookbook of recipes and things to do or encounters to have.

"I'm sorry to inform you, but this is an apparent suicide. We need to complete the autopsy for confirmation."

"Suicide?" she said softly. She knew he wasn't feeling well but not so unwell as to kill himself.

"We knew to call you because he had left this." He handed her an envelope with her name on it. Someone had already opened it, the seal broken. "Nothing of significance. It just asks for you to be called and notes that everything in his apartment is to go to you."

She smirked. Even in death he got violated. She guessed she shouldn't be surprised, nor would he be shocked.

"Did you have to open it?" She lifted the envelope.

"We needed to confirm who to contact."

"Right." She stared at the note in her palm.

"Here are the few items we found on him including what looks like a will and his apartment key."

Luna took the larger manila envelope and sighed. This wasn't supposed to be how they were going to end their days. They had started life together and she had always imagined that they would grow old together as well. They had been orphaned at a very young age, so she somehow figured the fact that their adoptive parents took them both meant that they would always be siblings. Even in death.

CHAPTER FOUR

Luna sat at her kitchen table. The intimate apartment was quiet in the midst of her internal turmoil. She wondered if she should have asked who found Daniel, how did he kill himself, when would the coroner confirm the cause of death, what did she need to do for his cremation, and a hundred other questions. But in the moment, she only wanted to confirm it was him, get his stuff, and get out of there. She knew the mortician tried to be kind but there's nothing that could have prepared her for seeing her brother like that.

She had called their adoptive parents and Javier on the drive home. Their parents were speechless. They asked if she was okay, and to keep them informed of whatever else needed to be done. They had understood, since they had first taken Luna and Daniel in, that the siblings had an unusual bond. Which also meant that they knew Luna needed to be allowed to grieve on her own.

"Whatever you need," their mom had said. Her voice small; grief entered her breath with each syllable.

Luna couldn't imagine what this was like for them. They

had adopted Daniel and Luna after trying to conceive for years. To bring two children into their lives only to lose one in such traumatic circumstances had to be devastating.

Luna promised to call them back as soon as she had more information on Daniel's service. For whatever reason, he had specified that only Luna was to coordinate the funeral activities and be allowed to handle his affairs.

Javier had offered to come over and sit with her, but something about it didn't feel right. Something about the way this all happened just felt wrong.

"I'll take off. It's not a big deal," he said.

The Camden County Hospital Emergency Room had been hit with a lot of violence lately and Javier had volunteered for the additional work hours. Even though the thought of his arms around her, his body next to hers felt comforting, in this exact moment, she didn't want to be around anyone. Not even the man she'd been with since freshman year of high school.

He'd seen her through Pastry Arts School and her apprenticeship at the bakery while she'd seen him through nursing school. Both worked their asses off to get to where they were. Even with that bond, she simply didn't have the heart to be around him or anyone else.

On the kitchen table before her sat the manila envelope Daniel had left her. She stared at it as if it had some mystical power. As if opening it would somehow unleash a darkness that she would be unable to put back. She knew that was silly, but still, her fingers simply hovered over the clasp.

Her one-bedroom apartment was sparsely furnished and dotted with simple gifts from her parents and Javier. They had gotten the wood and glass circa 1960s living room set from the furniture store downtown, the queen bedroom set from Costco, which had been a modest upgrade from her double bed set. And the kitchen pots, pans, utensils and silverware from the

Dollar Store. Proud that she had been able to buy most of these key items without assistance, in this moment, she didn't care about what she could and could not afford. She simply wished for her brother.

The last time she had talked to him, Daniel had complained about his hands shaking at inopportune times. She joked that he drank too much coffee. When he was diagnosed with Huntington's Disease, a rare degenerative disease that causes neorological and cognitive degeneration and results in death, he refused to tell her because he had been convinced that the diagnosis had been incorrect. All he'd tell her was that it was genetic and he needed to understand what exactly that meant. Was that why he killed himself? Did he discover something that scared him more than the shaking?

She knew he'd researched their family history. He'd gone to great lengths to understand their bloodlines in the hopes that within that knowledge laid a cure. And then he told her the original diagnosis of Huntington's Disease. A rare disease that could end in death with no known cure. Daniel had the symptoms of shaking, difficulty coordinating, paranoia, mood swings and depression. Still, he held onto the fact that he was only twenty-five and the onset of the affliction didn't typically happen until the thirties or forties.

"This isn't possible," he told Luna. "They had to have gotten this wrong."

His words echoed in her mind. As she sat on her living room couch, her own hands shook as she unclasped the envelope. Her denial was distinct, her emotions numbed. Her hope diminished while she watched her fingers lift the unglued flap.

She pulled out a note, a map, plane tickets and vouchers for a tour to Sweden.

Sweden?

What the hell was in Sweden?

The note apologized to her. For what, it didn't specify. Just that Daniel was sorry.

I've spent the last several months researching our family and there's some things I can't tell you. You'll need to find out yourself. To do that, I've arranged for you to take a trip to Sweden where the core of our family history sits. You have to take this specific tour with this specific tour guide. Don't fuck around, Luna. This is important. More than you may ever know. Tell the tour guide you're my sister, and he'll know what to show you.
Luna – I love you. You need to do this. It's the key to who we are and it's the cure. The only cure.

Luna refolded the note and put it back in the envelope. Suddenly, she heard the sound of a key turning in the lock. The sound startled her and something in the way the person entered told her this was a thoughtful heart, a true spirit. She looked and saw Javier.

"I know you said don't come, but I just needed to make sure you were okay," he said.

For a flash she was pissed at him but her anger quickly died the moment she looked into his soft mahogany eyes filled with empathy and caring. She got up from the kitchen table and hugged him as if she hadn't seen him in years, not hours.

"I love you," he whispered into her ear.

She kissed him, the tips of their lips touched, his tongue just tasted hers. In that moment, she wanted to make love to him. She wanted to be close to him like she'd never been close to another. And then Daniel's words resonated through her.

It's the key to who we are and it's the cure. The only cure.

18

She led Javier to the living room, paperwork in hand. She explained to him what had happened, what Daniel had left her, and what that might mean.

"I'm not sure I want to go," Luna said. Her hesitancy laid in the potential of what finding out could mean. What was their ancestry? What had they inherited from generations prior? In the vastness of not knowing the answers to these questions, she found comfort. She knew that was stupid, but she liked not knowing, at least for now. Maybe when her own symptoms became more aggravated, she would be driven to discover the truth or at least the truth that Daniel found in his own paranoia and depression.

"Minimally, you get a free vacation." Javier held her hand. Whenever they touched, an electric jolt traveled through her skin, making her want him more. Similar to how she immediately knew a person's preference in baked goods once they touched, she knew that they were meant to be together from the first time he had placed a hand on her bare skin so many years ago.

In this moment, she also found comfort in knowing that his hands cared for people, cured people, consoled the ailing, and gave her comfort.

"Optimally, he was right," he said. "And whatever it is that he had and you might have, I emphasize the word *might*, is curable."

"That's true." She fingered the plane ticket. "I guess I can get time off from Bizcocheria."

"You've both had so much sadness. Don't you think it's worth finding out?" He asked. "Besides, what could happen in Sweden?"

INTERLUDE 2 – FREYA MEETS HER FUTURE

I knew this day was odd as the rain pummeled our lands. It stormed here so infrequently that Papa closed up shop as soon as the charcoal clouds neared us. He commanded me, his only daughter, his only child to head inside. Begrudgingly, I obeyed as he headed towards the back to close up our metallurgy and armoury shop. I would rather remain at my father's side and assist with preparing our properties for the impending hurricane.

Electricity lightened the darkened sky. Just as I began to close our doors, I saw you wander down the curving mud road outside of our lands. The scent of danger and flooding had become prominent in the coming air. Your steps uneven, you looked confused. You had already been drenched as if the storm followed you and you were trying to outrun it. Only seconds before it caught up to you. You collapsed a half mile away from me.

I looked up as I shuttered the windows to see you fall to the ground. I ran to you and, in your half-awake state, shouldered you to our home, the rain poured down in unforgiving sheets.

By the time I got us inside, we were both soaked to the bone. I stoked up a gentle fire to ease our drenched state.

I placed you, half conscious, across from the stone fireplace. The one that Papa used to prepare the metals to be molded into whatever we needed them to be. Our family has had this as our core location for generations. The scent of charring wood provided comfort as the raging fire fought against the chill and fierceness of the electrified night.

"What's your name?" I asked as I eased a woolen blanket over you. Something to help prevent you from getting a chill.

You looked at me with the most complex brown eyes with green flecks. You seemed confused. You looked in my direction as if I was not there; as if you were someplace else in your head. I carefully put my hands on your skull to see if there was a fracture, something that would explain your hazy state, and yet I found nothing. Your nearly black hair had been matted against your scalp. Your skin had deepened to a stunning shade of darkened sand. You did not acknowledge my touch, so I lightly felt for fractures and broken bones. Your clothing shredded in parts; the skin underneath sliced as if you had been in battle.

"Where did you come from?" I whispered almost to myself. With those words, you showed a slight bit of acknowledgement, your lips moved, but not quite with an answer.

"I'll get you a cup of tea," I said.

I immediately ran to find Papa. I couldn't do this alone. I told him how I'd found you and our brief interactions. I shared the state of your body and mind. Without hesitation he followed me back to the hearth.

Papa checked you too. He pulled me aside, a bit out of your earshot and then advised me to be careful. "We don't know this man," he said. "He could have come from anywhere." Papa's eyes were gentle, worried. He knew more about the dangers of our lands than I. He had maintained the family stall in the marketplace in town. Just as he had worked for the king and the king's guards similar to his father before him. With these came deeper knowledge of the true ways of our people. Ways I knew he had spent years training and preparing me for.

And he was right to caution me. Papa was always right. I looked over my shoulder and back at you with his words resonating through me. But there was something about you, a gentleness evident even in your strong countenance, your sinewy muscled body. A body that clearly had encountered many battles based on the scars that mapped your skin. A body that should have caused me pause but did not. I thanked Papa for his help and guidance. I then put a kettle on the fire and prepared us tea with the hope that a good cup would nourish your battered self. Mama had always said a good cup of tea could reinvigorate the most beaten of souls even though most of our countrymen only drank coffee. With Ceylon black tea in hand, warm against my skin, I brought it to you and put your hands around the cup.

"This should help."

At first you didn't acknowledge me. You were still lost in whatever world had brought you here, whatever place you had escaped. I motioned for you to take a sip. With that, I saw a flicker of acknowledgement come across your face. That spark within your eyes came in sync with the evening sky which grew more powerful each moment with Thor's lightning.

I fell asleep beside you, hopeful that as the dawn came so would your voice. When I awoke, you were gone. I ran to find Papa who had already begun working on the latest request by the king. I found him gathering coal, wood, and other fuels to stoke the fire to a blue-hot glow. When I told him of your disappearance, he dismissed it.

"For the best," he said and motioned for me to return to work. I couldn't hide my frustration. None of this made sense to me. If you were of the king's guards, then we should have seen you before. But neither Papa nor I had recognized you. Papa sensed my hesitation and responded, "We discover what we need to know with time. Until then, we have orders to fulfill." He motioned for me to assist in gathering the coal. I tried to argue but he had none of it. He simply reinforced that all we needed came with time.

"Another day of metallurgy," he said as he piled wood within the hearth. "Another day of creating weapons and protective gear for the people, the king and his guards." He was sweating from the intensity of the heat. He wiped his brow. "This is a life others envy, my daughter," he said. "We must focus on what we have and what we can influence. All else comes with time."

With that, I agreed and assisted in the preparations. I looked out of the window to see our lands had been drenched and muddied by the receding storm. Excited, I ran outside to find your footprints in the soaked grounds. The saturated lands had captured muddied footprints. At first I thought these would lead me to you but your markings only led me so far. When I returned, Papa nodded his head and sighed, just as he did when I did something that was indicative of my youth. "Come, we have more work to do."

At dinner, Mama said you were an apparition. A figment of my imagination. But I knew you were true.

I knew you would be back.

"We have too many orders to fill to focus on this stranger," Papa said with his mouth full of Mama's famous Kroppkakor, boiled potato dumplings filled with minced pork. "Eric the Victorious has placed a fair order that we need to fulfill. His men shall be heading out in the coming days. We need to be sure they are properly armed."

I knew those words ended this conversation. He would have no more discussion regarding you. I bit into my own dumpling and quieted. In silence, I told myself to forget about you. I told myself that I must return, my full self, to our familial practice and trade. And so I did.

CHAPTER FIVE

"What could happen in Sweden?" Javier asked with almost a laugh.

They didn't teach Swedish history in New Jersey schools so he truly had no idea.

Luna almost said, "Lots. Isn't that where Vikings come from?" And then she thought better of it.

Instead, she took Javier's hand and led him towards her bedroom. The room was warm on this fall day with the baseboard heater rumbling with waves of comfort. This and the air electrified from the latest bout of storms had left the air crisp and inviting. In that moment, Luna didn't think to cry or scream at the world for the loss of her brother. She didn't think to pound the table or demand that they had already been through enough. She didn't tell whoever would listen that Daniel was an awesome brother who only wanted a fair shot. She didn't think to demand that he only wanted to understand who they were and where they came from.

Instead of rallying against the world at the unfairness of it all, she took the man who had kissed her their freshman year of high school and led him through the apartment. This same man who had known her since third grade when Luna and Daniel were first adopted by the Aubers. This man who had defended her when, being the new kids in school, they had been mocked and ridiculed. They had been questioned regarding their reddish-brown hair, green eyes, and Asian features. He had defended her when she was mocked for not "looking right." He had been there when they were cornered on the way home and were a heartbeat away from being beaten by bullies and sent to the hospital. Javier was there with his crew to intervene and stop the attackers.

He even walked Luna and Daniel home. At that time, Javier did it because, "It was the right thing to do." He'd been through something similar when his family moved to Camden from Guatemala, so he knew the pains of being the new kid, the awkward kid, the outsider.

That moment after he had intervened, even though Luna would always swear that she had it covered even if her bloody nose, blackened eye, and bruised ribs said otherwise, that moment he had looked at her with such caring, such tenderness and just a tinge of sadness had always stayed with her. So much that in this moment of shock and grief and confusion, all she wanted to do was pull him on top of her and feel his body against hers.

She guided him in the moment and closed her eyes. He knew not to speak. He knew that her hunger wasn't about him, it was about escaping the cruelty of the world and getting lost in the feel of him, the feeling of them. As they made love, she turned her mind off and simply felt the rhythm of them. The rhythm they had formed over the last ten years of togetherness. The rhythm that had begun when they were just fourteen and curious about what it would be like to kiss each other. To touch. Those awkward moves refined with time, exploration leading to understanding of each other's bodies. The study of his skin, his touch, his kiss, the way he melded into her. The way their hips connected. The way his whole body joined her when she put her hands in his hair and pulled him towards her. He moved downward to give her pleasure, an act that normally in her heightened state, she would beg him to do, especially since his lips and tongue had been well versed in what she craved. An act that she would normally beg for, but as mischief twinkled in his amber eyes, at this moment all she wanted was to feel him on top of her and to have their bodies crescendo together.

He took her lead and as they came, she kept her eyes closed, unusual for her. Normally she'd insist that he look at her, into her, as they orgasmed. Their souls kissing in that moment, this time she only wanted to feel him.

He laid next to her; they had been together so long that they were more comfortable naked than clothed. Her hands wandered his chest and arms, leading up to his half-shaven face. She wanted to say thank you, but didn't think he would understand, so instead she simply leaned in for one more gentle kiss.

"Swedish, huh." Javier returned to their previous conversation. "I would have lost that bet."

Luna smiled. She would have lost that bet too. When Daniel said his spit test from Ancestry.com came back with Mongolian, Viking, and Western European genetics, she was floored. She had even asked him if he was sure they sent along the right results. Insistent that they were accurate, she knew from his tone that this was the moment Daniel became obsessed with their origins. Luna shrugged at Javier's comment.

Instead of owning her own amazement at her genetics, she said, "Guess so."

"Are you okay doing this by yourself?" he asked. She knew what he meant. Fulfilling her brother's wishes set her off, made her numb. Although, she waited for the pain to hit her, floor her. She waited to burst forward with sobs. She even tried to force it but somehow she could only feel that deep pain inside. Each time she tried to show it, the tears, sobs, and screams of grief simply would not come forward. And because of this she simply must go forward knowing that the well of pain will break forth soon enough.

She nodded to Javier. A gentle nod but still an acknowledgement. The cryptic instructions Daniel had left intrigued her but also had her at a loss. She placed her hands through Javier's chest hairs and pondered that nothing about this day made sense.

She had only wanted to bake cakes since the first time she'd made a cake from scratch with her adopted mom, Olivia. Before then, no one had cared enough to spend time with her. To teach her anything one-on-one. No one had bothered to sit down with her and talk to her like she was a human being. The tone typically used with her by adults had been that of talking to an object, an empty cardboard box, something to throw away.

Baking with Mrs. Auber had been the first time Luna experienced the intimacy of a parent or an adult taking the time to care for her. The simple act of measuring ingredients and reading directions had become sacred mother-daughter time. Luna found excuses for them to cook together whenever she could. She volunteered to bring in cupcakes and snacks for her class. She sought any moment so she could revel in the pure joy that she got from sharing family recipes. Even the act of cleaning up had become a beautiful and sacred activity. The love, caring, and joy that came with the simple act of baking and the pure happiness that people gave and received from their sweet delights made her want to do it forever.

Luna returned her thoughts to Javier who looked at her with concern.

"Am I okay?" she repeated. "To be honest, I don't know."

That was the purest truth she had. She had no idea if she was ready to do this alone. Hell, she wasn't sure if she was ready to do this with a fucking army. The simple acknowledgement of her uncertainty brought forward a light shaking of her limbs.

Goddamnit. She glanced at Javier to see his reaction. This shaking had begun a few months prior. She had told Daniel and Javier about it, knowing they would understand. They had already been through the beginning stages of a similar ailment with Daniel which had turned out to be a physical affirmation of a more serious ailment. The trio had spent the previous two years investigating and researching what exactly his illness meant.

And they had wondered if, since Luna and Daniel were fraternal twins, it was only time before she had the same symptoms. So when her own shaking began, they weren't surprised.

That said, she prayed no one else had noticed, the reality of it possibly ending her career and all that she had lived for had become incredibly real to her.

Javier looked down at her. With a slight affirmation, he placed his hand over her arm. His gentle touch was one of support. She smiled in response, a light gentle smile that just kissed her lips, letting him know that she appreciated him and his caring.

"I need to do it, whether I'm ready or not. You know?"

He pulled his hand away and sat up in bed, the bedsheet around his waist, his chest begged for Luna to touch it. Even in this moment of grief and sorrow and uncertainty, she hungered for him. She loved to see him naked and for them to lay together.

"I'll go with you," he said. "If you want. I can make it happen."

Her hands steadied as she placed them on his pecs and then let them wander to his lean stomach. "This feels like something I need to do alone."

INTERLUDE 3 – FREYA'S FUTURE IN A VISITOR

Papa said not to expect to see you again. And that was fine, even though I kept thinking about you. I wondered what had happened after the storm. I hoped you were okay. Your mysterious exit left me curious since you departed before I could find out your name.

Imagine my surprise when Mama called me out from our home and towards where I worked outside of our Armourny shop. Mama approached us with her arms filled with cheeses and a bladder of milk.

"Freya, we have a visitor," she beamed.

I cleaned up a bit from hammering the latest armor into shape. I had been working on the ironworks behind our metallurgy and armoury shops which were directly behind our home. All of which was down a small path from the main road.

I had already tested the first batch of metals behind the metallurgy shop earlier in the morning. I had to make sure the weight felt right during my standard maneuvers. I did not like us selling our wares without testing them first. Like Papa, I took pride in our weaponry.

Our family had been in this business for a solid century and we had earned a reputation for amazing work. As I approached the shop, I noted your familiar outline hovering near Mama. When I entered, you came from behind her. I had never seen Mama look so giddy, her arms overflowing with your gifts.

You came into the daylight and shyly smiled. "I wanted to thank you," you said. It was nice to see you in the sunlight and animated. Your eyes sparkled in their welcome. I got lost in those eyes. Their depth captured me. I forced myself to look away and recompose myself. Not used to courting, and honestly naive, it took me a moment to understand your intent.

Mama coughed. "I will put these away and leave you two." She motioned toward the house and made her way to it. She nodded her encouragement for us to talk.

I wiped my hands on my skirt, unsure of how to engage you.

"You did not have to do that," I said more sheepishly than I normally would.

I did not anticipate you being so handsome in the daylight. I know that sounds odd but there was something about your spirit, your energy that made you glow.

Later Mama said you only glowed when you looked at me. I will take her word for it.

"It was quite a storm. It is the least I can do." Your words were followed by a silence filled with a longing I had never felt before. One that filled me with anticipation and serenity in your presence.

"Good to see you, young man," Papa interjected. His words surprised me. He must have been watching from the entry of our working space. He approached you and offered his hand in welcome which you eagerly accepted. "I do have one question for you. What is your name?"

For a second you looked confused, like you did not under-

34

stand. Then a moment of recognition and a chuckle. "My apologies. I am Ulf of Bjorn. I settled down the road a bit." You motioned toward the curving path that led to other lands.

"The Tulin place? I did not know they had moved on."

"They kindly sold a bit of their land, a few cows, and sheep to me. Just so I could get started."

"What brings you here?" I asked. This seemed the natural question. The Tulin family had been here longer than us and had the largest acreage around. I was surprised that they would give up any of their land if they did not need to.

You looked at me as you measured your next words. It was evident in your stance, in your look.

"My teacher, Liam of Krigsman, was an old friend."

You let those words hang among us. I could tell that Papa registered what that truly meant. Liam had been training the king's army for ages but he only worked with the local gentry. His specialty was to train the warriors who were taught to dominate battles. This explained your scars, your musculature. But it did not explain why you became a farmer.

As I readied to ask you those pertinent questions, the ones that piled higher with each exchange, you said, "I must go for now. I have work to do in the fields." You looked at Papa. "I would be honored to visit your family, on occasion." You glanced at me as if referencing the real reason you wanted to return.

To be honest, this surprised me. Most young women of my age and from our town were more feminine and demure in their demeanor. They wore brightly colored long skirts with long sleeved shirts that gathered around their necks. In comparison, my body tended to be more muscular due to the physicality of our work.

Due to our business, I dressed in tan stocking pants and a dark brown jacket that closed in the front. This was the same fashion typically worn by the men of our town. But this attire made my work easier. It was simply more practical.

When the opportunity arose to go to town, I was often mistaken for a boy unless my thick red hair was loose and down my back. Upon closer investigation my soft features, wide eyes, and full lips gave away my true gender.

Rarely did anyone come calling for me. Most men preferred a more feminine and genteel woman. One ready to care for the house and family, not go to battle or wield an axe with zeal.

It had also been presented to me that I could be a bit more forthright than expected of a lady. What did they think of a woman who would one day take over the family trade of armory?

I looked at you with curiosity.

Papa glanced between us, noting your interest.

"We would be happy to have you come by," he said. "On occasion."

CHAPTER SIX

L una entered Bizcocheria, the corner bakery that she called home, at her typical predawn hour. The day's orders had been neatly stacked next to the register. She smiled at their familiarity. She hadn't been in since she had left to identify Daniel's body. When the owner, Margarite, had heard Luna take the call, she had been kind and told the baker to take the week off.

"Family first," Margarite had said. "Whatever you need."

Luna had fought and said she wouldn't need the time off.

Margarite knew Luna better than she knew herself and Luna took the time away from Bizcocheria once she had seen her brother's body and began to feel the numbness, understand the pain.

Luna returned to the bakery approximately a week later, thankful for the home away from home. She loved the feeling of the bakery in the early morning, before anyone came in. She loved the scent of the fresh eggs, powdered sugar, flour, spices, milk, and cream. She loved the feeling of the empty baking area with bowls and measuring cups that had been scrubbed clean waiting to be used for the day's goods. She loved the feel of the paper slips which detailed the day's special orders and the rolls, cupcakes, and other bakery items that she'd lovingly make in anticipation of the walk-in customers.

As the sun came up, the light gently seeped in through the storefront windows highlighting the ingredients that had been delivered only moments before Luna arrived.

She admired Margarite's insistence that they only use the freshest of ingredients; a nod to the fact that it made a huge difference in the taste and texture of the pastries. Luna put the groceries away and thumbed through the day's orders, prioritizing them based on time to prepare, time to bake, and pick-up time.

She loved seeing repeat customers. She could tell by the order what they were celebrating and for whom. A quinceañera, a sweet sixteen, and a wedding anniversary topped the list. They were all for families she eagerly anticipated greeting when they picked up their special confections. Plus their normal cupcakes, puff pastries called quesitos, shortbreads called mantecados, Mango sweet cakes, and Mung bean pastry to name a few. They always made sure to have the local favorites on hand.

The back bell rang which signaled someone had come in. Luna looked up to see Margarite close the door behind her.

"*Hola. Como esta?*" She smiled sweetly; her cheerful demeanor evident in her movements; her mid-length wavy black hair tied back in a ponytail, ready for a day of customers. Margarite always came in dressed comfortably in jeans and a black t-shirt, but formal enough with red lacquered nails and a blazer so that when folks came in, they knew who was in charge. Not that anyone would question that. She'd owned the place since her *titi* had retired five years earlier.

"How are you feeling?" She handed Luna a cup of *café con leche*, a homemade favorite.

"Thank you." Luna took a sip and savored the smooth, warming drink.

"And? How did it go? You okay?" Margarite put her purse underneath the counter and started prepping for the day.

"Things are just weird, you know?"

Margarite had lost family members before. She was far too familiar with the grieving process that had to be managed along with the paperwork to care for the newly deceased.

"*Y tu mami y papi?* They okay?" She shook her head. "I can't imagine what they are going through."

"I guess they are fine. Mom's not talking a lot and dad's staying focused on the funeral arrangements. I think it keeps his mind off of other things."

Luna had spent the last few days talking with her parents. After a lot of convincing, she finally agreed to let their father handle the funeral arrangements, even though a part of her decried that Daniel had insisted she handle it for a reason. But for the life of her she had no idea what that reason was.

Luna was sure that when her parents adopted the twins more than twenty years ago, this was the last thing they anticipated would happen. Especially considering that of the two of them, Daniel had typically been the more optimistic and cheerful one. She had no idea how her parents were making it through all of this.

"I'm sure it does."

Margarite came up beside Luna and placed her hand on her shoulder. They'd been friends much longer than employer and employee. The neighborhood was relatively small, and though Margarite had been five years ahead of Luna in school, the moment Luna's gift for confections became known, Margarite was one of the first ones who showed up at her door.

At the time, Luna was pretty sure that Margarite's goal was to disprove the youngster's natural talent. Imagine her surprise that the rumored gifts were real.

They became fast baking friends, so much so that when it was time, Margarite's *titi* sponsored Luna to attend the best confectionery school in town.

"*Y tu?*" Margarite tried to make eye contact with Luna but was unsuccessful, though to no fault of Margarite. Luna simply couldn't look her in the eye, without the need to cry. The grief of it all so fresh it became overpowering at the most inopportune moments. And at this juncture, all the moments were inopportune.

"Me?" Luna stared at the order receipts as she figured out what to say next. She loved Margarite as if she were her big sister and in many ways Margarite had been one.

The coroner had called and confirmed her brother's cause of death the day prior yet only Luna had that information. Just like Luna hadn't shared her impending trip to Sweden with her employer, nor that Daniel had committed suicide.

Luna sighed. "I don't know. I mean, what do you do with the fact that your own brother, the only person you've known your entire life, is gone?" Her voice quivered which surprised her. She did her best to control it, but the feelings demanded to come through.

Margarite pulled up two stools and guided Luna to one of them. Before that, Luna hadn't realized she had been wobbly but the moment she saw the stool, she knew her legs were ready to give out from under her.

"Here." Margarite sat on the other stool as she took the receipts from Luna. "Are you sure you're ready to be here?"

Luna took Margarite's hand.

"I need this. This place. I was born for this." Luna's hand began to shake as did her legs. She pulled her hand away from

Margarite and put it in her pocket, in an attempt to hide it. The last thing Luna wanted was for Margarite to decide that she couldn't do her job anymore. The reality of that decision came as Luna's affliction became more prominent. She just wanted to delay that discussion as long as possible.

"That's not what I asked you," Margarite said. *"Tu es familia.* You are always welcomed here. But are you ready to come back to work?"

"He left me something, Gi. Something I need to do." After a pause, Luna told her about the manila envelope and the will and the trip to Sweden. She left out the suicide part. It felt too fresh and surreal to share. "According to the plane ticket, I need to leave on Monday."

INTERLUDE 4 – THE MATING OF FREYA AND ULF OF BJORN

You visited each week with gifts in hand. Mama loved your Hushållsost cheese the best. She loved serving it alongside her Tunnbröd flat bread, Papa's favorite. I loved the way you looked at me, each time as if you saw me for the first, an endearing smile crossed your lips.

You were never improper like what some of my friends had shared regarding their suitors.

Other ladies in the village had suitors who eagerly found ways for them to be alone together. Their hands wandered. Their mouths hungry. Their lust rampant.

But not you.

There was a point when your manners - your friendly distance - made me wonder if you were interested in me. Maybe you were simply in search of a friend. And if that was true, then I was fine with it. I had enough work with all that needed to be done for the family business, courting was not something I typically had time for. But, the more time we spent together, the more I felt our hearts intertwine. The more the thought of only being friends felt a hole in my soul, one that I did not believe I could fill elsewhere.

Our conversations jumped from our favorite season to foods, to our dreams and wishes. You were always optimistic and joyful in your projections for life in the coming months and years. Yet you rarely talked about your past. I should have understood the significance of that.

When I asked you why you had left the army of the king, your answer was brief and matter of fact.

"It was time," you said.

The way you said it let me know that there was to be no follow up questions. The topic was closed.

I must admit, I had asked the Tulins about you. Once we knew your name and the frequency of your visits had increased, I knew that I needed to better understand who you were and where you came from. They simply said that you had wanted to retire and they were happy to sell you some land that they had not been using.

"It's better to be used than left to waste," Mr. Tulin had said.

A simple yet understandable answer; I chose to accept it as the purest truth.

The day you went to Papa and asked for my hand, I was a bit surprised. At that point, I had figured that I simply had a crush on the most attractive man I had ever seen and I should leave it at that. I had decided that our relationship would go no further than friendship, even though the thought of only friendship deepened to a pain I never thought I would repair. I refocused on my plans to continue the family business. Possibly expanding it to include jewels and additional armory. Admittedly, my knowledge was deeper in the armory space.

How joyful I was when Papa told me of your intentions. I actually asked him if he had understood you correctly.

"Did he say it in another language? Was it lost in translation? Did he say it in Khalkha Mongol?" I asked.

Papa chuckled. "I understood fine."

"What did you say?" I asked him. Curious if he viewed this as giving up his legacy. Typically, family businesses were passed down from father to son so the perception of losing a valuable resource in his daughter had been a true potential. That or the potential that you would insist on taking over the family business when Papa readied for retirement. Either way, Papa could consider it a loss.

"I told him I could not give you up. We have too much work to do." Papa said this with an authority and seriousness that terrified me. I rarely heard him use such a tone.

"You said what?" I blurted out.

The last thing I ever thought would happen would be for me to marry. Not that I did not have potential suitors. Once men realized I was a woman in the clothing of a man, they often became fascinated. Add on the knowledge that I have the skills of a warrior as taught by my father and his father before him. Those skills necessary to properly test our wares, then they often became enamored.

Let us not mention if they saw me in standard clothing of a lady, then they tended to become even more curious. One had cornered me in an alley and insisted that I demonstrate my talents as a woman. Little did he realize that I also had the fighting skills of a man. I proceeded to leverage them and leave him curled up in the alleyway, clutching his manly parts.

Those who were more physically polite but verbally intrusive, I told to move on. They rarely captured my interest. This led me to decide that I would simply focus on the family business and find my pleasures in my daily activities.

Until we met.

Taken aback by my reply to him, Papa responded. "What

45

do you know of this man, Freya? He only came into our lives a few months ago. Has he been forthcoming about his past? What do you really know of him?"

These were valid questions and ones that, if I answered them truthfully, I would be disappointed. But still.

"He is a good man," I said. "Never improper. Very skilled. He would make a good addition to our family."

Papa smirked. "I am sure that is why you are interested."

I blushed at the thought of your bare chest glistening in the daylight as you worked your fields and cared for your animals. A view I enjoyed only once or twice, always sure to regain my composure before you saw me.

"Papa, he could help us with the business. He has the ability."

This was a truth that Papa could not deny. Where else would he be presented with a ready-made warrior who could effectively test our products? Most of the warriors either died in battle or chose to become traders and continue to leverage their navigation skills and relationships. Finding a warrior who wanted to till the land and care for cattle was highly unusual.

"I'll consider it." Papa returned to his chores, and made it clear that our present conversation had ended.

I visited you at your farm to ask you about it. You seemed surprised that Papa had told me.

"It was the proper thing to do," you said. "But not to come to pass." Your words tinged with sadness.

"Not necessarily true." I captured your hand in mine, surprised by your shaking. I had noticed the tremor before, but figured it was from hours and hours caring for your land. A new lifestyle that required you to use previously lesser used muscles. I assumed the shaking would naturally decrease as you became more skilled at your work.

Your eyes met mine and I saw the sadness deepen. I felt the

dejection of my father's words. You searched my face for a tic in my response, a flaw.

"Truly?" you said.

I nodded. "Truly."

At which time you took me in your arms and we kissed. At first hesitant and then deep, exploring. A kiss I had never dreamed I would experience. By the time we released from our embrace, I knew we needed to be one.

With your assurance that we would never go far from my family and Papa would inherit a son and worker instead of losing a daughter, we married in the afternoon on a gentle spring day, the air fresh with daffodils, tulips, and cherry blossoms. Our gathering was intimate with only the bishop to officiate, us, and my parents. At your request it was outdoors with the smallest number appropriate so the memory would remain precious and intimate. In my enamored state, I believed those sentiments.

I should have questioned it.

CHAPTER SEVEN

The flight wasn't bad. Luna had never traveled overseas so this was all new to her. Luckily, both she and Daniel had daydreamed of traveling around the world so she had her passport ready. Margarite had agreed for Luna to take the time off, no question.

Even so, when Luna thought of leaving the bakery, she felt like she had betrayed them. Margarite had discovered her and built the foundations of the specialty baking around Luna's skills. The last thing Luna wanted to do was put her boss and friend in a predicament.

"We'll be fine," Margarite had said.

Even though part of Luna believed it, part of her felt like she had only really discovered her true purpose when she and Margarite joined forces. And she couldn't let Margarite and the family down. She had never taken time off since she had begun, fresh out of school. She already felt like she had been gone for too long. She had left guidance for fulfilling the impending orders with her assistants. They should be fine, she told herself. As she exited the plane, she could feel the excitement grow within her. Yes, all of the guilt that she felt was real and so was the excitement. She had never been to another country before and simply placing one foot off the plane and onto foreign land gave her thrill she never thought she'd experience. She looked around the airport surprised at how similar it was to the Philadelphia International Airport. Were all airports so similar? The main difference was the names of the stores and the use of Swedish and Finnish alongside English on the signs. She wandered forward, quietly eyeing the airport markets and travelers as they too made their way toward the luggage stations. Once she had picked up her belongings, per the traveling instructions, she made her way to where the drivers with signs for their travelers waited.

A chauffour dressed in black jeans, a white buttoned-down shirt, and a black jacket met Luna and others at the Stockholm Airport, sign in hand, guiding them to the tour van. She'd read and reread Daniel's notes on the flight. The night before she had left for Sweden, she had finally braved her brother's apartment and found stacks of additional documents. She didn't know how relevant they all were but at that point she would take anything that might act as a guide as to why he killed himself. Just thinking those words made her inner world sink, the truth of his loss that much more real.

Something in her gut had said that she needed to go through his apartment before she left town. What she found in his apartment seemed sparse. It wasn't like him to send her on this wild goose chase without a more detailed guide. He had always been more detailed, more careful. Just the fact of his passing didn't make any sense. There had to be more that she didn't understand; more that was missing.

None of this felt complete. There were definitely missing parts to this story. She kept thinking that there had to be more than what he said in his will. More than what he left in his notes.

At his apartment, she had gone directly to all the places she knew he would leave things precious to him. Things that he may not want to share with others. Under the bed. Behind the couch. Under the kitchen sink. He definitely took his lead from their mom who tended to hide things in spots as dictated by old television shows like *The Dick Van Dyke Show* and *I Love Lucy.*

She didn't know why she thought he'd want to keep their origins a secret but she knew he did. She found research scattered throughout his apartment in his standard places, plus shoved behind the back of his couch, and even underneath the rotary phone that she knew he never used. Printouts from Ancestry.com and from online community boards. Pages and pages of notes from god-knew-where about who-the-hell-knew-what. But they were important enough for Daniel to retain them and hide them away, which meant she had to read them.

She spent the ten-hour flight immersed in the pages. She had even found his laptop and tried to crack the password. If he had this much stuff printed out then just imagine how much more he saved on his hard drive.

In the van, she listened to the tour guide tell them the history of Adolso, the town of the Birka. Her brother's instructions were clear.

Luna – you'll be at the Skytteholm hotel near the Birka grave and museum. Tell the tour guide who you are. He'll help you. He'll know what you need to do.

Why he went all James Bond, she didn't know. Why not just say why she had to be there? Her frustration grew as she looked down at her hands, their shaking became more prominent the greater her anxiety grew.

"Fuck," she said.

The couple in front of her turned, clearly annoyed at her outburst.

Luna apologized and then whispered to herself, "What the hell, Danny? Why?"

"It's the source of the cure," she heard his voice in her mind. "The only cure."

INTERLUDE 5 – THIS IS MARRIED LIFE? FREYA'S UNEXPECTED NEW LIFESTYLE

You had insisted that we sleep in separate beds. You worried that your nightmares of past battles would disrupt my rest. At least that is what you said when we first married.

Our standard evening routine was to lay together well into the night and then you left once I had fallen asleep. Your own bed called to you; you had said.

In the morning, I often found you up and restless. You were typically awake well before me, no matter the hour.

When I would ask if you were okay, you always responded in the affirmative. Then you would give me this gentle smile lit by your deep wanting eyes. Those eyes filled with sadness and complexity that I knew I could not fully understand while I also knew I would be here for you, forever.

Our day would then begin with the standard chores: you worked on the dairy farm, and I worked with my father on the metallurgy.

You joined us in the afternoons and assisted with the more complex workmanship. You even helped test out the products to be sure they were ready for looming battles.

Then the raids began.

I do not know how else to describe them. I traveled into our fields to check on the cattle and sheep only to find them randomly slaughtered. Trails of blood and flesh and tufts of fur scattered along the dirt and sand trails. Hunted. Slaughtered in the most horrific ways I had ever seen. This was more than a hunger; it was decimation.

I asked the Tulins if they had ever seen anything like it. Reliant on my ability to describe the treachery, not willing to drag them to the place of the bloodshed.

Mister Tulin said it had to be wolves. "It's not uncommon," he said. "For them to come late at night."

"That sounds like a pack," Misses Tulin said. "For that much bloodshed. They were rabid."

I did not ask Papa. I knew better. He had already been concerned because of your tiredness. I did not want to introduce any more doubt into his thoughts.

He wondered if you were made for this life. Somehow, he thought being a farmer had been more laborious than being a warrior. I eased his concerns with gentle words of assurance of how you simply wanted to be sure you did the best for us.

Which was true. Part of the total answer, but still true.

I would not have the complete answer for a bit. I had much more to learn.

You said not to worry, that you had seen this before. "It will pass," you said.

I questioned if it would harm you, harm us; my worry was prominent in my heightened tone. The uncertainty and potential of what these rabid animals could do to us raced through my mind. Fear grew by the moment. You simply took me in your arms and held me. "My love, they will never harm you."

I looked up to see your expression. Was it fear? Was there

doubt? Did you believe your own words of safety and protection?

"What about you?" I asked.

With that question you met my eyes, your voice steady, your look unwavering, and you whispered. "They have done all the damage they can do in our waking hours."

CHAPTER EIGHT

L una listened intently as the tour guide, Bo, expounded on the history of the area. She focused on each word to find an overlap with the information Daniel had left to her. Each syllable, every description had to tie back to each other. They simply had to.

As she focused on Bo's narratives, his stories of the area, she admired the landscape through the van's window. The land was a bright, almost surreal, green. She had never seen anything like it. Especially not in Camden where the streets were concrete and aged, tall buildings dominated the landscape across the river from Philadelphia.

She'd heard stories of race riots that burned the city down and seen the remnants of destroyed buildings in the center of Camden's city. An area that had been abandoned long before she had been adopted by the Aubers. A small city that had once been the hub of Southern New Jersey and due to riots and looting had become a painful afterthought. She doubted Sweden had seen anything like it. She hoped it hadn't.

When she had seen pictures of Sweden, she had thought

that they must have been touched up, the colors too vivid, the people too beautiful, the buildings too regal. But all that she saw in person proved that the images were real.

"Damn," she whispered in awe as Bo spoke of the history of Adelso. He expounded on the history of Vikings and invaders, the active trade with South Africa, Mongolia, and other parts of Asia. The trading included slaves. This explained a lot regarding her and Daniel's heritage and their features, she thought.

They didn't fit the stereotypical Swede. She had no idea why she assumed that the blonde hair, blue-eyed milkmaid image must have meant that their ancestors came from the same stock or why it had surprised her for there to have been slavery in this country as well as vast explorations across conti-nents. When she thought about it, it only made sense for anyone with a boat to have ventured beyond their immediate shores.

"And here we are at the Birka Museum," Bo said as they pulled into a parking spot. "Please make sure any items you are not bringing with you are secure and you watch your step as you make your way down the stairs."

He assisted the older tourists on their way out of the van.

As they exited the vehicle to begin their exploration of the museum, she pulled Bo aside.

"I was wondering." She stopped herself. What exactly was she wondering? How would she ask if her dead brother had reached out to him and if he had inquired about a cure to Hunt-ington's Disease?

"Yes?" The word trailed off as he waited for her to finish her thought. Luna searched his eyes. Deep blue almost purple eyes with black rims. She wanted to ask if he wore contacts and then tried to come up with something to avoid continuing the conversation she had begun.

She looked down and took a deep breath.

"My brother had set this trip up for me. We were orphans and well..."

"Was his name Daniel?" Bo asked. He said this nonchalantly like he had asked this question daily. His stance casual. He wore the standard tan pants and button down shirt that most tour guides wore. The only variant was his bright white sneakers.

She looked up. "Yes. It was."

"Nice man. We talked many times on the Nordic Heritage Boards. You have an interesting bloodline." He pulled up his phone and searched a bit. He seemed to have found something and then looked at Luna with curiosity.

" He had mentioned..." Luna replied but trailed off unsure where her thoughts needed to go. "I didn't have the chance to talk about it in depth."

"Interesting." He thumbed through his phone. "You'll want to pay special attention to this tour." He pointed towards the museum. "We're going to the Kista Library tomorrow. I'll introduce you to Birger. He's the librarian in charge of the special collections."

"Special collections?" she repeated.

She knew she sounded frustrated. Among the exhaustion of the flight, jet lag, and the realities of her traveling thousands of miles just to discover something that she should have been able to get over the phone finally made her hit her wall of bullshit. "I really just want to understand why my brother insisted I come here. Why he thought this was critical to my life."

Bo smirked. "Follow me."

INTERLUDE 6 – OUR WOLVES - THE TRUTH OF FREYA AND ULF'S LAND RAIDS

Papa heard about the wolves from the Tulsins. He brought it up while we worked on another order. This one for a neighboring sheriff from a nearby town.

"You have had troubles?" Papa asked.

His face was covered in a sweaty sheen. His body drenched from the exertion of the day.

I was not far behind him. We had brought the oven to its peak for the iron to be molded.

"Troubles?" I repeated. I knew what he referenced but I hoped that I was wrong.

"Tulsins mentioned missing livestock," he said "missing" like he meant "murdered".

"We have been managing." I pulled the iron from the oven and took it over to the pounding stone. I had been careful not to get close to the bright red metal. Our heavy leather protective frocks and gloves ensured that if by some odd chance we miscalculated, then the likelihood that we would be hurt was minimal. I knew this but somehow the topic at hand made me nervous.

"We can make traps. We have the designs." He pounded on the metal and shaped it to the form specified by the sheriff. Everyone had a preferred style. We made recommendations based on what they were going to do but, in the end, they made the final decisions. And this sheriff had a very distinctive style.

"I think we are fine." I stood far enough away so the flickers of metal that sparked off with each motion would not touch me. After years of working together, since I was a mere child, we had this down to precise actions.

Papa focused on his work. Only the sound of metal on metal filled the air between us. Just beyond our activities the day progressed. In a few hours it would be night and I would return home to jointly make supper with you.

"Your mama would appreciate it if we could assist." Papa said this with calm, but I understood the intention. If he could not convince me to let him help then he would use the worry of my mama as a key point; a convincing point.

"I will talk to Ulf," I said.

I do not know why I knew not to accept the traps. I should have been eager to get rid of the horrors that plagued our lands. I should have been eager to disable whatever brought horror to our cattle, to our sheep. But at the thought of it, I cringed.

* * *

I had returned from the labor of the day to find you ready with our evening meal. You and I dined on the breads mama had made, your soft cheese, and eggs we had traded with the Tulsins in exchange to provide them fresh milk. The evening sky was bright with stars like sparkling pins. A light breeze kissed our skins as we noshed on the fare.

"Papa offered traps," I quietly said. "To help."

You did not look up. Our eyes did not meet. I should have

known this to be the sign it was. Instead, you continued dining. I feared that you had not heard me.

Just as I was about to repeat myself, you spoke. "We will be fine. Please thank him." Your voice quavered with uncertainty and a tinge of fear.

"It has been months." I reiterated. Not with anger or frustration but you just restated the fact.

You paused and then took another bite of cheese.

"We will be fine," you repeated. Your voice darkened like it came from somewhere deep within you. A place I had never been.

I waited until you thought I was asleep. You returned to your bed and I took the opportunity to dress. The night was bright with a golden moon. I pocketed a dagger, a side sword, and sheathed a backsword across my back for easy access.

Then, I headed out to the last place one of our sheep had been killed. The moonlight was inviting. I smeared dung on my clothes so as not to be easily seen nor smelled and waited in the bushes. If this truly was a wolf, then my natural scent would betray me, without question.

As the night grew, I worried that the invader would not appear, that somehow, I had tipped the intruder off. Just as I readied to pack my gear and return home, I heard a rustling unlike that of our livestock. The shadows that flashed nearby were of another form. Not of sheep, nor of cow, nor of wolf, but of something else.

I readied with my sword in hand. I wanted something that could have a broader reach and did not require close combat like a dagger. As I positioned myself for battle, I heard the braying. It sounded like a creature being tortured. Not one of our animals, but of something that hungered. A deep soul-crushing hunger. I moved slowly towards the sound, only to capture a look.

In the distance a form writhed. It churned and rolled. Arms stretched wide and what looked to be hands with elongated fingers and nails shaped like meat hooks. The braying turned to panting as the creature went through significant exertion with each movement. A pained sound. Then the head that had been curled under and against a chest threw upward into the sky with a vicious howl. That is when I saw the face, your face, transform from that of the beautiful, wonderful, kind man I had married to that of a hideous monster.

The face of a hungry wolf.

I am thankful for the training Papa and Grandad had given me in both battle arts as well as in hunting. That enabled me to know enough to remain still and not react to what I saw.

Because what I saw made me want to run.

CHAPTER NINE

"I know you spent a lot of time in the Birka Museum yesterday. But I think this, this is truly going to be worth it," Bo said.

He guided Luna into his car and onto the main road.

The night before, Luna had followed Daniel's instructions to the letter. He told her to spend as much time at the Birka site as possible so that's exactly what she did. She read and reread each placard, every sign. She studied the drawings and recreations. She listened to the audiobooks and reviewed, book-by-book, every single item in the gift shop.

When the rest of the tour moved on with Bo, Luna stayed behind. Thankfully, Bo understood her desire to unlock the mystery of her brother's letters. Otherwise, he would have insisted that she stay with everyone else. But he had been in contact with Daniel through online chat and Zoom calls so he was quite familiar with the purpose and intent of her visit.

He simply gave her instructions on the best cab to get back to the hotel and his own personal cell phone number in case she needed it.

This morning, he wasn't surprised to find her in the hotel lobby. She was the first of the tourists ready for the second day. She had already had one cup of morning coffee and had begun her second. She sat somewhat impatiently waiting for the tour to begin again. She was convinced that the key to Daniel's death and her own ailment lay in these days of history and ancestry and correspondence.

"Technically," Bo said. "We are supposed to head to a neighboring town known for its Viking presence. But I arranged for another tour guide to take over this morning." He glanced at her. "There's someone you need to meet. Another person your brother had been in touch with."

She sipped her coffee. "Oh? Another piece of my brother's puzzle?" she said.

"You could say that," he said. "You could also say that he is the missing piece to a lot of puzzles." Bo snickered at his own joke, a joke that Luna chose to ignore. If this guy held the keys to her own personal mystery, then she was all for introductions.

She was almost too tired to thank him. She had been up most of the night trying to piece together the bits she had gathered from the museum, the texts, the printouts. She pulled the URLs from the printouts to dive deeper into their mysteries. She spent more hours than she wanted to admit trying to unlock the mess that she called her life.

Among all of the paperwork and clues, not a single thing mentioned Huntington's Disease. She tried to follow the fragmented patterns Daniel had left behind. She wished for the simpler times when they were kids and were just happy to have such great adoptive parents.

Even though she'd never fully thought of the Aubers as blood parents, the gift of having a steady home to live in with adults who loved and cared for them was tremendous.

They had been tossed into an orphanage at such an early

age that they didn't know what to expect when the Aubers came to visit for the first time. After a few false starts with other families, Luna and Daniel had concluded they would simply be wards of the state until they became of age.

Imagine their surprise when the Aubers arrived at the home and volunteered to take on the brother and sister for a weekend that then lasted the rest of their lives. At the tender age of eight, Luna didn't really remember much other than the warm smile of Mrs. Auber and the gentle guidance of Mr. Auber. Back then they didn't care about genetics or blood relations or Vikings. They were simply thankful for a home, a real home, to go to.

She called Javier, frustrated. "Why did Daniel do this? I've spent days diving deeper and deeper into stuff looking for... fuck...I have no idea." She leaned her head against the wall. Her coffee in hand. Her tired eyes were bloodshot red.

"I don't know, Ni," Javier said. "But based on everything we know, this was important to him, right?"

She sighed. "Right."

"And he insisted you do this, right?"

A long pause. One that even she thought may be a little too long. "Right," she whispered. "Why did he kill himself? This... it doesn't make sense." Her voice was small and in such a whisper Javier had to strain to hear her.

"Do you want me to come out? I can catch the next flight."

The thought was more than enticing. Luna nearly told him to get his ass to Sweden but then she thought better of it. She had no idea why this was so important to Daniel. But he had specified that she do this on her own. In all of their time together, she never knew of him to make a demand without a reason. A really good one.

"Are you still there?" Javier said.

"Yeah, I'm here." She sat back up in the chair and watched

as other guests walked past her. They seemed so enwrapped in the environment. So joyful. She wished she knew what that was like. Every bone in her body wanted to cry out in pain, in sorrow, in anger. Instead she said, "I need to go. I'll call you later, okay?"

"Ni, you need to rest," Javier insisted. "Please."

She hung up without further comment.

"You ready?" she asked Bo.

"I think you'll like the guy I'm about to introduce you to. He's been here longer than I have."

That doesn't really mean a whole lot, Luna thought. Especially considering Bo must have only been in his late twenties. Maybe he was a few years older than her, but it was doubtful that he was any more than a year or two.

She followed him to his car without additional discussion. After a thirty-minute drive, they pulled up to a seemingly empty field with a green mound in the center. He parked the car, they got out and she followed him along what seemed to be a winding hedge that went down the hill on the left side of the mound. She paused, uncertain if this was the smartest move and then her shaking hands reminded her that, fuck it, she may as well follow him.

He took her down what felt like a winding path to nowhere. The path was lined by trees and hedges that only allowed the visitor to see a few feet ahead. He must have seen the look of uncertainty on her face.

"I promise you, this will be worth it," he said.

Her intuition told her that this was the real reason she had traveled thousands of miles. Something in this field, in this small neighborhood library near the Birka museum that Bo insisted Daniel had wanted her to visit. Something with this man, Birger, was why Daniel killed himself. It was time to find out why.

INTERLUDE 7 – THE HOWLING – FREYA

You brayed. The howling echoed into the night sky. Your eyes changed from their deep brown with green flecks to a golden yellow.

Where did my love go?

You stretched and sniffed the air as if you readied for a hunt.

I called your name. Softly at first and then, not with insistence or demand, but with love. The same love that filled our wedding vows.

"Ulf." Hesitant at first and then again. "Ulf, please." My voice nearly a whisper. I prayed you, the *you* deep inside this creature, heard me.

You turned, surprised. You focused on the location of those three simple words and so I repeated them. I stood up in the long grass and said your name again with the same inflection. "Ulf. It is me. Freya."

I said my name with gentleness and hope. As if it was a long-forgotten language that you needed to hear in order to return to me, to us.

You abruptly turned in my direction. Your eyes fixed on me. At first you advanced as if you had found a lovely bit of prey and then I said your name again and the simple words, "I love you."

I do not know if you heard me. You continued your advance and before I had a chance to protect myself, you pounced and pinned me down. My arms held against the solid earth by your claws. You sniffed me, in search of something. Something I did not understand.

I could have killed you. I know that. Especially with you so close to me. I had the weapons. I had the skill but I did not have the heart. You were and are my love. Your nose against mine. Your teeth bared.

Just when I feared you would try to bite, I said, "Ulf. I love you. Please, come back to me."

My words said so intimately that only you could hear them. My lips nearly touched your skin. The tone, the inflection, every ounce of each word meant only for you.

In that moment, you paused. I swear I saw a bit of recognition, a realization of who I was.

You leapt from me and bounded off into the night. The truth of my Love, the truth of our existence had been borne before me with your transformation.

CHAPTER TEN

B o led Luna down the curving staircase and through a
gingerbread-like door that took them to an underground
passage. The passage opened up to a bevy of books which came
in all shapes and sizes. Stacked high along the walls and piled
up on the floors, she marveled at how it evoked mental images
of *The Hobbit*. And in the center of the space stood a man of
oddly tall stature, his head nearly touched the ceiling.

"Luna, I'd like you to meet Birger. Birger, this is Luna
Auber. She's the sister of Daniel Auber."

Luna extended her hand and the man greeted her. Waves
of cinnamon, almond paste, and vanilla custard flowed from
Birger to her. The sensation was one of warmth and comfort. It
reminded her of home although she couldn't explain why.
These were not dessert essences that she typically encountered
and yet they evoked exactly that...feelings of home and safety.

He seemed at ease with the enclosed space, something that
Luna didn't think she'd be so comfortable with if she were him.
Why in the world would anyone choose to work in such a
confined area, Luna thought. It wasn't so much the volumes of

books, although the place was definitely packed. It was more so that the ceilings were quite low and the space seemed to have been made for children, at least in comparison to Birger's size. This was one of the few times Luna was thankful for being of average height.

"Lovely to meet you," Birger let go of her hand and shoved his hands back into his jeans' pockets. "Daniel talked a lot about you."

"You spoke to him?" Luna asked. A little incredulous. "I had no idea."

"We were members of the same historical society, so we spoke quite a bit." Birger offered Luna a seat. "Bo is a member as well. That's how he knew to bring you to me."

Bo nodded. "Well, that and Daniel had mentioned something about you," Bo smiled. "I'll leave you two for now. I need to get back to the rest of the tour." He turned towards the main entrance. "If you need anything, just reach out. Good to see you, man." Bo and Birger fist bumped.

Luna looked on, surprised.

"What? You think you're the only ones with urban culture." Birger smirked. "How is Daniel?" He asked. "The last we spoke he was arranging for this tour, but I would have expected him to be with you."

"He's dead," Luna flatly said. She supposed she should have anticipated that news hadn't spread to here but for whatever reason the innocent question hit her in the gut.

"I'm sorry, what?"

She averted her eyes. The idea of meeting his gaze made her want to cry even more than talking about Daniel. "He died a few weeks ago. He left this trip in his will to me. Said I needed to meet Bo and you, I guess." She shifted in her chair; the awkwardness of the moment took over. She silently wished she had taken Javier up on his offer to fly out here.

Birger stood up to his full stature, his head only an inch from the ceiling. "No. This...this doesn't feel right."

"Tell me about it."

"That's not what I...did he tell you your ancestry?" Birger reached for a leather-bound book that had been stacked among several others.

"You mean Viking, Mongolian, South African, Western European? Yeah, it was a little surprising, I guess."

"No. I mean." He flipped through some pages. "You're a direct descendant of the Birka."

Luna stared at the handwritten document incredulously. "Wait, what? How is that possible?"

Not only had Daniel never mentioned it, he never even inferred it. He had been more focused on being diagnosed with Huntington's Disease. Would have been great if he would have mentioned they were direct descendants of the most famous Viking of all time.

"You are a direct descendant. There aren't many of you remaining."

She studied the document and how the lines from one name to another connected. Finally leading to the person she knew as her mother, according to birth records, and then to her own name. On this document it simply stated Luna and Daniel. No last name.

"We had been searching for you both for years. We had lost track of your grandmother, then got word of your mother's birth and then eventually your births. Not too long after we heard of your births, we lost track of you again. When Daniel reached out, we were ecstatic."

"Who are 'we'?" Luna said. Slightly concerned that this complete stranger knew more about her than she knew about herself. This all struck her as otherworldly. Borderline impossible. The Birka was mythological. No one was supposed to be related to it. Folks came by on tours to ogle it. "I mean, what you're saying can't be right." She stared at the page. "This doesn't make sense."

Birger lifted the book and took it in hand then turned the pages to begin the tale of her ancestry. "Let's start at the beginning with Freya and Ulf."

CHAPTER ELEVEN

"You're telling me that Freya found her husband in the field, he attacked her, and then he ran away?" Luna had just spent the last two hours having Birger retell the documented stories. These tales were only shared with brethren. And only in person. Birger made that very clear when he began the retelling. So this was why Daniel insisted that she travel to Sweden and visit the Birka.

"According to Freya of Bjorn's letters to her husband. The ones she had relayed to her children and then to her grandchildren. In short, yes, that's what I'm telling you." Birger placed the leatherbound book down on the table before him. These stories had been shared verbally from generation to generation until they had been written down to be kept in the familial library. Only to be shared with fellow family members. Birger's family had been identified as the historians for The Lycanthrope Society to ensure that the heritage was never lost among brethren. This remote neighborhood library was dedicated to local tales. If someone was introduced as a member of the ancestry then Birger was authorized to share the more confidential history associated with shapeshifters.

Luna looked at her mildly shaking hands. The shock of the realizations Birger just provided had nearly been more than she could absorb. She replayed in her mind all that he had shared. Freya's discovery of Ulf, his courting of her, their wedding, and then Freya's unraveling of her husband's truths.

"I'm a..."

"He was a shapeshifter," Birger said, his tone neutral. He had several visitors a year inquiring about the Birka but only a select few, a handful, had appeared since he took on this role from his father. And those who inquired were direct descendants.

INTERLUDE 8 – HOW WE CAME TO BE - FREYA

I ran home after seeing you in the field, hoping that I arrived before you. Unsure, considering the depth of night and whether you registered that I was the one you saw. That I was your wife. Thankful that the moonlight had been bright this late hour to guide me on my way, I locked the door behind me, needing time to understand what had transpired and to figure out what to do next.

My love, my life, the only man I had ever considered marrying could have killed me with the simple swipe of his claws, the clench of his jaw. All I wanted was to be in your human arms so we could figure this out together. I knew that somewhere in that wolfen body, you were present. The human you. The real you. The man who fell in love with me. If that person was not still within the beast version of you then I know that I would be dead right now.

Yes, you were still there, no matter the carnage that had occurred to our livestock.

In the morn, I sought out your fellow soldiers who resided

only miles away from our home. Those of the elite guard who would have known you in your darkest times. Dressed in neutral toned tunics, leather belts, trousers, and leather shoes, I found your cohorts preparing for an impending attack. They smashed against straw and clay figures, driving spears through their hearts. The field tucked away down a winding road and barren except for them and their gear. I am thankful I knew of this private field for the guard of the king because of my father. Otherwise, I would have never found them.

Once I got their attention, at first, I asked them politely to tell me about you. To share what they knew of their kinsman. One, who went by the name of Chago, led the others in the conversation. With much hesitancy, he finally revealed that you were of the private guard for the king and his family. When I said I knew that, we had shared that much, he said that I did not understand.

"The king," Chago said. "He has special guards. Ones that are trained and others that are appointed because they were born for it."

The one gentleman, the one who had been the most hesitant, the one who seemed to hold the most back, finally spoke. "Ulf could not have been anything else. Even if he craved the life of a farmer." The sadness in his eyes spoke more than those words.

Ulf, I knew, based on his comments, that he had seen your pain. He had experienced it. And I knew that he must have been of the same heritage. Caged by the same fate.

"Then why did the king let him leave?" I asked. More so because this did not make sense. If you were fated to be among the private guard then typically the king would not have allowed you to move on. I knew that warriors often retired but not to be a farmer.

The one who spoke up last, coughed. "I cannot speak to the king's logic. I can say that your husband craved the gentile life, a quiet life, and had done much for the king and our lands to deserve the opportunity to have what he pined for."

CHAPTER TWELVE

"Oh, hell no." Luna, who had paced the small space as Birger debriefed her, had finally sat in a small wooden rocking chair and placed her head in her hands. She did her best to absorb all that he shared as she got up from the miniscule chair. "This is why. Holy shit, this is why Danny –" She couldn't finish her sentence, she couldn't finish her thought.

They were werewolves? What the fuck!?

Never in her life could she have imagined that she was a descendant of the Birka and of werewolves.

"This is real?" she mumbled as she stumbled out of the library. Her body felt weighted, her emotions dense. She tried her best to say more, to acknowledge more but all she could do was mumble. "This is real..."

The hour had grown late and she made her way into the evening. She had no idea how far she was from the hotel and she didn't care. She just wanted to run, run as far and as fast as she could from that place.

She wanted to go home and make pastries and bake cakes. She wanted a random customer to make her way into the bakery and to challenge her to guess their favorite flavor combination. She wanted her Friday night movies with Javier and Daniel to come back. Even though she hadn't seen her brother in months, those movie nights had been the highlight of her weeks. She wanted their homemade popcorn and dorky movie jokes. She wanted to lay on top of Javier and touch his stubbly face. She wanted café con leches with Margarite in the early morning hours. She wanted birthdays and holidays and anniversaries and family gatherings. She wanted all the things that made this world wonderful and that somehow magically converged at her place of work.

She wanted her life back. She didn't want this.

Anything but this.

"Luna, stop."

Birger followed her from the library. She looked back to see the Hobbit-like structure immersed in the side of the hill and Birger coming forward from an entry at the base of a series of stairs that emerged from the bright green grass. She turned back away, unable to absorb what he had just shared and her environment. If someone would have told her last week that she'd be in the real-life equivalent of The Hobbit with a taste of Lord of the Rings, she'd tell them they were insane. She turned back around, clutching her jacket to her and randomly made her way through the jade green field in the darkened night with only distant streetlights and the interior lights of remote historic homes to guide her.

Birger continued forward towards Luna. He was careful not to be too abrupt. He knew what he had shared with her was traumatic. His father before him and his father before him had been given the same remit. They had never questioned the importance of it. A hidden race, a hidden culture. A secret world that he knew he had to protect. Lives and realities that had to be kept underground otherwise they would experience severe persecution. He had volumes of evidence of it. Of the lycanthropes being demonized, terrorized, murdered. He took his job as the gatekeeper, the Historian of The Lycanthropic Society, very seriously. He couldn't let her careen out of the library and into the night without ensuring she was okay - both her physical safety and her emotional well being. For some, these discoveries were devastating.

"Please, Luna!" he cried out.

She stopped. Not because he called for her but because she was out of breath. She just needed a moment to get herself back together. It wasn't every day she ran out of a building and dashed away. Okay, she never did that.

"Luna, please. You need to be prepared. There's a reason Daniel sent you to me. I can help you. There's a lot to this and –"

"Have you lost your mind!" She hollered and continued down the emerald green expanse. She couldn't deal with this right now. This was too much. The stories, the trip, Daniel's passing. She continued forward. She just couldn't talk to him right now. She hurried in her movements, eager to make it back to the hotel. Needing to be alone.

As she drove forward, the scent of the evening breeze filled her nostrils. Her skin became coated in the night's mist.

Maybe this was real. Maybe Daniel really did kill himself. She drove onward, her steps haphazard.

Her mind a haze.

Maybe for once her instincts were wrong.

INTERLUDE 9 – THE LYCANTHROPES
- FREYA

Papa did not ask why I looked frazzled or distracted in my efforts. I tolled by his side at the fireplace of his work space as we prepared the fires. The workshop in the distance of our home, set off from the primary road, which allowed us to remain focused on our efforts.

The metals had been placed in the depth of the fire so that they could be melted and then molded into weapons.

As he checked on the status of the materials, I am sure he wanted to ask why I looked distant or frightened. And I was not willing to share. Not everything. Not yet.

He relied on Mama to inquire. When she brought us our afternoon meal, she asked where you were.

"Much to do on the farm," I said, enjoying my meal of Falukorv sausage, a dense smoked veal and beef meat, and bread. I smiled around my bite of sandwich.

"You have not been looking good," Mama said. "You sure everything is okay?"

I glanced at Papa waiting for him to chime in. He remained silent but it was clear that he intently listened for my response.

He had been concerned about the impending marriage of myself and Ulf. My father worried about the differences in our backgrounds. Concerns regarding potential demands from the king. The differences in your daily needs compared to what I was used to providing.

I did not worry. I knew the life of a warrior after having studied it under my papa. I understood the needs of one who may live in the battlefield for days or weeks at a time by working with so many of our dedicated customers. I understood your needs, at least the needs I knew of. And I understood what we needed as a couple. The last thing I wanted to do was to confirm his concerns.

"All is fine." I reached out and touched the hand of Mama. "Not to worry."

"I need you to be good for our chores. There is much to do," Papa said. "We will need the assistance of Ulf soon as well. The weight of the impending efforts will require his muscle, his strength."

The unspoken part of Papa's statement was that this was the agreement. He would not have approved of the wedding if you were not willing to work alongside us. He had always wanted, felt like he needed, a son in addition to his daughter, to carry on the family business. I had spent my life dissuading these concerns and thoughts. The last thing I wanted to do now was reinforce them.

"He shall be here next week," I said. "We shall be here next week."

CHAPTER THIRTEEN

L una panted as she closed the hotel room door behind her. Once she had made her way through the field, she had walked down the road in the evening light from the library to the hotel. Thankfully it had been less than three miles away. She chose not to look behind her or pay attention to Birger. She needed to be alone.

Daniel wasn't kidding when he said there was a big benefit to staying so close by. It's like he knew she would freak out. And why wouldn't she? It wasn't every day that she would be told she's a werewolf or shapeshifter or whatever the hell he said she was. Her body was still sweaty and achy from the exertion, but the effort also felt good. She needed that physical release after so much chaos and turmoil. She needed some way to let go of the physical and emotional pain and trauma. Walking five miles in the middle of the day was a good start.

Later, once she had returned to her hotel room she considered calling Javier and her parents but what would she say?

Guess what? I'm a werewolf!

Great news! Danny didn't have Huntington's Disease. He was a shapeshifter!

This'll be great for Halloween. I'm thinking next Halloween season I'll try on the skin of a deer. What do you think?

These exchanges didn't quite go over very well as she rehearsed them in her head. She needed to find a more tactile way to approach the topics so that they didn't sound so bizarre. Yeah, she thought. Good luck with that.

She showered and changed. The tour group would return to the hotel for dinner soon and she figured she'd seek out a little normalcy by rejoining them for the evening meal. When she saw Bo, she didn't know what to say. Did he know? He must have known.

"So?" He approached her. "How did it go?"

She searched his face for signs of a deeper knowledge. She found sparkles in the core of his eyes. Little bits of light that betrayed his understanding. She debated within herself whether she should open up this conversation with him. Was she ready for it? She honestly wasn't sure. And with that thought she said, "Good. I'm sure I'll go back sometime tomorrow."

Bo nodded. "Sounds good."

"Out of curiosity," she began. "How frequently do you bring tourists to meet Birger?"

"You mean for a similar purpose of yours?" he asked.

She nodded in affirmation.

"Not often. It's pretty rare actually."

"Then how do you know?" Even as she asked this question, she wasn't sure what she really meant. It just felt like there was something that must flag him about other shapeshifters.

He looked at his watch and pointed to the dining area. "That is a much broader conversation and possibly one that you may want to have with Birger first." She observed the rest of the tour members take their seats. "In the meantime, may I recommend that we have our evening meal, enjoy the folk singers who have been arranged to entertain us and revisit this possibly tomorrow?"

Luna watched as the servers brought forward the first course of the meal. Bo led her to a chair at a nearby table. She took this as the break it was intended to be.

Later that evening, after she had devoured the traditional meal of Kalops, a beef stew with potatoes and carrots in a gravy, and then enjoyed the entertainment, she readied to return to her room. She noted that Bo doted on the other tourists in their group. So much so that she wondered if he was avoiding her. Just as everyone was wishing each other a good night, Bo approached her.

"You may want to check your email before you sleep," he said. "I believe there's a note for you that you may be eager to read." And without another word, he ascended the stairs to his own room.

Intrigued, Luna made her way to her room, and plopped down on her bed. Her mind alive with the discoveries of the day, she was far too wired to sleep. She pulled up her phone and went through her email. She didn't find anything major at first. And then she found one note from Birger with the subject line of, "When you're ready." In the body of the email was a secured link to a private site for The Lycanthrope Society.

Nope. Not ready.

She almost deleted it and then thought better of it. At some point she would be able to look her new life view in the eye and make peace with it. Even if that day wasn't today. Instead, she thought avoidance might be the best road forward.

She investigated exchanging her plane tickets so she could return home sooner. She had technically fulfilled what Daniel wanted her to do, so she could return to her old life without any regrets. At least that's what she believed in the moment. She knew her fate or whatever she should call it, so she could go home. And do what? Randomly turn into a shewolf? That couldn't be right. That didn't make any sense. There had to be more to it than this. She understood the misdiagnosis of Huntingtons and that Daniel and her shaking were actually precursors to their transformation, their shapeshifting. But there had to be more.

Daniel had been specific that the cure to their shaking was in Sweden, at the Birka site. Which meant either Birger or Bo or somebody had more to tell her, or to give her.

But what? What the hell could they do for a genetic variation that condemned her to a life of howling at the moon. Damnit. That thought was definitely as crazy as it sounded.

Ok, she didn't know if howling at the moon was an actual thing, but according to the old school horror movies they'd watched on Friday nights, it was definitely in her future.

Luna peeled out of her clothes and tossed them in a corner. With hopes that it would help her relax, she hopped into a steaming shower and enjoyed the feel of the water against her aching muscles. She allowed the water to glide over her skin and through her hair until she felt the tension leave her body and puddle into the bottom of the shower, swirl the drain, and then disappear down the pipes.

She toweled off and wrapped up in a cozy white fluffy robe, provided by the hotel, and returned to her bed. At her bedside remained the stacks of papers that Daniel had left. Even though she wanted to go home, she knew she couldn't. There was still too much about this that didn't make sense.

If Daniel insisted that the cure existed here, then she needed to find it. While the cure was busy revealing itself, it could also let her know why he killed himself because self-mutilation was not on the short list of Daniel's "must do's". And yes, she acknowledged that making light of this was a coping mechanism and at this point she was just happy to have a coping mechanism at her disposal.

She could understand if he was distraught at the thought of not being human. And even horrified at the idea of potentially being a human flesh eater. She even understood if he was afraid of the future. But suicide? That still didn't make sense to her.

Luna couldn't piece together a logical explanation of why Daniel would have killed himself. She wasn't convinced that this affliction wasn't manageable. In order for their bloodline to make it this far, then they must have found ways around all the cliched howling and barking and attacks. And she knew her brother, and there was no way that he didn't come to the same conclusions.

Instead of "What Would Jesus Do," she asked herself how did Ulf make it through? In order for her and Daniel to exist, Ulf and Freya had to have had children. And if they had children that meant they stayed together and that implied he figured out how to control the inner wolf.

The question was how?

The other question was how long before her shaking became full-fledged changing? If this was a progression, then when, and how, did this maturation finish? Did this mean she was in the puberty stage?

INTERLUDE 10 – THE WOLF GUARD - FREYA DIVES INTO ULF'S ORIGINS

I could tell when I came home after talking to your comrades that you did not remember the night before. You seemed at ease, if not a bit exhausted. I hinted at your nightly excursions, but you did not respond. You acted like you had no idea what I talked about. And you probably did not. I had no idea what or how this worked.

I only knew I loved you and there had to be a way, some way, to get you through this.

You promised that you would help Papa a few days a week, even though it took you away from our farm. But you understood that this was a promise we had made to Papa. We needed to keep that promise although you never understood why he did not trust me with the armory duties. I loved you for that. I loved you for your belief in me.

"It is not that he does not trust me," I said. "It is more so that we have some orders coming that require a stronger arm."

You nodded in comprehension.

My mind returned to my interactions with your former cohorts of the special guard for the king and their words. One had mentioned a seeress named Hiwa. I had never met nor heard of her but knew that I needed to find her.

I told you I would be back after running an errand for Papa. You did not question it. You simply nodded. I promised I would be back before dark.

I asked around town about Hiwa and where I could find her. There came a point in which I swore she was simply an apparition. She had become the stuff of legend, of mythology. I made it home before dark as promised, and I gave up on finding her.

But then a quiet man visited our family's stall in the market one day. He had heard that I had been searching for Hiwa. His guidance odd, he directed me to wander through the expansive fields and into the neighboring woods and then listen for her calling. I would hear the song of her voice on the day's breeze.

Uncertain but desperate, I followed his advice. And at the end of the song of the day's breeze, beyond the neighboring fields, just at the other side of the woods, I found a small dead end street that resulted in a circular driveway. A thatched hut at its epicenter. Trees, shrubbery, and vines enclosed her home while overgrown plants encroached on every inch.

All of this seemed like it was done intentionally so visitors would simply walk by. I looked up to see a slight stream of smoke come from the chimney. Someone was home.

I knocked on the door, unsure if this was the right answer. But truly I did not know what other answer I had, what other choices may be available. As far as I knew, this was the only choice.

She answered. A small in stature woman, slightly plump but more in a soft way like she did not do hard chores. Most of her work must have been in the healing arts based on the little that I knew of her. Her body was covered in a gray overcoat that kissed the ground. Her skin a light mocha Her eyes a deep chestnut.

"May I help you?" Her voice was melodic and welcoming. She was younger than I had imagined. For some reason I thought all seeresses were old and hunched over. Perhaps I had read too many children's fairy tales.

"I am here to help my husband, Ulf of Bjorn."

Her eyes lit up when I said your name, her familiarity was clear. "Ah yes. I was expecting you." She opened the door wider and motioned for me to enter.

CHAPTER FOURTEEN

"What is this?" Luna waved freeform pages in the air. Pages that described The Lycanthrope Society. "What the hell? Why didn't you mention this last night?"

Birger shushed her. They were not the only two people in the library. He had been busy reshelving books when she came in.

Luna had spent much of the night and early morning continuing her research. She was disappointed in herself for not looking up the foreign words before now. She had done what many readers do when they encounter words from a different language embedded within her native language, she skimmed over them and moved on.

She lowered her voice a smidge and read from the top page. 'Lycanthropy means werewolf or someone who believes that they can change into one.' It's all over my brother's paperwork. Why the hell didn't you mention this before?"

Birger quietly continued with his chores as she confronted him. Even though it was a weekday afternoon, she still had to observe the library's rules. Or at least behave like she'd been in a library before.

"Please lower your voice," Birger whispered. "I know this is a lot to take in, but there are other visitors trying to read." He motioned towards a young mother and her small children in a sitting area across from them. "This *is* a library." The mother glanced at Birger with slight annoyance. He nodded in acknowledgement and placed his hand to his mouth.

Flustered, Luna almost argued with him. She knew it was a library, but this was potentially life or death. Or at least it felt that way. Flummoxed, she wondered how he expected her to behave after being told such otherworldly stuff.

"I deserve answers," she whispered and flopped the stack of pages onto the book cart before him.

He simply blinked at them.

"I'll tell you whatever you want." He paused. "I just ask that you listen."

"Isn't that what I've been doing?" she said, flabbergasted, her tone raised, forgetting she had run away from Birger yesterday.

Birger motioned for her to lower her voice. His own voice focused and directive. "I need you to truly listen and absorb what I'm about to tell you. If what I've told you so far enraged you then you need to be prepared for the rest."

"I'm ready," she said defensively. She stood up straighter as if that would enable her to take on even more otherworldly topics.

Birger smirked. "No," he said. "You're not."

He continued with his work.

As the historian, he had seen her type of behavior many times before and for much less dramatic discoveries.

He had only begun revealing the truth of her family's legacy. If her response was this over-the-top for the simple truths, then he couldn't trust her to have a calmer reaction to the bigger secrets.

"I need to know." She pushed the cart away from him and stood in front of him. "I need to know why Danny did what he did and what the hell is about to –" her voice rose again.

"Please be respectful of the others here," he interrupted her. "Or I'll have to ask you to leave." His tone was quiet yet serious. This was a different Birger than the man she had met yesterday. Something in him had become more adamant, graver.

She searched his gaze and only found the something indescribable. Something she didn't understand. She knew somewhere deep within him were the answers that she needed.

"Fine," she whispered. "I'll listen." She took the nearest seat and folded her hands in her lap, signaling him to begin again.

Birger shelved the last of the books, forcing Luna to wait. She needed to calm down. He wasn't convinced that Daniel had killed himself, but she wasn't ready to hear that. She needed to better understand the rest of the history as well as The Lycanthrope Society and what it stood for. Until she had that information, she wouldn't be ready to hear about his exchanges with Daniel and how, if Birger was right, Luna's exploration of her heritage was about to go much deeper. Her life was about to change in ways even he couldn't explain. She would have to experience it. He observed her as she slowed her breathing and forced herself to calm down. Once he was certain that she was ready to receive what he had to provide, he sat across from her. "Let's begin where we left off with Freya."

INTERLUDE 11 – A SEERESS AND A
WARRIOR; HIWA AND FREYA

I entered the cottage to find Hiwa crouched in front of a stone fireplace where she must have been brewing the beginnings of her evening meal. Steam rose from a caldron as she stirred the liquid within it.

"Come in, come in," she waved. "It is nice to meet Ulf's chosen love."

I had never heard anyone name me as yours and it made me smile. She pointed me to a thatched chair next to the fireplace; a chair that looked like it had been used on many a chilly evening.

She welcomed me to her home and she told me of you. All of those things you had never shared. Whether because you did not remember or did not want to share, I would never know.

"Ulf, he is a rare one," she began. "He had been an orphan who happened upon the royal guard's lodgings. They found him outside of the main gate wrapped in rags and hope and took him in."

She handed me a warm cup which I thankfully took.

"He had originally been a houseboy and they discovered his

gifts when he was of age. That is when they changed his name to Ulf for wolf, as a nod to his natural abilities. His first shape being a wolf. Only later would they discover other capabilities."

She shared that she worked with the royal guard on a regular basis. She trained the special forces to help them mature and understand their gifts. The captain of the guard had called her to help Ulf, just as she had been called upon to help the other special warriors.

"They have their battle training and then they have their life training." She sipped from her own cup. "The life training begins shortly after the battle training. It is to help them control their gifts. If only the rest of us were so lucky."

"Control them?" I asked.

"So they can have a normal life." She stirred something in the pot as if to keep it from boiling over. "I credit the king. He could have been selfish, demanding his elite warriors stayed with him until death. Instead, he insisted that they were rewarded for all that they gave up in order to protect our lands and our people. But to do that, they had to learn to control their gifts."

What she said made sense but based on all that had occurred, it did not make sense for us. What happened to your training? How come you could not control your abilities? Or could you and you simply did not? If not, why?

"Each warrior is given their own unique set of divining runes. They must be kept on them at all times. The runes are blessed to protect the warrior and keep him from changing. He has been trained how to use them for when he needs to use his gifts for battle."

"There are no divining runes," I said. I stared into my cup, searching my memory for anything that might resemble the objects she described. I came up with nothing. "At least none that I have seen."

I explained how we met in the midst of a storm. How you were wandering in the darkness of night with sheets of rain obstructing your view. How I questioned if you had been injured. "We have now been together through multiple seasons. He definitely has no runes."

CHAPTER FIFTEEN

"What do you mean that Freya is the Birka?" Luna questioned. "I don't understand." She knew her brother had researched the historic warrior and that the warrior's gravesite was a key part of her tour through Sweden but how could they be direct descendents of the historic figure?

"The story becomes more complex after Freya met with the seeress," Birger said. "The key to controlling your gifts lies at that gravesite. The Birka's gravesite."

Luna studied Birger's expression. He remained serious, adamant, clear.

She wanted to blurt out more questions but did her best to keep her promise to stay calm and listen. To absorb all that Birger had to share.

"The divining has to take place at the gravesite. It's the gift from Freya to her descendants to help control the shifting."

Luna nearly got up from her seat and headed back to the grave which had been relocated to the Birka Museum. If all she needed to do was some incantation at the Birka's gravesite then he could have shared that before. At first she was annoyed but then she thought back on his words, on his promises, and she sat back down. There had to be more. Much more.

He looked at her with an acknowledgement of her eagerness and he motioned for her to wait.

"This is the gift that she has left for you, but with anything, there is a cost. There is always
a cost for the divining."

INTERLUDE 12 – THE SEERESS AND THE BIRKA - FREYA

"You love him," Hiwa said to me. "This is evident."

I nodded affirmation.

"You must share your gifts in order to protect each other," she said.

Hiwa wandered to the back of her hut, to a corner hidden in shadows. She dug into a bag made of animal hide and brought forth runes, two sets.

"You must take these." She took a piece of the hide and wrote on it with a dark liquid. "You must take these words and repeat them, in this manner, in this order, so you are both protected."

Hiwa relayed the instructions and forced me to repeat them, over and over again, until she was sure that I had them memorized.

"You must use these the next time you see Ulf. It is imperative that you do this for you. For him. And for your child."

I paused and then looked up into her eyes. "My child?"

She placed her hand upon my belly. Her touch, gentle. "You are pregnant."

I was not sure if I should be happy or panicked. I had always envisioned Ulf and me as parents, but the timing of this was surreal. How could this all be happening at once? I needed to focus on getting my husband back and safe. And now I had to be extra vigilant due to our child. I could not put her at risk. I placed my hand over Hiwa's and nodded. A sigh escaped from my lips.

CHAPTER SIXTEEN

B irger gave Luna a translation of instructions for how to use the incantations at the gravesite including where to find them, how to record them, and how to use them.

"The store where you will find your runes has been around for centuries. Family owned."

He handed her the instructions.

"You've done this before?" she asked. She shouldn't have been surprised by his preparedness.

"You could say that I'm well-versed." He smiled. A kind and endearing smile. One that made it clear he was more than used to this situation. He refocused her on the instructions. "You must get them from this exact shop," he said. "The runes you need must be blessed in a specific way and this is the only shop, at least that I know of, in which you can find them."

She smirked. This sounded like something out of a novel. That said, she was willing to try anything to help her alleviate the shaking and eventual transition. Who knew what actually waited on the other side of the transformation? She didn't really want to find out.

"And once I've done all of this?"

He noted her excitedness, her eagerness. He had seen similar responses many times before, but there was something extra in her actions. She seemed almost overeager to blow out of the library and head off into the night.

"You will need to return," he said. He spoke with a tone of direness.

"Ok, I will," she said with a hesitancy that made him repeat the instructions with greater pointedness.

"You must return, Luna." He handed her the papers. "The only reason I'm letting you go is so you can make it to the shop before they close. If you don't make it then you may need to extend your trip. They are only open during certain hours."

She smiled. "No worries. I'll make it." This was too important for her not to make it. Her brother had died before he could learn how to control this changing.

She was still torn as to whether to consider these as gifts or a curse. She leaned towards gifts and with that leaning, she'd be damned if she would go forward without the ability to control them and use them to her advantage. She refused to view them as a curse and wished her brother hadn't.

"Luna, your cure. There's more to it than this. This is simply the beginning, the starting point."

He held her hand in his, not the way lovers do but the way an instructor holds onto a key student. An urgent lesson. With this she sensed apple cake and she also noted a protectiveness in his touch.

"Of course," she said, the instructions in hand. Her anxiety and tumult of emotions surpressed throughout their discussion. She did her best to retain a calm demeanor. He gently let her go but without breaking eye contact.

"Then, tomorrow, yes?" Slowly, he allowed her to move ahead of him as he escorted her to the library's door. He grabbed his own coat and laid it over his arm, the library's keys in hand.

She nodded in agreement. "Tomorrow." She would have nearly said anything if he would just let her go on her way. His point had been made. She had to return.

She made her way to the small homeopathic shop a few blocks from the library. If Birger hadn't told her of it, then she doubted that she would have found it. The simple white single story building nestled among tall trees off the side of a remote road. From the roadside, the front door peeked out from behind the trees. She tried to act nonchalant once inside the shop but her glee was difficult to contain. If all of this was real, if she could truly change into a wolf, then what else could she do?

She found the interior of the shop to be reminiscent of the homeopathic and mystical shops back in New Jersey with small stations of cards and incense and natural oils and other ingredients. She would have normally spent more time searching through the shop but her focus remained on her task at hand. She did her best not to dominate the place by insisting the shop owners help her and insist that they show her exactly where the runes were kept immediately.

She searched through the displays and started for the front desk. She didn't want to make too big of a scene. Her goal wasn't to be remembered for the rest of her life by the shop owners but rather to get her runes and go.

Thankfully, the runes weren't hard to find among their stacks of cards, dreamcatchers, healing oils, and incense. She picked up the exact ones that Birger had pointed her towards. Ones made of bone with ancient signs etched within each one. Signs she wished she knew and understood but figured she would look them up later when she had more time. She walked over to the register.

The owner took the runes in hand. "I haven't seen these in

ages," the older gentleman said. His long white hair and beard obfuscated his face and demeanor, so much so that she couldn't really tell his facial expression. "People rarely come in looking for these."

He turned them over for the price and then tapped it into the old-fashioned register. A register of metal with scrollworks along its sides. It clicked with each touch of the keys.

"They look interesting." She tried to say this nonchalantly but guessed based on the owner's second glance that she didn't quite pull it off. She handed him her credit card without thought, and then thanked him for his time.

"Where are you heading?" he asked. He pulled out an ApplePay card scanner and handed it and her card.

"I thought I'd check out the Birka Museum." She approved the transaction and put her credit card and the runes into her bag.

"You should probably head over now. They close in a bit."

She thanked him for his helpfulness and attention and then she began her walk to the museum. The sun going down, she admired the rolling hills and gorgeous green acreage of lands.

Once at the museum, a converted airplane hangar, she waited outside until it was about to close before entering. Birger's instructions were detailed and quite precise. She needed to ensure that she entered only when almost no one else was around. She shoved down her nervousness. She had played through her mind different ways this could play out. She considered not going through with it. But if she didn't try then what? All of this sounded insane. Unreal. But if she didn't try then she'd never know. And what if she got caught? What would they do, arrest her? Probably not. They would probably just kick her out for trespassing or staying after hours. She could live with that.

Inside, she admired the wide open space with high ceilings. The main area had been broken up with glass case displays and miniature reenactments of Viking towns, villages, and everyday scenes like a manikin woman cooking over a fake fire.

Luna hugged along the outer walls and made her way towards signs indicating a bathroom was only a few feet down an intimate hallway.

She tucked into the vacant customer bathroom, her feet on top of the toilet lid, her body scrunched in a ball. She did her best to remain quiet and still. She repeatedly checked her watch for closing time. Once she heard the final footsteps echo to the exit, the door close, the lock fall into place, she came out of the stall.

Once back in the main space, the wide open expanse creeped her out with its layered shadows and the echo of quiet within the silence. Somehow, without any living creatures, it felt otherworldly. For a brief moment, she considered running away. But it was as if the shadows guided her to remain and fulfill what she had been directed to do. She took a deep breath and refocused on her purpose for being there.

She thought of Daniel and how she had to do this for him. She had to get it right for him. She made her way to the Birka gravesite and took out the bone runes and instructions. She couldn't risk getting it wrong. Not after all that she had done to get here. Not after losing Daniel.

Birger had specified that she absolutely had to perform the beginning of the ritual at the Birka's gravesite, otherwise it would not work. She followed the instructions, forcing herself to focus.

Once done the ritual, she took a second to see if she felt different. She assumed there would be something that would indicate her success. In the expanse of space, she felt no immediate change and questioned if she had done it right. She reread the instructions and acknowledged that she had performed them exactly as specified.

With that she gathered her things and made her way out of the museum. There was a second part to the incantation that she needed to fulfill in her room. Maybe she wouldn't feel anything until after that segment was done? She forced herself to be patient, or at least try to.

Continuing forward under Birger's guidance, she made her way out of the museum. He had even told her the best way to exit after hours so that no one would know that she had been there.

She walked the darkened dirt path in the evening hours back to her hotel. She questioned if any of this was real. Had Birger simply played a joke on her? Some kind of trick on a gullible tourist?

Annoyed, she snuck up the stairs of her hotel towards her room. At such a late hour, not many people were in the hall-ways but even so she was careful not to interact with anyone. She didn't want someone to note or question her late-night activities.

In her hotel room, she sat on her bed and reviewed the directions for the second half of the ceremony. Fuck it, she thought. She had taken it this far, may as well complete it.

As she had been instructed, she continued the second part of the spell. She thought of how she needed to do this for Javier and for Margarite. She reminded herself that she needed to do this so that she could continue with her life passion of giving people joy through her confections. She reminded herself that people died for this; that others gave up all that they held dear so that she and a select few others would be able to live their life dreams.

She repeated the instructions over and over, exact in each movement, every word, each syllable. In her mind she could see

Freya performing a similar ritual to save her husband. She saw her ancestors giving up their lives to save the lives of others. She repeated the incantation so many times that she had it memorized so that the words simply spilled from her tongue. The runes felt like they were augmenting her own limbs. Entranced, she repeated the guidance over and over and over again until dawn. Her body had become a simple extension of the incantation, the runes.

Birger didn't tell her what to look for but she figured that instinctively she would know once the gifts of Freya and her daughter had been fulfilled. Entranced, she felt their energies and spirits joining her as she continued to implement the gifts that they had provided.

And then by the dawn's light, in the midst of her repetition, with the feel of her ancestors surrounding her, holding her, guiding her, she looked on in glee at the fact that her hands no longer shook.

Only then she knew that her renewal was complete.

INTERLUDE 13 – THE WARRIOR AND THE WOLF - FREYA

When I returned home you were nowhere to be found so I waited for you. I kept watch next to our front door. And I waited. The hours grew long. And I waited. My body tired, my spirit fearful, but I knew this needed to be done.

The evening came. And I waited. I was greeted by the scents of the dark hour, the sounds of the earth as it transformed into a world intended for the dark arts.

I dozed off. I awoke to the dawn as it neared me with the sky turning to pinks and golds. And I waited more. The promise of a new day, a new world, a new life came with each sound of an awakening spirit, the scents of hydrangeas and roses as they opened to greet the dawn.

Just as the dawn came you returned. Not in your human form but in your animal form. Your fur matted; your face somehow reminiscent of your human face. I could see your desire, your intelligence. Your eyes remained the same beautiful colors, but with gold and rust at their core.

Yet I knew it was you. You moved slowly down the path to our home, in a stealth-like manner. You moved as if you knew you were coming home, as if this land was familiar and yet you were careful. As if your intention was to be here.

For that I was grateful. I needed your interactions with me to be gentle, genteel. I needed you to want to be here. I needed you to not fight me in my efforts. I needed you to remember me.

I approached you with hands palms up so you could see that I hid nothing. Like I would with any animal I needed to tame. I came in peace with the intent to save. Slow and purposeful in my movements.

You neared me and sniffed my hands. You let me touch your head and then pet your fur. You purred with my touch.

You leaned into it, desiring it.

This is when I began the incantation. The words of transformation, of control. At first you continued to purr and lean into me. Then with the repetition, you became dazed, like the spell had begun to take effect.

And then something in you changed. You shook your body like you were trying to get rid of the magic. Like you wanted to remove it from your hide. You shook to extricate me from you. To rid me of you. I tried to keep my hands on you as you worked to shake me off.

I repeated the words louder, with greater urgency, increasing the rhythm. Your movements became more and more aggressive, clear in your intent.

You stopped moving and turned towards me. A deep growl came from within you.

Your teeth bared.

Your eyes glared.

Your back arched.

I continued the incantation as Hiwa had instructed. I did not know what else to do. With no other option, I continued. And as I did so you arched your back more, revealed your sharp fangs then took one step back and lunged.

CHAPTER SEVENTEEN

Luna, half awake, came down the staircase to the main hall of the hotel. Her suitcase in tow. She had spent the evening and the early hours completing the enchantment, fulfilling the cure. Her cure.

The lobby was full of her fellow tourists' luggage. Bags of all shapes and sizes had been piled up near the entry. Today being their last day of the tour, she anticipated even more bags filled with presents and remembrances from the travels. She thought the timing of the historian's revelation was perfectly aligned with her return home. One more day, and Luna could have found herself staying in town for weeks.

She marveled at how steady she felt. Not just her arms and legs, but her core. It was as if she had been transferred from her old broken body to a new healthier, more stable, more robust self.

After being awake most of the night, she fell asleep with the dawn and was now late for breakfast. She knew at any moment Bo would arrive with the tour van and escort them back to the airport.

She approached the breakfast nook, a closed porch filled with gorgeous streaming daylight, intimate white wooden tables and chairs. She nodded at her fellow travelers as they finished their coffees and teas. She felt a smirk on her lips as they made eye contact. Although she had spent little time with them, her brief moments of interaction must have left an impression because the woman who had sat in front of her in the van on their very first day looked at her, a bit surprised.

The woman took a sip from her tea and made eye contact with Luna. She tilted her head in curiosity. "Are you okay? You look different."

Luna's smile broadened. She felt herself glow with excitement. In her pocket she rubbed her fingertips against the runes. She didn't want to risk having them in a bag. She needed them as close to her skin as possible.

"I never felt better." Luna requested an espresso and took a seat in a corner. Her back to the wall, she faced the rest of the guests. The room was bright white and overlooked the sun-filled landscape. The perfect backdrop to her future, she thought. A foreshadowing of the dawning of a new day.

The waiter brought her the morning beverage. She swallowed the bitter liquid and silently thanked her brother for this gift. She wished he had waited. She wished he had joined her for this trip so that he too could have revelled in the gifts of their ancestors.

Bo came through the main entry and gathered the guests forward to pick up their luggage and get into the van.

"I'm surprised you're joining us," Bo said to Luna. No sarcasm or mal-intent in his tone. "I thought you'd have more that you'd want to do before you left."

"I'm fine to leave," Luna said. "I've done all that I've come for."

Bo looked at her with inquisitiveness. "You may want to

stay one final day. I believe there may be some additional information that the historian can provide you."

Interesting, Luna thought. Had Birger spoken to Bo? She guessed she shouldn't be surprised if they had. She appreciated his concern. Luna picked up her suitcase and headed towards the van. "Thank you for your kind words and consideration but I'm fine. It's time to go home."

INTERLUDE 14 – THE WARRIOR AND THE WOLF CONTINUED - FREYA

You used your weight to put me off kilter and then you forced me to the hardened dirt. I could smell the musk of you and the tinge of your recent kill. I knew there must have been a reason you had come without hunger in your heart and without the need for a feeding. I knew you, my love, were in this body and with that knowledge I forced any fear away. As instructed, I continued to repeat the incantation. I had taken the runes out of my pocket and into the palm of my hand, rubbing them, feeling the etched images on each of the shaped pieces of bone. Knowing they would guide me. They would bring my Ulf back to the surface.

You growled close to my ear, nearly overwhelming my ability to hear my own words. Yet I continued. Even with your sounds overpowering mine, I continued. I allowed the movement of my lips, the feeling of the vibration of my own voice to guide me. Swiftly, you moved to sink your teeth into my neck. Involuntarily, a gasp escaped my lips, fearful that this would be the end. I forced that fear back.

I had to succeed; for us to be together.

I repeated the incantation, faster and faster. I felt my voice heighten with fear so I forced it back down. I knew the animal you, the beast, would not allow your human form to come forward if I showed signs of panic.

I felt your fangs break the flesh of my neck. The beastly form not allowing the human form to come forward. The beastly form protected himself by moving in to eliminate the threat.

I shut my eyes with force and sealed them from the daybreak, from the dawn. I continued saying those words without thought and just as I felt you going in for the kill, I blurted out, "I am pregnant, Ulf. Please." I said this with as much love and caring and desire as I could through the fear of death. I held my breath and anticipated that at any moment you would make the move that would end my life.

You paused.

"We are pregnant," I whispered and closed my eyes tighter, waiting for that final strike.

With that, you pulled back. I felt you slowly move off of me. Your growling quieted and then stopped. A whimpering came forward. One that combined the sound of a wolf in distress and that of a man who was lost.

I opened my eyes to see you next to me, your body in the throes of changing. I placed my hand over my throat where your teeth had just been. I felt the cuts, the blood. I returned to repeating the incantation as you turned.

CHAPTER EIGHTEEN

Luna walked through the Philadelphia Airport International terminal, her luggage in tow. She reflected on the days prior and couldn't believe it. So much had happened in such a brief period of time. The tour, the museum, the historian, the heritage, the history, the Birka, the cure.

The Cure.

Holy shit, the cure.

If someone would have bet her what Daniel had left for her and the secrets that waited for her in Sweden, she would have told them they were insane.

"Hey!" She looked over to see Javier with a handmade "Welcome Home" sign. He beamed at the sight of her. His thick jet-black hair pulled back. The waves accentuated from brushing. Still in his nursing scrubs, all she wanted to do was run into his arms. She had to admit to herself that she had missed him more than she had ever thought possible. She nearly ran to him and kissed him, long and lovingly and with a passion that she didn't even know she had.

She missed him so much as a friend and as a lover. She

couldn't wait to tell him all about her trip, about her revelations. Although she knew she couldn't be completely truthful even though she wanted to be. She highly doubted that he would understand, that anyone outside of the situation, outside of her ancestry would understand. If anything they would either not believe her or see her as a freak. She had rehearsed on the flight back the story she would tell him. The version she would share with anyone who might ask.

She pulled into him and hugged him, reveling in the feel of him. Enjoying the musk and spice of his cologne. The one that he only wore on special occasions. Knowing that her return warranted a special occasion, made her smile. This was the same cologne that always made her hungry to kiss him, to touch him. She looked up and lightly pressed her lips against his and sighed. Now this, this was what she had really dreamed of, returning to her life. She couldn't wait to get back to her place, have amazing "I missed you" sex, and then return to the bakery.

She had already listed out the cakes waiting for her. Juliana's pistachio with vanilla icing, Harry's chocolate icing with peanut butter cake, and Alfredo's cake de ron which was normally made for Christmas, but that he loved for his own special days. She could already feel the heft of the flour bags and the enchantment of the precise measures, the rhythm of the standing mixer, the warmth and comfort of the ovens.

She looked into Javier's eyes.

"I missed you," she whispered with an urgency that she didn't know was in her.

"Really?" he smiled. His eyes searched hers. They had never been separated for this long, at least not since they were in third grade. "Well, that's good to know."

With one hand he took her bag and with the other, he held her hand as he guided her towards the car. "How was the flight?"

"Flight?" She had already mentally pushed forward to their lives together. Not just to what she wanted to do that day but what she had planned for them to do for the subsequent days and weeks and months. She couldn't wait.

"Yeah, you know, the whole reason we're at the airport."

She laughed. "Oh right, that flight." She squeezed his hand. "Guess what?"

He led her to his car and loaded her luggage into the trunk, the airport alive with travelers. Luna mused at the families greeting one another; the couples holding each other as if they had never seen one another; the kids bright with excitement that their father had returned home; teenagers returning from trips to be greeted by their parents.

"Is this a fun what or a 'I better look out for something' what?" he asked.

"What do you want it to be?" She asked with a mischief that let him know he was about to get a whole lot of lovin' quite soon. Before he responded, she blurted out, "I'm the descendant of a Viking warrior."

"No joke?" He opened the passenger door of the gray Honda Civic for her.

As she got in, she replied, "No joke. And not just any warrior. THE warrior. The Birka."

"Nice." He said that as if he wondered if this was something that he should be familiar with. "You mean you are going to dress like a Muslim?"

"Not a burqa. A Birka - B-I-R-K-A," She laughed. Hell, she hadn't known what a Birka was until Daniel told her. Why the hell would she expect him to know it? She just assumed Daniel had told Javier everything he had told her.

Javier got in and started the car. She put her hand on his lap and began to tell him the official story of the Birka and how Daniel had figured a bunch of this out and the reason she needed to go to Sweden was to talk to some folks in person. Just when she was about to fabricate a cure for her "Huntington's Disease," he interrupted her.

"You're shaking," he said. "Is it —"

"Gone." She interrupted with a glee that seeped from every pore.

"Really? So, the disease..."

"It's cured."

INTERLUDE 15 – THE LOVERS RETURN - FREYA

Once your changing completed and you returned to your manly form, you laid on the dirt before our home, unconscious. The dawn was fully present. The sun smiled on us. The nearby finch's birdsong swept the morning breeze.

I wiped the sweat from your brow, your body gleamed from the exertion. I curled against you; our bodies hugged one another.

I needed to feel you, taste you, smell you, and let you know that I was there.

No matter what, I was there.

As the sun shone overhead with the kiss of clouds passing through, I drug you inside. Similar to the night we had first met so many months before, I pulled you into my bed which had become ours. I put you under our covers and there, I curled against you. Feeling your sleeping breath, I ran my hands through your hair as you dozed. Once I knew that you were safe and well in our home, I returned to the guidance of the seeress and followed the exact instructions of Hiwa.

CHAPTER NINETEEN

Luna and Javier had spent the last few days getting back to normal. In the days since she had returned from Sweden at no point had she experienced shaking. She silently thanked Hiwa, Freya, Ulf, and Daniel.

Javier had shared that he had taken on the overnight shift at the Camden County Hospital Emergency Room. While Luna was away, the emergency room had been hit with wounds stemming from a gang fight and many of the standard crew had requested transfers. Paul, the head of the ER, had asked for Javier to help. Paul had been an old friend, an advocate of Javier's since his internship days. Someone that both Javier and Luna credited for much of Javier's success in medicine. When Javier had heard that Paul had lost two of his closest friends and coworkers during the fight, Javier knew that he needed to be there for his friend and mentor.

"I want to be sure he's okay," Javier had told Luna. And she understood, even though she was naturally fearful that he would be hurt. She also knew her fear may not be totally warranted considering the hospital didn't get hit with a gang fight every day.

She knew that Javier wanted to make sure his friend eased through this trauma with help. A proud man, Paul would never admit how much it pained him to lose such good people, both friends and coworkers, which made it even more important for Javier to be there for him. The shift, from midnight to noon, which spanned four days a week, was one of the toughest rounds at the hospital.

Knowing all of this, Luna wanted to take him a treat.

She sipped from the *café con leche* that Margarite had brought her. She reveled in the bitter and full comfort of the warm drink. They had finished the previous day's orders and for the first time in a while, Luna had nearly a clean slate. Margarite had taken care of the orders that hadn't specified Luna as the baker which meant Luna could make a special treat. One that she had planned the moment she and Javier had kissed on the drive home from the airport.

The bakery had filled with the warm and pleasingly soft scents of the coconut cake in its final stages of cooking. The standing mixer blended the ingredients for Javier's favorite whipped coconut vanilla icing. Once the cake had finished baking and then had enough time to cool, she would lovingly ice it with the frosting. Then she would trim it with shredded coconut and almonds.

As Luna worked on Javier's surprise, Margarite took a phone order while random passersby checked out the delights in the window. The doorbell jingled when the treats enticed them to come inside. A part time helper guided them through the pastries, helping them pick out the best ones for their tastes. Luna was happy to see the routine settle around her again, but she was even happier to settle back into the routine.

Luna loaded the iced confection, one of the best cakes she

had made, if she did say so herself, into the bakery's standard cake box. A white box with the name stamped on the side. As she lowered the cake into it, she was amazed by her steadiness.

"I won't be long," she said to Margarite. "I just want to get this to him before his shift ends."

Margarite nodded in acknowledgement. "Tell him I said, '*Hola*,' It'll be good to see him soon."

INTERLUDE 16 – ARE WE WARRIORS OR WOLVES? - FREYA

You awakened in the early evening hours, like your consciousness came with the night's stars. You gazed at me with a softness I had never seen. The love and tenderness poured through every inch of you.

"You are pregnant?" you asked. You reached out to touch me, your touch gentle.

"We are pregnant." I placed your hand on my belly so you could feel the bump, the forming of our first child. "The seeress, Hiwa, confirmed." I thought hearing her name would make you happy. That knowing we had the backing and help of a long-standing friend would bring you joy.

I did not anticipate what would happen next.

You flustered. "You cannot," you said. "Whatever it is, you must change it back."

"She said we would be fine –"

"No," you said. "No, you don't understand—"

"It is to help us."

You got up from the bed and paced. "Meeting with Hiwa can mean only one thing."

Lost in your emotions, your movements reminiscent of your wolf form. You became lost in your racing thoughts.

Confused by your response, I showed you the runes, so you could see what I had done was good. That it would bring you back to us forever.

Your expression changed to that of shock.

"You cannot do this, Freya." You stood in front of me and then kneeled before me. Your eyes met mine as placed your hands on my shoulders. "You do not know what you have done."

CHAPTER TWENTY

With the boxed coconut cake in hand, Luna entered the ER through the sliding double automatic doors. The ER hummed with the sounds of the television monitors in each corner blaring *Good Morning America* and the receptionists registering new patients.

Even though the emergency room staff could never truly predict when they may get slammed with patients, Luna seemed to have arrived at a nice quiet moment. The waiting room, lined with simple metal chairs, plain and sterile, was nearly empty except for a few patients getting registered. Optimistic and cheerful that the morning would be uneventful, especially considering the mental image she had of a room full of chaos, blood, and sadness, Luna approached the front desk. The woman behind the glass divide seemed distracted like whatever was on her mobile phone was more important than what happened in the room.

"May I see Javier Rodriguez, please?" Luna rested the cake box on the edge of the counter.

The crew member was someone Luna had never seen before. A rotund woman with abrupt grey and brown peppered spiked hair and too-bright-pink lipstick. She looked at Luna with questions.

"I'm sorry, who may I ask is here to see him?" She picked up a pencil as if she was about to take a bevy of notes.

"Luna. I'm his fiancée." She said this with a slight tinge to her voice, annoyed that this woman wasn't being more pleasant.

The crew member looked at her with disbelief and then picked up the receiver of the multiline phone in front of her. "You can go ahead and sit over there. I'll tell him you're here."

Great, Luna thought. Who knows if Javier would be available. She smiled and then took a seat across from the nearest television monitor. The smell of her cake reminded her that she hadn't yet eaten that day. Her stomach grumbled in response.

As she waited in the nearly bare waiting room, the television monitors revealed the morning's top stories. She looked through the passageway and saw Paul spy her and head in her direction.

"Luna!" He came through the doorway which divided the waiting room from the patient's rooms and greeted her. "I didn't expect to see you here. How are you?"

She stood up and shook Paul's hand. Even though he was good to Javier, she didn't feel like she knew him quite well enough for a hug. There had always been something about him, a stiffness or formality that bothered her.

She made sure to keep her distance.

"I came with a gift for Javier." Luna showed Paul the box.

"May I?" He pointed at the lid. She lifted it and he leaned in for a sniff.

"Wow. A Luna Special. That looks fantastic!" He took the box from her. "I'll show her back," he said to the receptionist. "Javier is helping a patient in 6B."

Paul pleasantly waved to her to follow him and then guided her back. Luna could see Javier in 6B chatting with a patient while reviewing something in the patient's folder. He looked up to see Paul and Luna approaching. The moment he saw the box and his fiancee, his demeanor changed from serious concern to brightness.

He put away the folder, said something to the patient, and motioned that he'd return.

He raced to her. "I can't believe you came." Javier hugged her.

"Am I disturbing you?" She nodded towards the patient's room.

"Hm? Oh no. He'll be fine. I was finishing up."

"Look what she brought for you." Paul handed him the cake box. "A Luna Special."

"It's for everyone," Luna said.

Javier opened the box and his smile widened even further. "Now this is going to be a killer breakfast." He leaned in to kiss her.

"I figured with everything going on, you guys could use a treat."

"When you're done, I could use your help in 8A." Paul read an inpatient report. "No rush. It's just something I'd like your opinion on."

Javier stood up straighter, his disposition returned to one of formality. "I'll just put this in the break room."

Luna couldn't wait for him to bite into the treat and share it with his coworkers. They had more than earned it. She could only imagine how difficult the overnight shift was. This was the least she could do.

"You," a voice demanded from behind them.

Luna turned to see an overly thin woman in sullied jeans

and a once-upon-a-time-white t-shirt, her blonde hair matted, her expression wild.

"Can we help you?" Javier asked.

The woman reached into her waistband and held up a gun.

"Fuck," Luna mumbled.

INTERLUDE 17 – NOW WE ARE
WARRIORS - FREYA

You seemed frantic. Your eyes harried. "You are an ulfr hyrða."
I did not understand. "Hiwa said that this would put you back in control. That the runes and the incantation would bring you back."
"We are bonded," you said.
"Yes, that is good."
"No. The enchantment, the words, the runes, the blood. You are now a wolf guard."
I smirked. "That is not possible. I am not of your blood line. I cannot be 'Of the Wolf'."
You sat next to me on the bed. Your tone continued to be serious. "There are guards that are of blood and ones that are of bewitchment. Most are of bewitchment. They are warriors who excelled in their arts so the captain identified them as the elite. He has Hiwa enchant them so that they can gain the strength and powers of the wolf."
You let me sit there for a moment, absorbing your words, our truth.
"Why?" I asked. "Why have me do this?"

The reality of this new normal was still sinking in. How could I be a wolf? Why would she do this especially if I was pregnant. How would this affect our baby?

You pondered this for a moment. You held my hands in yours. "Hiwa is good. She is a protector. Without her I would never have been able to lead a normal life."

"But how I found you –"

"I had been attacked and left for dead. When I awoke, I did not remember what had happened nor where I was. Only in the later days did my memory mostly return. When you mentioned Hiwa I recalled her and her purpose."

We sat in silence for a bit within our cottage. Still in bed, our hands in one anothers. The day outside had forced away the night. With the daylight came the sounds of the morn.

Your revelations both excited and terrified me. Thankful that you had regained your memory and that you were still willing to share your life with me. Terrified at what this bonding meant and afraid of who would have attacked you. The implication that whomever did so also stole your runes. And if that was the case then why would someone do that? What would they gain?

"Where are your runes?" I asked.

You thought for a moment. "When I awoke, they were gone."

"To what end?" I asked.

"Not everyone believes in the wolf guard. There are those who deem us unnatural and seek out ways to destroy us." You shifted towards me. "Freya, we are linked at the soul. With the help of Hiwa I can teach you how to control your powers. We need to do so for our child."

CHAPTER TWENTY-ONE

J avier came up from behind Luna. "We don't want any trouble."

The woman's hands shook. Luna wasn't sure if it was due to fear or adrenaline or withdrawal, but whatever the reason, this introduced a whole new level of complexity. If this woman panicked then she could easily toss off a shot and who knew where the bullet would land and who would be harmed.

"Fluff," the woman demanded. "Now."

Javier stood in front of Luna and headed to the secured cabinet. "No problem. Just give me a second." He typed in the code on the security panel and the light turned red which implied that the code was wrong and the cabinet remained locked. Javier looked confused and tried again. Again it turned red. He looked over at the addict. "One second."

"Don't fuck with me!" she yelled. "I don't have time for this shit." Her hands shook more vigorously.

Javier tried the panel again. Luna looked beyond the woman and saw Paul behind the central nursing station. His face distorted with fury. It looked like he was pushing a button.

Was he pushing an override? An override that kept the cabinet with all of the prescription drugs locked? The cabinet that Javier tried to open without success? Luna knew that the hospital had installed an additional security procedure of an override for the narcotics cabinet but that was only supposed to be used in case of extreme emergencies.

The ER crew had been trained that if they were attacked at gunpoint to go ahead and give the intruder what they wanted and then call the police who were already on site. That way everyone stayed safe. The look on Paul's face let Luna know that he had reached a new threshold of determination, of anger, that she'd never seen before.

"Just one more sec." Javier reached over to try the security code again.

"Bullshit," the addict responded, and before Luna could register the subsequent sound, she saw the addict jerk back and Javier go down.

At first, Luna thought he was playing. What else would he be doing? In her shock, she thought that for whatever reason he figured it'd be funny to play dead in the middle of this chaos. Maybe he thought that it would distract the intruder, and him falling to the floor would provide a distraction for someone to overpower the malnourished, ill being. And then the reality of the situation hit. It hit as Javier's blood began to pool from under him.

INTERLUDE 18 – FOR OUR DAUGHTER - FREYA

Your face. Such pride. Such caring. Such tenderness. When the midwife handed you our daughter, freshly cleaned from birth, you looked like you could hold onto her forever.

This was why we had to bond.

This was why we had to fight.

For our daughter.

For our family.

CHAPTER TWENTY-TWO

Luna looked towards Paul. His face hard, resigned.

That fucking bastard, Luna thought.

Paul reached under the desk and pulled out a gun. How did he keep a gun under the desk without anyone knowing? Holy shit, Luna thought. Things just got a lot more real.

"Try it," Paul said. His voice became ten octaves deeper than his normal talking voice. His gaze trained on the addict. His stance practiced. His aim true.

The way he held the gun, Luna swore that he must have been at the shooting range. Like he had been given training on how to handle it. In that moment, maybe that was a good thing.

The druggy's eyes grew wide when she saw Paul and his aim trained on her. The realization that she wasn't about to get the narcotics and that here was someone equally armed must have put her in a panic. She tossed the gun and ran. She made her way right past Paul and toward the main entry. Paul proceeded to shoot at her. Just the fact that this doctor was shooting a gun in an emergency room put the staff in shock.

Luna raced to Javier. She heard shots fired but didn't look

up to see what happened. Instead, she focused on Javier who was face up on the emergency room floor. A pool of blood spread from his back. The entry wound prominent with the spreading blood. She tried to focus and remember what Javier had taught her after he had had one too many nights of treating gunshot wounds. How to stop the flow of blood. How to keep him from dying.

What really worried her was that his eyes were closed and his breathing shallow. So shallow she could barely register it.

"I'm here, baby," Luna said. She placed her hands on his chest to see if she could feel his heart. "I'm here."

She searched his face but he didn't acknowledge her. His breathing grew faster and shallower with each moment. She looked around the ER for someone, anyone who could get them out of this, but in that moment all eyes were focused on the addict and Paul. She started to call out for help and then thought better of it. No one would be able to help him the way she could. She knew he could be nearing his final moments. All they would do was put him in the operating room and pray that they had gotten to him in time. That wasn't good enough, damnit.

That wasn't even close to being good enough.

She had the cure.

She knew what she needed to do.

INTERLUDE 19 - WE ARE A FAMILY OF WARRIORS - FREYA

We named her Lovisa. We could feel her strength with each movement. Her body strong, her voice solid. Our pride vast.

We took her to Hiwa not long after her birth. We both needed to be sure that we had the blessing and encouragement of Hiwa. She opened the door to her intimate hut and held her arms wide. I placed Lovisa, swaddled in a woolen blanket, into her arms. She held her like our daughter was her own.

"Such a beauty," she cooed. "She will do great things."

"Will you help us protect her," you said. In your eyes, in your stance, your concern, your hope was evident. I reached over and held your hand knowing how much this moment meant to you, to us.

"Come," Hiwa motioned for us to follow her inside. The darkened hut aglow with a hearth fire. A pot atop the fire with something brewing. The steam of the dish rose from the lid of the pot. She led us to wooden chairs facing the hearth and encouraged us to sit. She cradled our girl and whispered words of sweetness.

"Hiwa, you have always been kind to us," you said. "We want to ask for your help in raising our Lovisa."

She looked up at you with a tenderness rarely seen and nodded. "It would be my honor. Starting when she can walk, we will begin our training. This child will fulfill her destiny of greatness."

Hiwa kept this promise and treated our beautiful girl like her own grandchild. Taking her in from an early age and teaching her the arts. Not just to control her natural gifts but the enchantment arts. The arts of the Seeress.

"She may need these as well," Hiwa said. "I will not always be here to protect her. Therefore, I will teach her how to protect herself."

She swore that she would not tell the king of Lovisa's existence. Our fear that he would want her to be his. That he would insist she join his guards, his pack.

When she made this declaration of protection, you believed her. You said she had never betrayed you. And I too believed.

My concern was with the others. Those who thought the Lycanthropes were meant to be gods and those who believed that they must stop all with the gift to transform. Destroy them.

You had not told me of those with the belief that we Lycanthropes are gods nor of those who existed to stop us. You had always been too humble. But I knew from my conversations with Hiwa that such believers existed. I guessed that one of those believers was the one who had stolen your runes and left you for dead. The believer, thinking that he had neutralized you, therefore, considered himself more powerful. And I knew that since the attacker had not shown himself that he must have believed he had killed you and that one day he may return.

His return and those like him, they were the ones I feared.

CHAPTER TWENTY-THREE

L una reached into her pocket and pulled out her divining runes. She had no idea if this would work. She had read and reread the enchantment and the instructions. She took a syringe and drew her own blood, then dripped it into Javier's partially opened mouth. And then she began the spell. She whispered it into his ear. Over and over. She imagined them as one, their souls intertwined. She felt for his heartbeat to see if it had steadied. In the chaos of the moment, no one approached. She looked around them, aware of the potential for someone to come forward. She knew at some point someone would.

But in those few seconds no one questioned.

No one approached to help.

And for once she was thankful for this. She didn't want anyone questioning what she was doing. She simply wanted to heal her soulmate. His eyes didn't flutter. His breath deepened a little and because of that she was encouraged. So she continued. She looked up to see others scurry by them as if Luna and Javier weren't there. She wondered if there was something to the spell that made them invisible to others. She hoped that she would have at least a few more seconds to continue the spell and to be that much closer to saving him.

"Please, Javier. Please," Luna said, her heart breaking. She renewed the enchantment, the runes held over his heart. She figured that Lovisa and Freya had left these instructions for moments like these. Of anyone she knew, he deserved this gift. He deserved to live a long and prosperous life.

She opened his shirt and placed the ancient runes against his skin, while she continued to repeat the words. The only words she knew to make him return to life. In her mind she prayed, she begged to Freya, to Daniel, to Ulf, to Hiwa, to the gods, any gods who could intervene.

She imagined him returning to life. She saw them together, as a family, with their children. With the descendants of Freya and Ulf who deserved to be of the earth.

She saw her family happy and joyful and alive. Javier at the center with a child in his arms and another clutching to his leg, eager to play with his papa.

"Please," she whispered. "Please."

His eyes fluttered open and he took a huge gasp of air. His back arched forward.

"Thank you," she prayed. "Thank you."

She put her hands through his hair and met his eyes.

"I love you," she said.

She held him in her arms for a moment and then kissed him. In that moment she knew that this was truly a gift of her ancestors and that they had provided this cure exactly for this moment. She felt them both returning to the moment with the chaos of the emergency room coming forward. She kissed him and cried, "Here! Help him, please!"

INTERLUDE 20 – YOU MUST MOVE ON - FREYA

My love. Our days together were long. We enjoyed our quiet life on our dairy farm. We cared for our cattle together. We sheared the sheep. We milked the goats. We helped Papa in his business. After Papa passed, we made sure that his workmanship and quality of wares was stellar and continued the fantastic craftsmanship, as expected by the king.

Our nights were spent in the arms of one another. No longer needing to fear the random transformation to come at night. Instead we found comfort with one another. The feel of you in my arms, our bodies intertwined. The taste of you deep into the night. Our beautiful daughter swaddled in blankets, sleeping in her crib, only a few steps from our sleeping quarters. The blessings of awakening to her hunger cries and our joyful days of her laughter. And as she grew, our love grew exponentially. The peace and normalcy you had craved, we were able to find and live.

We made sure Hiwa taught our daughter the fine arts of the Seeress. And then we begged my papa to train her in the arts of metallurgy, weaponry, and battle. Not that he needed convincing to spend time with her. His love for her and desire to see her take on the family traditions drove his acceptance and passion to teach her. And so he taught her until his death.

Lovisa believed that all children had knowledge of such wonders. And we wanted it that way. We needed her to accept all that she was and all that she could be, instead of questioning it. As far as she knew, this training was simply part of a normal upbringing.

She grew up curious, strong, and joyful. She grew to be a fine youth. If she asked to learn of something, we encouraged it. If she asked to visit a place, we took her. If she showed interest regarding something, we fulfilled her wonder. We made sure that our beautiful daughter felt complete and that all of her intellectual desires were fulfilled.

And then one day, you passed. A natural death. You died in your sleep. We gave you a proper burial. A quiet one with only the closest of kin. My heart broke on that day, but I knew I had to continue to protect our family.

In my grief, I began to change. I did not realize that was what happened. Our daughter found me in our field next to a shredded cow. Its body savagely ripped apart. Horrified, our daughter initially feared that I had been injured by whatever had destroyed the innocent animal. My body covered in the bovine's blood and muscle. Panicked, she awoke me and felt every inch of my body to check for similar injuries. She only found minor cuts and bruises. I spent the remainder of the day calming her worries as she cared for me. She had yet to begin her own transformation.

That would come soon enough.

Shocked that the transformations had renewed, I knew I had to return to Hiwa for guidance. I did not tell Lovisa of the cause of the death of the cow. I could not share with her the reasons for the destruction and why she found me in such a state. I simply had to ask her to trust me and allow me to stay with her godmother, Hiwa, for a time. Lovisa took me to the home of her godmother and then, with concern and caring, left me there. Her sadness and fear dripped from every pore even as Hiwa consoled her and told her that I would be fine.

"This is a natural part of grieving," she told Lovisa to ease her concerns.

"I will be fine," I encouraged her.

Your loss must have truly hit our daughter harder than I had anticipated. She did not want to leave me alone, even with the one person besides us who had raised her. The three of us were in the cottage of Hiwa. The night encroached. I wanted to be sure that our daughter left before the possibility of me transforming.

"Are you sure?" Lovisa asked. She held my hands as they shook. Hiwa looked on with concern.

"I will care for her," Hiwa said. "We will have time to focus. The king is away with his warriors so we will be alone. I promise that I will return your mama when she is whole."

Our beautiful, confident daughter left without another word but her mannerisms betrayed her deep concern. Her uncertainty evident in her slow progression to the door and eventual exit. Once Lovisa closed the door to the intimate cottage and we were alone, Hiwa more closely inspected me. She took her healing crystals and waved them over my body, murmuring incantations in a language I did not understand. She then performed a cleansing with ancient herbs that I had only ever seen in her garden. Once done, she sat me down next to the fire. Her look was not one of completion, but one of complexity. She poured herself a cup of tea and handed me one as well. We sat quietly for a moment and then, gazing into the flickering light of the fire, she began.

"In your grief, the bonding must have flawed. I've never seen such a tight joining as this."

She did not speak again for a time. She sipped her tea of mint and lavender and honey. She eyed me and then put her cup down. She got up and checked me again with her eyes, hands, and crystals. Her focus double what it had been previously.

Afraid to break the spell, I quietly sat and awaited her declaration. She was the only person I knew who could help me. She was the only person who ever knew that I had become a wolf warrior as well. In faith and belief in her gifts, her powers, and her friendship, I waited. Once again, she finished her incantations, the words seemed to blend together to form something beyond words, beyond emotions, and then she stood overlooking the fire. She dumped the remainder of her tea into the flames causing them to steam and sizzle, but not go out.

"We must retrain," she declared. She did not expand. I took this moment to make a request I had asked for before, hoping that in this instance she would be more open, more welcoming.

"Can you teach me?" I asked. "Like you've taught Lovisa?"

She looked at me with curiosity. I was a little surprised others had not asked for this. Later, I would discover that many had asked but Lovisa was the first time she had agreed to teach.

"Why?" she asked. Her look was one of abrupt intensity. Like she did not trust those who made this request of her.

"I want to protect us in all ways possible." This was true. I worried that as Lovisa aged she would be held accountable to protect all of us. I did not want our daughter left alone with such demands, such responsibility. I also did not want to be left alone in our home without as many tools as I could obtain. I wanted to be sure that I fully understood the mystical elements of the transformation gifts so that no matter what arose, I would be able to address it.

She waved me off. "You have many means of protection," she said. "You are more skilled than most in this life."

I looked down at my hands and at their shaking and pondered the years we had together in relative quiet. Yet I knew that many threats remained only a stone's throw from our humble homes.

"I fear they are not enough."

She observed me. She looked for signs of something I did not understand. "I will consider this." She then placed her hands over mine. "Let us begin your rebonding."

Days passed and Hiwa performed the ritual upon me several times. Each time she checked again to ensure that the bonding had succeeded. Each time she seemed concerned. "I must bring in Lovisa. We must bond you together."

"Why?" I asked. I had never heard of such a thing. Among the tales shared neither you nor Hiwa had mentioned such challenges.

"Your spirit and Ulf's remain bonded to one another, even in his passing. Your spirit wants to return to the beast-self which some believe was Ulf's natural state."

"Oh." Surprised, I did not know what else to say. I had never heard that your natural state was of the beast. I had only ever thought of you as my soul, my life, my breath. Together we had always felt whole. Together we had transcended all else, including the wolf.

"Some believe that this is true, that the natural wolf warriors are actually beasts when they are in their true state. I had never known why but this may be the reason."

"Others have been through this?" I asked, trying to digest all that she had shared.

"These gifts were handed down to me from the king's previous seeress who handed it down from another, and so on. In my time, I had never been witness to such complications, but yes, based on what you are experiencing, others must have had similar problems."

We called in Lovisa and described what needed to be done. In order to safely perform the ceremony, I was forced to reveal our truths. I explained to our daughter that her shapeshifting powers would naturally begin to come forward in the coming year.

Hiwa explained the purpose of the bonding, including that my own transforming had gotten out of control. We told her that she and I needed to be bonded in order to complete my healing process.

"You must understand," Hiwa said to our daughter. "This will bring forward your own transformation."

At first our daughter was silent and then her expression changed to that of certainty.

"Of course," she said.

This additional information frightened me a bit. I did not want to harm our daughter in any way although the Seeress had insisted that it would not. With that assurance, I agreed.

Once done, we were bonded. Lovisa and I thanked Hiwa and returned to our home. We returned to our normal lives. The random transformations had stopped, the bonding effective.

We returned to our typical chores and lives including a visit to the village market to sell our wares. Since I had taken on Papa's swordsmith shop and Lovisa managed our dairy farm, we had a cart of dairy products from the farm and metalware from the smithery. We returned to our stall with the cart behind us and welcomed our long-standing customers who had become friends over the years. It felt wonderful to be back to our normal lives.

Deep in conversation, I looked up to find three masked men on horseback. Invaders. The masks of simple black cloth. Their horses raged into the village. A darkening night sky came in behind them as if they brought the clouds and impending storm with them.

They used the height of the stallions to their advantage and sat upright. They wore dark leather battle armor and demanded that they be treated like the royalty they deserved.

"You shall bow down to us!" One declared, his voice dark and triumphant.

It was clear they knew the king and his warriors were away to lay claim to other lands and therefore left our own lands at risk. Their mannerisms confidently displayed their aggressiveness.

A neighboring stall owner, a fisherman who had sold much of his goods already and had been preparing to close up his stand, looked at them with disgust. "Why do you deserve special treatment?" He asked. "Who are you to make such demands?"

The lead invader glared at the fisherman and without a word, tossed a knife through the air that hit the tradesman squarely in the heart with a precision that was rarely seen. Aghast, Lovisa began to move forward, but I motioned for her to wait. The handle of that knife looked familiar. It had been one Papa had forged for a special arm of the guards when I was a child.

These men knew how to fight.

At first, the townspeople responded in a flurry of fear, screaming in terror, running in a panic. The invaders motioned them to be quiet.

"Silence!" demanded the leader.

The townspeople slowly complied. I felt the waistband of my pants to grasp my own knife and reached with my other hand underneath my coat. I prepared to draw my sword, always hidden and at the ready.

I waited for the right moment to strike. I motioned to Lovisa to stand down until absolutely necessary. We had not allowed others to know of her powers, and I did not want these ignorant fools to force our hand.

I was thankful that we had encouraged our daughter to dress in the same clothes as Papa and me when we had to run our stalls at the market.

They stole from the sellers with a ferocity and hunger rarely seen. They overturned carts, tossed whatever they did not want, and ravaged what they did. They treated each of us like their personal slaves. They inspected the women as if they only existed for their own pleasure. My stomach turned at the sight of such behavior. The townspeople were terrified.

I waited for them to be distracted enough by their own hungers to launch at the nearest invader. I unsheathed my sword while I tossed my knife at another. The knife nicked one of the bastards while I battled a third. His swordsmanship was well-honed.

We fought with ferocity.

It was not enough. Their numbers seemed to have doubled. From where they came, I did not know. I nodded to Lovisa that it was time. I scrambled away from my fight and guided our daughter to behind one of the houses, out of eye shot of the townsfolk.

"My daughter. I have waited long to reveal our truths," I said. "It is time."

In that moment we brought forth the gift of the wolf.

CHAPTER TWENTY-FOUR

Once Luna knew that the emergency room nurses would care for Javier, she turned her focus to the cause of the horror. The demon who had allowed the addict into the space. The asshole who had begged Javier, her love and the only man she had ever wanted to be with, to work this insane shift. The jackass who dared to bring out a gun and threaten an addict. The idiot who, instead of following procedure, decided that he would make himself the law.

She hid within an empty room and stood tall, shoulders back, staring in the direction where Paul had chased after the invader. He thought he was the law.

Well, now Luna was the law.

She tore her shirt off in readiness for the change, eager to feel her teeth lengthen to their hungry fangs. Her hands arched into sharpened claws. Her legs began to get longer, they were ready for the pounce. She held her runes tightly in her fist and focused all of her energy on this fucking devil.

Luna went on all fours and within her mind she enabled

the change. Her spirit was eager to chase the man who nearly killed her heart.

In partial transformation, her eyes turned a burnt yellow. Her limbs began to elongate. Her face had begun its shift to be more wolfen and bestial. When she felt the spirit energy become her dominant lifeforce, she leapt from the room and chased after Paul.

Her stride so long that others merely felt the blur of her pass them as she dove after him. In a few moves, she caught up to him in the parking lot. He had stopped in his pursuit of the invader and she took him down from behind. His gun flew from his hand and across the parking area.

"You fucking bastard!" she growled. Her voice gravely and deepened. "You kill him. I kill you." She did not yell. She did not scream. She simply stated her truth.

"Who the fuck are you?" he said. His own voice filled with anger and a tinge of confusion. She wanted to hear fear in his voice. She wanted him to anticipate the impending attack and pray to god, any god, for his life to be spared.

She raised her extended claws, her arm high in the air. Her stance made it clear that the strike was meant for death. He tried to turn his head to see his attacker. She slammed his head against the concrete. He tried to wiggle away from her, but she pinned him with an even greater force.

She did not answer him. She did not acknowledge him. Her intent to kill nearly completed as she readied to tear out his throat. Her focus and purpose were pure. She felt something shove her off of her prey and rip her away.

UNTITLED

INTERLUDE 21 – DANIEL'S SEARCH FOR TRUTH - DANIEL

I honestly took the spit test, aka DNA test, because I was curious. I mean, it didn't matter where we came from. Our adopted parents took great care of us. It wasn't like we had a reason to run away.

But I wanted to know, you know?

We'd taken so much shit because people couldn't figure us out. They always had some nasty shit to say like, "What are you?" or "Where'd you come from?"

We didn't deserve that. We were just kids. But in that anger, in the alienation, I needed to know.

Then I got the results from Ancestry.com, Luna. Imagine my surprise when it said we had Mongol (okay that wasn't surprising based on some of our features), Western European, and Swedish, specifically Viking. Viking? Now that's cool as all hell. They even gave some potential blood lines and relatives.

I wasn't expecting that.

So, I joined a few online boards, you know? Can't hurt. I thought maybe I'd run into a cousin or something. Might be kinda cool. Maybe have a family reunion.

Then that fucking shaking. At first it happened every once in a while. I figured I drank too much. Like the shaking was a kind of hangover. No biggie, I cut back. Should have taken care of it, right?

Nope.

Then I figured it was stress. That seemed reasonable. I got stressed out and the shaking showed up. I picked up Tai Chi. That didn't quite do it, so I picked up yoga. I thought they'd help alleviate the stress so the shaking would go away.

Nope.

It reduced but it didn't go away.

That's when I went to the docs. I must have missed something. Something I didn't understand.

Man, he checked me out. I mean a ton of tests.

Meanwhile, the shaking got worse. I woke up in the middle of the night with sweats and arm and leg cramps. The weirdest fucking thing. It felt like I had been running all night. I'd be totally exhausted. Crazy shit.

Then the doc said he thought it was Huntington's Disease. He never saw it happen at such a young age. Blah, blah, blah. Not much he can do, there are some experimental treatments, blah, blah, blah.

I looked it up.

Fuck, it's a death sentence.

After that diagnosis, it made the heritage boards mean a lot more.

I got a hold of our birth certificates to confirm our birth parents' names. Just in case we got something wrong. I needed to be absolutely sure.

I started posting on the boards about our birth parents and

the results of my spit test. I asked if anyone knew anybody from these bloodlines. Asked if anyone knew anyone with Huntington's Disease.

Turned out it was a purely genetic disease so the more folks I could find the better.

That's when I found this group on Ancestry.com's boards. Turned out our parents were members of this community or at least our dad was.

It seemed cool.

They talked a lot about how everyone existed for a reason. I could get down with that. One guy posted about how no species was supreme. Uh, okay. That's a little bizarre statement but sure, I could back that. Some talked about Huntington's Disease and their own symptoms. How they controlled it or tried to. So that was cool.

This was how I met Birger. The guy I set you up to talk to. He's pretty cool. Also a member of the same society. He's typically quiet on the boards but when he saw who our dad was, he messaged me on the side and we started chatting.

Dude had some crazy good knowledge about us. I mean CRAZY GOOD. Some stuff he said he couldn't tell me on a board which was fine. I mean, I got it. He said it's probably not Huntington's Disease that was causing the shakes. He said, what I got was hereditary but it was not that.

I asked him what it was.

I mean, if he was going to lay that on me then might as well go all the way.

He reiterated that the boards weren't secure. This wasn't the kind of stuff that he could share in a virtual environment.

He said, "Who knows who reads what you post, even in a private chat."

Sounded a little paranoid to me, but, fine. I respected his privacy.

Birger mentioned that the society was actually bigger than a message board. He said only a few of the people were on it. That the society, The Lycanthrope Society, was a very private group and like a community or a family.

I loved our adopted parents. I mean, they were dope.

They'd done so much for us, but I must admit that I'd always wanted to have a real family, you know? I'd never quite felt like I was a part of something big.

So I was like, "I guess these Lycanthropes are like Greenpeace or the Order of Friends or The Freemasons." They must have been something bigger than me, bigger than us. Something that could really mean something in my life and for others.

He invited me to join. Said I had to do some stuff first, but he said he had no doubt that I could do it. Without hesitation I told him I'm in. Plus what a cool name, The Lycanthrope Society.

CHAPTER TWENTY-FIVE

Paul laid in a panic, near Luna. She had been tossed only a few feet away from him. Just far enough away to put him out of reach. She looked over to see his unfocused wild eyes. His fear, confusion, and anger all broiled into one expression. He looked between her and something above her. Or someone. She tried to lift whatever was on top of her, off of her.

"Motherfucker, fuck him," she murmured. Luna didn't care what he thought or felt. He had no right to do what he did. "Get off," she said.

She tried to get up and finish what she had started. Teach this overprivileged sack of shit a lesson but she couldn't move. The more she tried to get up, the more who or whatever had her pinned kept her down.

"Get the fuck off!" she yelled. She continued to struggle and looked up to see what seemed to be another shapeshifter in partial transition. His body was larger than hers. He localized his transition so that it focused on his arms, legs and torso, which allowed his strength and powers to come forward in those areas. His face was a bit hairier than she would expect.

She guessed that his nose wasn't typically so large and distinctive. His eyes were grey with yellow specks. She needed to learn how to do that, she thought.

"No," the stranger growled, his voice more human than animal. "He's not worth it."

The shapeshifter nodded to Paul and then towards the police in the doorway. They were currently taking the drug addict into custody and not paying attention to them. Paul had nicked her with a random bullet which made her stop long enough to get a hold of her. The police had the addict cuffed. They were finishing up and Luna knew that at any moment they could turn to her.

"Your man. He'll need your help," the stranger said.

Luna searched his eyes and looked into him, then at Paul who was slowly getting up, and finally at the entry to the emergency room where she would find Javier. She thought on the stranger's words, on his guidance. She knew Paul wasn't worth the possibility of being put away but she also knew that Javier wouldn't be in this predicament if Paul hadn't overridden Javier's ability to unlock on the cabinet.

"Fine," Luna said, half-heartedly. "I'll stop." She said this in a way that was almost believable.

The stranger raised an eyebrow. She kept his gaze to make it clear that she would not continue after Paul. At least not in that moment. The stranger flexed his arms as if considering to let her up. His facial features were more human than wolf. His control truly was impressive, she thought.

"If I get up, then you will not attack him again, correct?" he said.

Luna squirmed underneath him. She could always lie and say that she would leave Paul alone and then go after him anyway. What would this guy do? Kill her? She explored his eyes to see if there were signs of a killer. A bloodthirsty, hungry killer. Even though she didn't think he was the type, she knew she couldn't be sure. Hell, she didn't even know another shifter existed in Camden.

"Fine," she said. "Promise." Slowly, he allowed her to get up. Her curiosity peaked, she promised herself that she would get the question that hung between them answered. "Who are you?"

INTERLUDE 22 – DANIEL DISCOVERS
A NEW WORLD

I got invited to this party one day. I was just wandering the boards, seeing what was going on. It sounded pretty cool. One of those happy hour things. I figured I'd never been to a Lycanthrope Society party so why not?

They held it in some fancy place in the 'burbs of Southern New Jersey. One of those old mansions that'd been converted into a party place for rent. Set back from the main street, circular driveway, away from anything else. I guess about ten acres surrounded it, easily that much. Driving up to it was pretty dramatic. The white mansion had more than fifteen rooms (Yes, I counted), huge windows, and double doors for the main entry. I walked in as a twilight sky set behind the Colonial structure. The circular driveway had already been lined with lots of cars of all shapes and sizes. Everything from Maseratis to Porsches to Hondas. Heck there was even a VW Bug.

I was pretty sure they usually held weddings there. I think one of my coworkers mentioned checking it out. Anyway, it was pretty cool at first. I got out of my little Honda and went inside. They had suited waiters serving drinks and appetizers. Those little finger food kinds. Like tiny sandwiches and those mini hot dogs. I ordered a beer, and another guest came up to me to chat. This plain looking guy in dark jeans and a button-down white shirt. Looked like he hit the gym a lot. Come to think of it, most of the folks there were pretty buff.

Anyway, I told him I was surprised by all of the people. Who knew we had so many relatives!

He laughed. "Where did you come from?" He asked. "How'd you find out about the Society?" All that kind of stuff.

I told him about my spit test and the boards. Nothing dramatic.

He talked about his heritage. Vikings, too. A touch of Malaysian. When I mentioned our family lineage, he was all kinds of impressed.

"Not many of you around," he said as he tossed back a vodka.

The waiter came over and handed me a beer so I took a few sips. Didn't want to seem too eager. I had no idea why this guy was impressed but I figured I'd go along with it.

In the meantime, he talked about how he found out about The Lycanthrope Society, his own blood lines, who he was related to, how his family got to the States, that kind of thing.

He even offered to show me around. He said the basement of the joint was the main headquarters. I thought this was cool but a little weird. Really? The basement? I sipped on my beer and didn't say much in response. Just nodded to confirm that, yeah, I'd like to check the place out.

He leaned in and whispered something about them moving around. I guess that was normal. I'd never been a member of anything like this before, so what did I know?

We talked like it was no big deal. All casual-like. I figured I'd enjoy a few drinks, grab a couple of those mini dogs, have a little fun, get a good laugh, and then head out. No harm, no foul. They seemed like nice people.

Good people.

A couple of hours passed and it got dark outside. I chatted with a couple of other folks, just to see what they were like. When I realized the time, I thought I might stay a few more minutes and then jet. I didn't want to outstay my welcome. Maybe have another appetizer and a beer and then head out. Maybe talk to one or two more people and exchange some phone numbers. I wanted to stay in touch with some of these folks. Something about the vibe in the room made me feel like I had met our family, like I belonged. Something neither you or me experienced before. Not really. Except for with our parents and Javier. Otherwise, nah.

Just when I shoved a mini pizza bite in my mouth, a guy got up in front of everybody and talked about how we're a community and how great it was to get everyone together. How we'd been related for thousands of years so we needed to pay homage to our heritage.

K. I was down with that.

In the middle of him talking, the room broke out like an old school *Mission Impossible* movie. You know, the ones with Tom Cruise. The younger Tom Cruise. Out of nowhere, people dressed in all black flew in through the windows on these long ropes. They jumped folks in the room and held them at knife point.

I was like, "What the hell?"

One guy in all black yelled, "TRG!"

I was like, "What's a TRG?"

I swallowed my pizza bite nearly whole. Thought I might choke on it.

Then this feeling came over me as a sensation filled the room. My arms and legs started shaking.

I thought, "Fuck, I can't have an episode now."

I could almost see this vibration, like an invisible contagion had come across everyone. Folks started shaking and gurgling and making these weird sounds. I crawled on hands and knees into a corner to get out of the way. I didn't want to be a target of these robbers plus who the hell knew what else was going on.

That's when it happened.

Everyone started changing.

I never saw anything like it, Luna. One minute they were humans and then they were these beings. Some turned into wolves, others into bears, and others into I don't know what.

And then I felt it too.

I looked at my hands and legs and felt this shifting. It was uncontrollable. It hurt but didn't hurt. I mean, it was like my body knew what to do.

At one point, at the peak it felt like someone was ripping my insides out and I screamed but it wasn't my voice. It was a deeper, huskier, more bestial voice. I was terrified.

The last thing I remembered, a fight broke out among these creatures and one guy who looked like a cross between a bear and a bodybuilder came right towards me.

I thought, "Oh fuck!" because I couldn't fight that guy.

This was definitely a time I wished we had taken Kung Fu or Jiu Jitsu when we were kids instead of spending our time sneaking into the movies.

That guy or thing bared his teeth and just as he dove at me with claws drawn, I blacked out.

Fuck.

I woke up in the middle of the night, naked and covered in dirt and what looked like blood. I looked around and realized I had been laid out among some bushes about a mile from the mansion.

My god, Luna. What was I supposed to do? What the hell did I do when I was blacked out?

I made a run for it and got back to the mansion. I swear the place was nearly abandoned, except for the bodies. No joke, Luna. Tons of bodies.

They were in all forms. Some human, some animal, some barely alive, some dead, some unrecognizable. I mean like, I saw these masses of blood and flesh like it had all been ripped apart by something. When I saw that, I puked up my pizza.

The ones that were still alive looked like they were in a daze. One guy was transforming from a hairy, fanged creature to a naked bald guy. Once his transition back to human form had been completed, he just laid there, unconscious. I looked around for the guy who had invited me or the guy I had been talking to and didn't see them. I didn't know this guy who just changed so I knew better than to touch him. I mean, who knew what would happen if I did.

I scrambled to find my clothes or what was left of them. I didn't bother to look in the mirror to see how I looked because I knew I was a mess. A hot mess. I threw on my clothes and found my car keys in my pants pocket.

I ran for it. I needed to get the hell out of there.

That's when I knew I had to leave this for you. I had to protect you from all of this shit. From whatever the hell we are.

CHAPTER TWENTY-SIX

"Who are you?" Luna asked. She brushed herself off as the stranger handed her a shirt. "Thanks."

"I'm Chago."

Much taller than her, his build was narrow yet muscular as if it was meant to be the shape of a wolf. Once he was done transforming back to a human form, in a quiet, subtle and clean transformation, it was as if he had never been a beast. She marveled at how he could shift back to a full man form with short dark hair, light skin, and chiseled features with such ease. She noted that he wore stretchy clothes which didn't tear in his change. Smart. She looked around them and no one seemed to notice their transformations, neither his nor hers.

Interesting, she thought.

"Birger asked me to look after you," Chago said. "He was concerned when you didn't return."

Birger? She had no reason not to believe him. How else would he even know who she was or what she was?

"You do realize that he," she pointed at Paul, "is a murderer." She pulled on the shirt. Not self-consciously at all. Probably helped that it didn't seem like anyone had any idea that she had been topless. Not a single person looked at her sexually or with surprise, including Chago. He acted like it was every day that he saw a woman rip off her shirt and go after some guy.

She really needed to better understand what happened when they changed. There had to be something about it that blocked people from being aware of it. She would be surprised if literally no one, other than Chago, had seen her transformation, including her toplessness.

"From what I saw, you prevented that," he said this in a flat matter-of-fact tone and then brushed off his clothes as if he had been covered in soot.

"Fine," she replied. "As far as I'm concerned, he had the intention of being a murderer. I witnessed it. I saw him pressing the override button. I saw the gun, even if he tossed it."

"Needless to say, whatever he attempted to do, didn't work," Chago dismissed her comment. He seemed nonplussed by Paul's actions.

"Fine." She didn't need him to agree with her. She knew the truth.

"Don't you think you should return to your fiancé?" He motioned towards the Emergency Room.

Luna looked at him quizzically. Javier and Luna had never officially gotten engaged, but she had intended to propose to him shortly. Actually, within the next few days. All of the drama of the last month had made her realize how much she loved and needed him. In the past, he had inferred that they should get married, but Javier was never one who had to follow cultural norms. He cared more about their relationship and that they were together, no matter if a piece of paper declared it or not. That said, she knew his family and her family would adore their nuptials, even if it was just a small ceremony, preferably in his parents' church, The Cathedral of the Immaculate

Conception. Hence her change of heart. Even with the renewed focus on their officially tying the knot, she still debated whether she should tell him she's a werewolf, but that question was for another time.

Beyond the fact that she intended to marry Javier, how did this stranger know so much about them? She looked at him a bit more closely. She knew she saw him somewhere before and then realized she had seen him at the airport.

At least she thought she had.

"You look like," she made herself stop. If she was correct and Chago had been at the airport when Javier picked her up then that meant that Chago most likely knew about her trip which made sense considering his reference to Birger. Still, something about this didn't sit right. Birger didn't strike her as the kind of person who would secretly send someone to follow her around. He seemed a bit more direct than that. Like he would have told her he had sent someone to help her.

She made a mental note to reach out to Birger. She knew she had taken off sooner than he liked, but hopefully he wouldn't take it personally and would return her calls.

If she could only get into Daniel's laptop. He must have some of the missing pieces to this. And there seemed to be tons of missing pieces. Like, who was this guy?

She brushed aside all of these unanswered questions and refocused on the moment at hand. "I need to check on Javier," she said. "Thanks for stopping me from making an ass of myself."

"You mean committing murder?" he said. His tone remained neutral. His stance strong and authoritative.

"Well, I guess." As she made her way back inside the hospital, she felt her phone buzz.

Margarite.

It would have to wait.

INTERLUDE 23 – DANIEL'S GREAT ESCAPE

I don't think I ever drove so fast in my life. It's a miracle I didn't get pulled over. Probably helped that it was, like, three in the morning. All the cops on patrol had probably fallen asleep.

I got back to my apartment and locked my door like my life depended on it, because I fucking well knew that it did.

That's when I started writing this and making the arrangements for our trip to Sweden.

For now, at least until we can get to Sweden and find out our truth, I'm going to lay low. I know you won't like it, but I'll have to miss our movie nights and weekly takeout nights. I'm not going to answer my door or the phone. Too many people seemed to know a shit-ton more about me than even I knew and that's not good.

That's terrifying.

I know this sounds asinine and all conspiracy-theory-ish, but I am not sure who to trust. For now, I'm going to disappear. You are the only soul I've known my whole life. I truly hope that the fucked-up stuff I saw was just some freakish once-in-a-lifetime thing that has nothing to do with you or me. Something inside me says that when you finally see this, you will probably be reading this alone.

Tell Javier I miss him.

I love you, Luna. Thank you for being my awesome sister.

CHAPTER TWENTY-SEVEN

She sat outside of the operating room where they worked on Javier. The hall was abuzz with patients being wheeled from one room to another. Nurses with assistants tagged along to make sure the patients got to where they needed to go. The air filled with sounds of monitors and pagers and the urgency of care. Moments before, it had felt nearly vacant with her focus on the invader and subsequent gun fight. Now as she waited while Javier was operated on, she felt like she was in the thick of the action. Admittedly, action that she put herself in the center of.

She couldn't stand the thought of being in a waiting room. She was thankful that no one made her sit in one. She needed to be as close to Javier as possible.

After careful consideration, she called Margarite.

"I know this sounds crazy but we were held at gunpoint." Luna paused. She left out the bonding to Javier part, the changing part, and the getting knocked over by another shapeshifter part. Those bits of information didn't need to be shared or acknowledged.

"What?" Margarite said. "Oh my God. Luna. Is he okay?"

"He's in surgery now."

Luna hoped that Margarite's kindness would hold out. She felt like she had asked her employer for a lot considering Margarite had willingly let Luna have time off for her brother's death, then let her have off to go to Sweden, and now this. Fingers crossed no more crazy drama came up anytime soon, even though Luna didn't hold her breath. She had a sneaking suspicion that much more was coming. When and what, only time would tell.

"Please, take care of him and you," Margarite said. "Just keep me posted, okay?"

"Thank you."

She hung up her iPhone and looked over to see Chago approaching. His gray t-shirt tucked into black stretch jeans. His body was much more fit than Luna had previously noticed. In reality, she wasn't paying attention to his body before. She was more focused on getting him the hell off of her so she could continue with her unmasked avenger routine.

How the hell did this man get into this part of the hospital? Typically, only close family was allowed back here and this guy wasn't even a known commodity. He must have said something magical and incredibly endearing to get to this point. Looking at him, she wouldn't be surprised if he had charmed his way in. He evidently had the ability to warm-up-to and enchant the cold, rule-following nurse at the desk who had stopped her earlier. She wasn't surprised at all. He smiled, a small comforting grin, and then took a seat next to Luna.

"You must be careful," Chago said. He looked away from her and allowed his words to travel to her brain and sit within her mind. She felt them inside of her. The surreal nature of their presence gave her pause.

Were these the words of a threat? What did he mean by

them? She knew that what she had attempted with Paul was dangerous and illegal but, at this moment, she didn't care. Her priority was Javier, one of the few people in this world she cared for incredibly deeply. She didn't even know this naysayer who sat next to her.

"I know you don't want to hear my words, Luna Auber, but you must be cautious. There's much more going on here than you are aware."

"Really?" No shit, Sherlock, she thought. She didn't need this odd guy to show up on her doorstep in order to come to that conclusion. Fuck, if anyone was tracking all this mess, they would have told him to stop stating the obvious because...well...*duh*.

"Excuse us." A police officer approached Luna and Chago from the ER entrance. His uniform was clean and tidy. She would have expected him to be a bit more haphazard after the morning's events. "I wonder if I could ask you a few questions."

"Sure," Luna said. She figured it was better to share all that she knew, at least all that she could share, with the officer. Plus she bet that he had no idea what her intentions were regarding Paul. Based on everyone's lack of response to her actions, she also bet that there was something about her changing or rather, any shapeshifter changing, that acted like a cloak of invisibility so that either regular folks didn't see it or they didn't remember it. Something she planned on testing out later, in a less stressful and safer environment.

And then she began sharing her version of the morning's events. She shared as much as she thought she could.

Chago sat in stunned amazement, like he couldn't believe Luna's candor. Once or twice he gave her a warning look when they reached a part in the retelling that could involve shapeshifters or bonding or something else of their otherworld. Of course she didn't share those details. She knew better. The officer took notes with ferocity. It was like he thought she gave him the secret to The Holy Grail.

As she relayed information, Chago primarily acted preoccupied and texted someone on his phone. When Luna finished up, the officer thanked her.

"Sir," he said to Chago. "Would you like to make a statement?"

Chago finished texting something and then said, "My apologies. I need to leave. I have a personal emergency I need to take care of." He put his phone in his jacket pocket. "Nothing for the police to be concerned of, but something that I need to address immediately. Besides, I arrived after all these events, and would provide nothing more than Miss Auber told you."

Chago stood and turned to Luna. He pulled something out of his back pocket. "Here's my card. If you need anything then reach out. Either way, I'll be in touch." He handed her and the officer his business card. Underneath his name and phone number were the initials TRG. As he made his way down the corridor, she swore she saw Chago and Paul acknowledge one another. She made a mental note of it and then refocused on the efforts at hand.

INTERLUDE 24 – DANIEL IN HIDING

The last few weeks have been bizarre. I never believed in conspiracies, but damn. There is so much I want to tell you, I truly do. There is so much for you to know. So much I swear that I still don't understand. One thing I'm sure of, it's time for me to prepare for the worst. There's been so much weird shit. Odd cars with strangers hanging outside my apartment complex at all hours of the night. Bizarre phone calls with no one on the other line. People pacing back and forth outside my apartment door like they are just waiting for me to leave. People I don't know messaging me and asking questions and when I try to find out who they are, they suddenly disappear. Like the text literally disappears from my phone like it never happened.

And that guy who invited me to the party in the mansion? Yeah, his account on Ancestry.com has been shut down and half those people who were at the party either disappeared from the site or they just aren't showing up anymore. It's like a fucking ghost town on those boards. Every once in a while someone pops up and is all friendly. Then the person starts asking questions like they're digging for info. When I call them on it, they disappear.

I went ahead and created alias accounts just in case someone's tracking me. You know, so I can still get info but without them knowing it's me. At least that's what I thought. I'm too scared to use my own accounts. I don't want anyone knowing what I'm doing or where I am. Even then, I swear they know. Every day this just gets weirder and weirder. I'd go someplace else but I'm afraid that if I step out of my apartment someone's going to follow me. It's safer to stay here and lay low.

Luna – I've set up my last will and testament. I know you think I'm overreacting. And that's okay. I just want to be sure you're covered. In it, I've left you instructions. I gave up on the idea that we're going to Sweden together. I'm almost positive you're going to need to do the trip alone. If it means that it saves your life, then it'll be more than worth it. If it means that you discover about our heritage, our birthrights, then I know it'll be worth it. I just want to be sure you are okay.

I reached out to Birger, you know the guy who told me about The Lycanthrope Society and asked me to join, and I told him it was time for me to find out what was really going on. I let him know about you and hinted to him about what happened at the mansion. I couldn't get into too much detail because I have no idea who is monitoring my email and my activities on those message boards. I hope he understood what I was telling him.

He hooked me up with Bo, a tour guide who specializes in the Birka and everything in that town. He told me exactly what tour to take, what to ask for, where to stay. He even told me to find Bo so that he can go with us to see Birger.

Luna, I hope you're reading this with me by your side. I hope we are safely in your living room and enjoying our Friday night takeout. Especially my favorite, the veggie pizza with cheese stuffed crust and pepperoni bread. I hope Javier is with us and we are saying our farewells before we get on the plane. I hope that we find the cure together and discover the truth about The Lycanthrope Society and all that it means to us. I hope I'm just being paranoid and all of this is my imagination.

I have a meeting tonight that should either confirm that we're good or, well, we'll see. I love you, sis. Fingers crossed, see you soon.

CHAPTER TWENTY-EIGHT

The officer looked down at Chago's card and asked Luna, "Who was that guy?"

"Damned if I know." Luna pocketed the card and looked over the policeman's shoulder and into the waiting room. She noted two people who seemed very familiar. One of whom she swore she saw at the airport. Was he with Chago? The more she thought about it, the more she swore she had seen them both at the airport when she got off the plane. What the hell? Neither of them noticed her. They were preoccupied with their phones.

At least she didn't think they saw her.

Just as she was about to get up and question the guy as to who he was and why he happened to be wherever she was, Javier's doctor came out of the surgery room.

He noted Luna. Thankfully, she had been a known entity at the hospital for some time so he didn't hesitate in giving her an update.

"At this point, I think he'll be okay," the doctor said. "He's lucky to have such a great partner in you."

"Thanks," Luna said. "Is it okay for me to visit with him?"

The doctor was a guy Luna knew tangentially. Javier had worked with him a few times but he hadn't talked about him at length. A kind man, Luna felt comforted that he was the one to perform the surgery on soon-to-be fiancé.

"We're wheeling him into the staging area now. Once we're sure he's absolutely stable, he'll be moved into his own hospital room. I'll have the nurse call you as soon as it's okay to visit with him."

"Thank you," Luna said with a relief she hadn't felt in ages. The thought of losing Javier on top of everything else nearly brought her to her knees.

She called her parents to let them know what happened. "Could you call Javier's mom? I want to stay with him as long as I can. I'll call them later, okay?"

"Of course," Luna's mom replied. "Are you sure you're okay?" Her tone softened with concern.

Luna hesitated. Should she tell the truth or what she thought her mother needed to hear? "I'll be fine," Luna said. She split the difference. "Mom?" Luna started. With everything that had happened, she needed to know. "Did Daniel tell you about what he was doing?"

"What do you mean? Do you mean exploring your heritage?"

"I guess," Luna said. "I guess you could call it that." She bit her lower lip.

"Your father and I have always believed that you need to discover your own path. You need to decide what's right for you."

"Right." Luna held these words in her mind and mulled them over. She knew that this was true and that she had to discover what was right for her, but it didn't entirely answer her question. "He didn't mention anything else? About any societies or groups or clubs?"

Her mom paused for a moment like she contemplated the question a bit more. "Not that I can remember," she said. "Hold on a sec." Luna heard her mother talk to her dad in the background, repeating the questions. "No, dear. Nothing like that."

"Ok–"

"That said, your father did mention that Danny had been acting weird for a bit. Not answering the phone. Only responding to brief texts. Not coming to the house like he used to. I guess we should have seen it as a sign." Her mother's voice trailed off.

"I guess so." Luna looked down the hallway at the waiting room and noted that the two strangers had moved on. Maybe their presence was just her imagination. Maybe they had nothing to do with this mess. "I love you, Mom. I'll come by later this week. Please tell Dad I love him too," Luna said and hung up.

She returned to the stiff and cold plastic seat next to the operating room. She wrapped her arms around her chest and snuggled back into the chair. The jetlag and long days had caught up with her and she swiftly fell asleep. Her body's need for rest outweighed her mental activities. Within moments, her dreams filled with Freya and Lovisa.

INTERLUDE 25 – FREYA BECOMES THE BIRKA

Day after day, I readied for the renewed fighting. Each day brought more contention with additional invasions to the intimate village. The townsfolk needed our protection and so we offered it.

I wore my favorite battle armor Papa had made for me so long ago. The chest, arm, and leg protection proved necessary against these intruders. This had been the same battle armor we used as a model for Lovisa's gear. With each fight, our daughter and I stood side-by-side. I had always been proud of her and I was doubly proud of her on these days. Hiwa had taught Lovisa a spell to identify a shapeshifter, even if the fighter had not changed yet. We used that to our advantage. It enabled us to know what techniques would be successful in the throes of the latest threat because we knew what we were up against. It also allowed us to only shapeshift when absolutely necessary.

We led villagers and other warriors into battle, at least those who had volunteered to help. Thankful for their presence, without them we would never have been able to fight off these devils. We used swords, knives, and fists to keep the intruders at bay. With each fight, the feeling of metal sunken into flesh filled me with sadness. Even if they attacked us, the loss of life is something that I would never find solace in. I looked behind me as we left the battlefield, the greenery littered with bodies. The metallic scent of blood filled the air. The stench of anger, fear, and hatred covered our bodies. I looked to our daughter to be sure she was alright.

Her own stance filled with despondency.

She asked what we could do to prevent such loss. How could we avoid this tragedy. My response was for us to simply pray for the fallen. And so we did. Each night we gathered our fellow warriors and prayed for those who lost their lives. We clutched each other's hands and lowered our heads in deference. No matter if he or she be a friend or foe, the loss of life needed to be acknowledged and grieved.

On this day, although our souls were in grief, our bodies were ripe and energized from the exertion and thrill of blade against blade and fist to fist. Our limbs shook from it. Our fellow warriors did their best to rest nearby. Not knowing what the future would hold, they needed to rest in preparation for the potential of additional fights.

The initial invasion, the day that Lovisa and I sold our products in the town market, had been temporarily unsuccessful. The attackers clearly were unaware that Wolf Warriors had been left behind, which made sense considering you and I never revealed my and Lovisa's abilities. During that initial fight, we fought the bastards back, in wolf form, and returned to our shop.

That is where we regrouped and found other warriors, both villagers and king's guards who had similarly retired from the elite guard or from the standing guard. We reached out to Hiwa and obtained her assistance in potions and spells to assist in the battles.

The way these invaders came into town with such confidence, my instincts told me there were many more behind them.

Sadly, they proved me right within days.

I prayed that the king and his men would return shortly. We needed all of the assistance we could obtain. I looked over at our daughter covered in a sheen of sweat, her breath heavy from exhaustion. I am incredibly thankful that our daughter grew to be such a skilled and talented warrior.

Ulf, you would be so proud of her. She has grown to be a mirror of you. Her height tall, her figure lean, her hair a long beautiful black that flowed down her back. Her jawline of a similar chisel, her eyes stunning with flecks of gold. With her amazing warrior spirit and spiritual soul, she is definitely our daughter.

She looked up at the sky as it filled with clouds. In the distance, they came alive with thunder. Beyond the hills before us, lightning struck repeatedly in the darkening sky. Behind us, the village had been locked down. Around us, our fellow fighters rested in preparation for the next insurgence. Our fellow warriors began to rise as they saw new daemons come over the hills before us. Lovisa whispered a prayer and readied her blade for the impending fight.

An attack renewed. With a fierce yell, a bastard moved on our daughter who proceeded to slash her blade against him, their battle gear clashed. Neither's blow was successful. Our daughter's look changed to that of anger and determination.

With a cry, I barreled forward and slammed into the warrior who tried to take down my child. I ripped his helmet from him and saw the face of a familiar. Of one I had grown to consider family. The face of Chago.

He had been our advocate, one of our tribe and yet here he tried to eliminate our daughter. Another of the Wolf Guard, Chago had once been a dear friend to us. When I had first sought out answers to your shifting, he had been among the guards who guided me. What brought him to betray our land? Betray us? He had ushered this faction through our lands and against our people. The treachery drove deep within me. I moved forward to terminate his threat. How dare he do such things? No matter what he had done for us in the past, this warranted his death.

The stun of his face kept me in place for a moment too long as it provided time for another invading warrior to come forward to interrupt my killing blow. The other warrior drove me to the ground and took me off kilter. Chago motioned to leave me. The warrior then made his way towards our girl.

"How dare you!" Chago declared, his attention fully focused back on me. "There will be consequences for your actions."

I sat up. "Who are you to believe that you have the right to make such judgements?"

"You must do as I say, dear sibling." Chago regained his composure and towered over me. "We are meant to be in charge, not the fool king. We are meant to be gods."

What was this foolishness? "Gods? We are meant to live in tandem. To protect and care for each other."

Chago laughed. "You believe the false words of the king. He says this to keep us in line because without our belief in him, he cannot rule." He locked his eyes on me. "Freya, join us. This is the first of many lands we will rightfully overtake. We are meant to be the ruling species, not humans."

I had heard Chago utter similar sentiments through the years but never so adamantly, never with such derision. Before now his intonation was such that I simply ignored his words as those of folly. But today, his tone was filled with passion and conviction. This did not intimidate me.

Behind him I saw Lovisa. She took the distraction of Chago and my interaction to eliminate the other warrior. The one who had knocked me over. She did so with a single clean slash that took off his head. It was the only clean way to eliminate his threat considering he wore armor.

I knew, based on the craftsmanship of the battle gear, that I had most likely molded it when this traitor had been with the king. It saddened me that one who used to be like kin turned out to be a monster. He only wanted power and to destroy.

After all that we had seen, I should have been used to such truths and understood that no matter what, there would always be beings like this in the world. But I did not.

Unaware of what had occurred behind him and in my absence of a response, Chago must have known that I did not agree. My expression revealed more than I had intended because Chago's face turned sinister. His teeth lengthened, sharpened. His eyes darkened to a deep blood red. I turned away from him and lept up to act as a distraction to allow Lovisa to perform the final blow. She stood behind him at the ready. But, in that moment when I was turned away from him, Chago slashed at my throat as if he brought forward lightning and was eager to perform the final strike.

CHAPTER TWENTY-NINE

L una screamed awake and nearly fell out of her chair. She was startled, dumbstruck, as she slowly recovered from her dream. She looked around and realized she was still in the hospital. Before her, a nurse in scrubs who had clearly recently finished a procedure in the operating room, leaned in to offer help. "Are you okay?" the medical practitioner asked.

"I'm fine." She meekly waved off the nurse and proceeded to shake off the lingering feelings of the dreams. Luna ran her hands through her hair and stretched to regain her composure. "Sorry about that." She softly smiled.

She had become aware of the ever-present announcements over the loudspeaker, the tell-tale monitors beeping at patients' bedsides, the lingering smell of bleach and antiseptics.

She checked her phone and found a text from an ER nurse specifying Javier's room and status. Luna took this opportunity to go to his bedside.

The room had a standard setup with two beds. Javier's bed was closer to the window, the shades shut, the room nearly dark with a small bit of light seeping in from the hallway. The neighboring bed was neatly made and clearly unoccupied.

Luna entered and quietly made her way to his side. Remnants of her dream continued to haunt her.

That dream had felt so real. It felt more like a memory than a dream. She wasn't sure she believed in such things, but it felt like she had somehow inherited Freya's memory. Was this a gift? A warning? If it was an inherited memory and not just a dream then how the hell did Chago live this long? That couldn't be possible, *could it?*

If it was possible then was this all a result of some fancy spell that Hiwa had cast on him? Or maybe he stole the abilities from the seeress? Maybe he was a seer? Her questions piled higher and higher. She felt for his card in her pocket as Javier shifted in the bed.

Unsettled in his sleep, Luna refocused on Javier. Her need to comfort him and verify he was okay overpowered the lingering questions and thoughts. She stood over him and gently brushed the hair from his face. She had missed this face, even though she had seen him only moments before.

His body bore an overall sheen of sweat. She hoped he didn't battle an infection. She made a mental note to point the possibility out to the nurse when she made her rounds.

"I love you," Luna whispered.

She knew she didn't tell him this often enough. In this moment, she wished she had shared her feelings with him more. Her gaze became tender with the thoughts.

"Luna." The surgeon stood at the door. Chestnut hair with swarthy skin, Luna swore his heritage must have been of Mediterranean descent. Average height and weight, what made him striking was his calm demeanor. In such a hectic environment, he brought forward strength and calm where others might be overpowering. He motioned for her to come into the hallway.

She lightly kissed Javier on the forehead. "I'll be right back."

The doctor greeted her, clipboard in hand. He had been reviewing Javier's charts. "I thought it was important to tell you that he will recover but it will be some time."

"Oh." Somewhere deep inside, Luna hoped that the little infusion of her blood may have given him superpowers. She had no idea what superpowers because she didn't actually understand what all of this meant.

"I wouldn't tell a regular visitor this information, but since you practically live here and Javier has it specified in his paperwork that you are to represent him in times when he cannot represent himself, I figured it was okay." He paused. Luna was surprised that he remembered her. She never thought that she left an impression. She simply visited her boyfriend when he had a shift. "It's a miracle he's alive."

A slight grin came across her face. So there was more to this Lycanthrope stuff than she knew. In her bones she figured this was true. She prayed that the infusion of her blood along with the incantation would only continue to help him heal.

She needed to better understand what these new powers were. She needed to talk to Birger and get into her brother's laptop. There had to be more information. She suddenly regretted taking off from Sweden so abruptly and not staying to learn more. She only hoped Birger would be willing to continue to teach her and guide her.

"Do you understand?" The surgeon asked adamantly. He must have misunderstood her grin for something sinister or childish.

She frowned and made an extra effort to demonstrate concern. "Yes, sir. I understand. I'm just thankful he's alive."

The doctor eased back and returned to his calmer demeanor.

She motioned to Javier. "I need to take care of some things. Can you have someone call me if his status changes?" she asked. "I won't be long."

CHAPTER THIRTY

Luna got into her car, a small beat-up gray Mazda her parents helped her buy when she had graduated from culinary school. They got it used and it had already seen more than ten years, but she didn't care. They didn't have a lot of money, so she was incredibly grateful for their help. She made sure to pay them back within the first year of graduation. She loved this little putt-putt car more than she could describe. As she maneuvered the streets to Javier's parents' home, she noted a vehicle trying to remain obscure.

It didn't work.

Even as she got out of her car and walked up to his parents' modest two story row home in the heart of East Camden, the black car stayed at the corner of the street, just within eyeshot. She decided to let them observe her. The time would come when she could approach them but for now she focused on her tasks at hand.

Javier's familial home had been occupied by his parents and his mom's parents before them. Luna felt bad that she hadn't called them directly, but, in the moment, she really wanted to keep her focus on Javier and what was happening in the hospital. So many weird things, so many unanswered questions.

Including the question of who tailed her and hovered at the end of the street.

She figured they didn't realize she had seen them, but after growing up in this town, and considering her career, she pretty much knew everyone and everyone pretty much knew her. So the black Hyundai Accent which had been on every block really stood out considering no one in the neighborhood had a similar car.

Plus she drove the "Luna way" by zigzagging through streets and following the same directions she followed when she walked. She didn't take the easiest or the shortest paths. These facts made the Hyundai Accent an even more obvious tail.

The brick row home had only two bedrooms - both on the second floor. One for the parents and one that had been shared among Javier and his siblings. The first floor had a kitchen, a common sitting area, and a backroom. The yard was small and gated. Plastic-covered windows kept the heat in during the freezing winters. Luna opened the gate, walked onto the porch, and respectfully knocked at the front door.

His mama answered. His dad, a foreman for PECO Energy, must have been at work.

"Luna!" The small and stout woman with nary a wrinkle and long salt and pepper hair hugged Luna in the threshold of the open door. "Please, come in. Come in."

Just looking at Mrs. Rodriguez gave Luna comfort. Luna had spent many afternoons as a teenager hanging out in this intimate home being fed the most amazing tamales and plantains.

Mrs. Rodriguez waved her into the living room and they sat

on the couch, all of the furniture covered in plastic. This was an old habit that many of the older families in Camden had. The clear plastic ensured the furniture lasted longer while reducing the amount they had to clean it. When she sat down, Luna's butt made the couch cushion's resistance squeak in protest.

"Where is everyone?" Luna asked.

"Errands, working. The usual," Mrs. Rodriguez answered. Luna was thankful for this. It meant she could spend focused time with Mrs. Rodriguez. But part of her felt guilty like she should be doing more. What else she should be doing, she wasn't quite sure.

She waited for Mrs. Rodriguez to sit and then reiterated what she had told her mom to tell them. His mom's face looked concerned, nearly grave. Luna didn't know what else to do but she couldn't leave her soon-to-be-mama-in-law like this.

"The doctor said he'll be fine." Luna reached out and held her hand. "I'll make sure of it."

Mrs. Rodriguez, nearly in tears, squeezed Luna's hand. "Thank you for being there for him. You've been together so long. I know he can feel you with him."

Luna nodded her head in thanks. She knew she had left out key information in the retelling of what the doctor had said, but as she told Mrs. Rodriguez of the dramatic scene with the drug addict and the doctor, she knew she had to go back to the police and tell them what she saw Paul do. Even though she had been candid when she spoke to the one officer in the hospital, she simply couldn't go any longer without telling him everything - well, everything within reason. Could she trust him? That question lingered. Even with it present, she knew she had to at least test the waters.

Javier deserved better.

She thanked his mom for talking to her and suggested she wait a day or two before visiting.

"The last time I saw him, he was still unconscious. You may want to wait until he knows you are there."

"He will know, *mi amore*. He will know." Mrs. Rodriguez smiled and hugged her. "Let us pray for his fast recovery." They lowered their heads in silent prayer. Luna was thankful that she could be there, if even in such a small way.

Once the prayer was done, she politely excused herself and made her way to her car. As she opened the car door, she looked around to see if that Hyundai was still present. At that moment, she didn't see it.

Good, she thought.

Maybe they had given up. She checked her phone as she started the car and saw that Margarite had called.

She knew the bakery had closed for the day, but Luna needed to let her know she'd be back later that night. She had too much to do to leave Margarite in the lurch. The bakery had been too important to both of them. She prompted Siri to call her employer.

"Is everything okay?" Were the first words out of Luna's mouth. She didn't even bother with hello.

"Of course, I just wanted to check on you. How's Javier?"

Luna turned the corner towards the police station. "He's stable, thank god. I can't even describe how awful today has been. But I will be back tonight. I have a few more things to do to prepare for tomorrow."

"You don't have to," Margarite said. "We have it covered. You can handle the rest in the morning."

"It's too important. I can't let our customers down." They need us, Luna thought.

Even though others may have thought their jobs creating confections was not important, Luna would never agree with that assessment. Customers waited impatiently for a holiday or anniversary celebration to order a specialty. Some virtually created holidays to have an excuse to have Luna create a special dessert. The joy it brought to them was invaluable. More than one customer had returned explicitly to tell them as much. That was the real reason Luna did her job, to make people happy.

CHAPTER THIRTY-ONE

At the station, Luna hunted down the police officer she had met in the hospital. She had to dig for the card he gave her - "Officer Alesandro Carlin." She didn't know what she expected when she found him, but he was sitting at his desk reviewing something on his computer. He looked surprised to see her.

"Hello, Ms. Auber. May I help you?" He motioned to the green cushioned chair positioned at the side of his desk.

Not wanting to lose her drive, fresh from seeing Mrs. Rodriguez, she allowed her passion to fly through every pore as she described the scene and what she saw Paul do.

"You have to understand, Paul was like family," Luna said. "How could he use the override on the medicine cabinet when we were being attacked by that addict? How could he set Javier up like that?" She asked the rhetorical questions of Officer Carlin who simply nodded in acknowledgement.

She didn't know why, but she had hoped he would agree. She wanted him to be as impassioned as she was. She wanted him to show the same level of frustration, horror, and disbelief. Instead, he simply listened.

In her pocket she thumbed Chago's card and her runes. She knew Chago had said not to do anything, but what did he know? She still didn't understand what he had to do with all of this. And how did he know Paul? Him being in her dream freaked her out, but it didn't really mean anything, right? It was only a dream. Probably a sign of how overtired she truly was.

"Thank you for coming out, ma'am." The officer wrote a few words on his notepad, just like she saw in old detective shows. "We appreciate the time."

"Does this mean you'll bring him in?" She had no idea if this was pertinent. She didn't know if police brought people in like they did in the movies or if that was a made-up thing. Either way, she wanted to know if they were going to do something.

"We can't promise that we will take him into custody," he said. "We will talk to him."

"But that's not enough!" she exclaimed.

Did he simply say whatever he thought would calm her down?

"He needs to be arrested," she continued. "There needs to be justice!" She slammed her fist down onto the desk, just like she saw in Dragnet. The officer's look of surprise made her take a step back.

"I'm sorry," she said. She quieted her voice. The disappointment dripped from her words. "I just can't believe that he won't be arrested."

"I understand your concern, but unless we get more to go on than this, then unfortunately there's nothing we can do. You can't be sure of his intentions or if he was pushing an override alarm. Your boy - fiancé - was shot by a drug addict, not by a coworker."

Luna clutched Chago's card in her palm as the runes rested against her fingers.

"Fine," her tone determined and her voice clipped. "Thank you."

She abruptly got up and headed for the door. She returned to her car and sat down behind the wheel. She needed to clear her head. Just as she took in a deep breath, a few spaces away, she saw the same Hyundai. She had a few choices. She could let this go, she could take care of things herself, or she could call Chago. She had to admit that taking care of things herself, now that she had a chance to really think it through, wasn't the best idea.

Something in her gut told her that Chago may have an alternative idea. So she called. What should she say? That Javier deserved retribution? He had already made it clear that he sided with the police, that he, too, viewed Paul as innocent, and Luna's reactions as being extreme. Even with these truths, she hoped that she could change his mind.

"Interesting," Chago said when Luna relayed the officer's statement.

"This isn't right," Luna said. She controlled her voice from escalating, knowing that keeping her tone regulated was more effective than freaking out.

"And?"

"We need to do something." She said this as a matter of fact. But if she was acting like she knew of something they could do, in the grand scheme of things, she did not. At least nothing legal. She hoped with all of her being that he would reveal some magical something that would make everything alright.

Chago inhaled deeply through his nose, slowly exhaled, and replied. "Fine. Meet me in an hour."

CHAPTER THIRTY-TWO

Luna followed Chago's detailed instructions of where to go and how to get there. On the way, she stopped off at her place and picked up Daniel's laptop. She figured she'd play with the passwords while she fulfilled orders later in the night. Too jazzed from the day's activities, she knew she'd be up late.

She drove up to the dramatic four-story Colonial brick home with a circular driveway and fountain. The day had flown by and she glanced at the sun as it lowered behind the home.

"Damn," she muttered. She walked up the stairs to the front door. Without a word, the door opened inward. She looked up to see a security camera on the outer door frame.

"Yeah, like that's not creepy," she said to herself.

She entered the main hall with white marble floors and a winding staircase like something from *Gone with the Wind*.

"Double damn."

At the top of the stairs, Chago leaned forward onto the railing. She could just see him raising an eyebrow.

"You left too soon," he said.

Before she could ask what the hell he talked about, he continued. "Sweden. You left too soon. There was a reason Daniel sent you."

INTERLUDE 26 – CHAGO'S TRUTH – HIS FIRST MEETING WITH DANIEL

I had seen Daniel in the Lycanthrope Society's gathering, Chago began. Our engagement had originally intended to be an informal drop by. This had been our opportunity to talk and possibly recruit some members of TLS which you may be more familiar with as The Lycanthrope Society, to TRG or The Righteous Group as we are formally known. TLS had been much more successful in unearthing shapeshifters through social media and online so we often leveraged their gatherings to further blossom our membership. Our own organization's methods for identification remained grounded in word-of-mouth and through familial gatherings. In the modern world, this resulted in very limited successes considering the number of our kind who had been abandoned or orphaned by their families. The long history of shapeshifters has been complex and bloody.

Something I will share with you another time.

I quickly realized that Daniel had been new to our kind when, during the Group Transformation, he seemed out of sorts or rather panicked. The GT was a common method of greeting among our kind. A symbolic showing of acceptance and transparency, if you will.

While the rest of those present had greater control of their shifting, Daniel's change seemed chaotic, frantic. His emotional response was sheer terror.

Unfortunately, that expansive energy resulted in a ripple effect among those present. The younger shapeshifters who hadn't been thoroughly trained lost control of their natural hunger which then resulted in unintended and saddening consequences. I won't go into details but what I can tell you is that we went to great lengths to clean up after the tragic activities.

That said, as soon as I saw Daniel, I knew his origins. It was indicative in his stance, fur, and bone structure. There are key indicators of a pureblood versus one who has been given our gifts. He was definitely a pureblood. And based on his responses to all that had occurred he had no idea what it meant to be a lycanthrope, let alone to fully shapeshift among peers.

Once we had taken care of the consequences related to the TLS gathering, I inquired for Daniel at his residence. He did not answer his phone and was not responsive to inquiries via email or on the community boards. I knew I needed to talk to him to help him gain a greater understanding of his abilities. Someone with that much raw power needed guidance, a mentor, a coach. Very few among our kind would have the ability to properly train him. And so I visited him at his home.

At first, he refused to answer the door, which initially seemed quite odd, but on reflection, considering he had fully shifted with no guidance nor training, his hesitancy made perfect sense.

"Daniel, I'm here to help you," I had said through the door. "I know of your origins."

That comment got him to peer through the door's peep-hole. I waved.

"I'm Chago Allard. I have spoken to Birger. He recommended I visit with you."

That was a lie. I hadn't spoken to Birger about Daniel. I didn't need to. I knew from reviewing the Ancestry.com community boards that the one person Daniel interacted with the most was Birger and Birger's bloodline was more infamous than my own. Well, almost.

Upon hearing Birger's name, Daniel began unlocking the main door, which he'd clearly fortified with additional locks considering the amount of time it took to finally open it even a tad.

"Who are you?" he asked. I could feel his fear vibrate the space between us.

If I didn't know any better, I'd bet he had a weapon on him, which wouldn't be too wise considering my skill with nearly any object, lethal or not.

"Chago Allard. I have been asked to visit with you. To ensure you were okay and to possibly *help*." I put my emphasis on the word "help" since, based on his behavior, he definitely needed it. "I believe the events of the prior evening may have been a bit unexpected. I can help you understand them and prepare for them in the future."

"I'm never going to one of those again." His voice quavered.

"That's not the type of event I am referencing." I let him sit with that clarification for a moment. He waved me in and nearly slammed the door behind me. He shuffled me into the living room which contained an oversized denim blue couch and matching loveseat, a glass-top coffee table, and not much else.

He looked uncertain as to what to do with me so I asked if I could sit. He nodded in affirmation and then he took the seat across from me.

"First, may I ask, how did you come to attend the community event?"

"I was invited," he said, defensively.

"Interesting." No one from one of the more established families would have invited someone who hadn't discovered his capabilities yet, so this was quite doubtful. "I only ask because typically membership is required before one can attend. It's my understanding that you're still taking us under consideration."

He pondered that bit of information for a moment. He eyed me, I'm assuming, for a twinge of something that may have caused him not to respond with the utmost clarity and transparency.

"It was a general invitation. On one of the community chats."

"Ah," I leaned back. I'm sure the individual who put forth that note didn't realize a fledgling had access to the postings. I would need to follow up with the community board facilitators to ensure that they were clear on what could be posted and by whom. We could not have another instance like the previous evening. There are too few of us already to take such chances.

I took a moment to consider how to move forward. His mannerisms were agitated and he seemed to be having difficulty with his shaking, a telltale sign that he had not been trained in how to control his emotions and his shifting.

I wondered if he had shifted since the previous evening and if he had, would he remember? In some cases, those who are early in their transformations will shift in their sleep. Emotions from their dreams may trigger a full shift and their bestial selves may need to fulfill certain hungers while in that state. Once reawakened in human form, he may not have any idea what had occurred while in his alternate self. At least not until he was properly trained.

I cannot emphasize enough the importance of proper training. In this instance, I decided to be straightforward.

"You are royalty," I began. "You are one of the few purebloods. A Righteous One."

"What does that mean?" he asked. He wrapped himself more tightly in his sweater as if the room had suddenly plummeted in temperature.

"It means you have abilities you have not even begun to explore. And before you begin doing so, whether intentionally or not, you need to be true to your Lycanthrope bloodline. Understand it. Accept it. Embrace it. Honor it."

CHAPTER THIRTY-THREE

L una made her way up the interior staircase to Chago. He looked down upon the main hallway, his focus away from her, or so she thought. Her footsteps echoed the nearly empty expansive space. The interior of the home was dark except for the moonlight that broke through the windows and the second story doors. Luna had only seen places like this in movies. Someone's dream castle, she was sure that it had at least ten bedrooms, maybe more.

Chago dressed in dark denim pants and a tailored black shirt with silver buttons. He continued his gaze outward towards the main circle.

"You left Sweden too soon. Birger had more to tell you." Chago slowly turned towards her. His eyebrow raised as if he assessed her movements and reactions.

"What are you talking about?" The words came out more abruptly and confrontationally than she had intended, but she was tired and in light of Daniel's death, Javier's near-death, and the recent discovery that she wasn't technically human, well, she had had it.

"I'm sorry," she said. "I didn't mean to say it that way."

Chago stood up straight and motioned towards double doors leading to an outdoor patio.

"Nothing to be sorry for. I am sure these days have been traumatic. You called asking for my assistance. In order for you to understand what can and cannot be done, we must start with the information you did not obtain due to your hurried exit from the Nordic region."

Realizing that she needed to keep it under control and listen, she followed Chago's direction and headed out to the patio. If she thought the moonlight was bright from the inside, she was shocked at how much it glowed when she got to the patio that ran the length of the house.

Multitiered, the first story had stone stairs that led to the second story where Chago and Luna stood. He motioned for her to take a seat on the cushion of a metal chair, part of an outdoor patio set. A set that definitely did not come from the pages of a Costco catalog.

Chago made his way to the staircase leading to the lower-level patio and faced Luna.

"There is much to know about us, our history," he said. "We have existed alongside humans for time immemorial. Not just werewolves, but many forms."

He looked out over the field below. A manmade lake remained still in the gentle, quiet moonlight. A delicate ripple appeared as an insect lightly landed on the pristine pool.

"We Lycanthropes were often misunderstood. Those humans who observed our changings, our transformations, were terrified by the sight and the potential threat. Our kind were hunted down and murdered without a thought." Chago's voice turned softer and more ominous as if he remembered moments of deep pain. "Each country has its own legends and mythologies regarding our kind. In English, we appeared in the

Epic of Gilgamesh, in Greek mythology with the Legend of Lycaon, in Nordic mythology with Saga of the Volsungs, just to name a few. We are in Japanese legends, German legends, French. The list goes on and on."

Luna wondered where this was going. Why was he providing this information? So she wouldn't feel alienated or unique? What did this have to do with punishing Paul?

"You are from a long line of shapeshifters," he continued. "One that's considered of the rarest and purest bloodline." His gaze returned to her. "I come from a similar heritage whose last known origins was France. You and I," Chago's voice became pointed, drawing her in. "We are the rarest of the rare. With that comes much strength, power, gifts, and responsibility."

CHAPTER THIRTY-FOUR

L una listened. For her this was an exercise in patience and concentration. She wanted to jump up and tell Chago that she'd heard enough. She wanted a simple answer to a simple question – how can she get Paul to pay for his betrayal of Javier? Having faith that Javier would be okay, she felt as though she needed to do something to help him and the one thing she knew she could do was reveal Paul's disloyalty.

She observed Chago's movements, listened to his tone. He continued speaking about their bloodline and richness that came with the centuries represented by their ancestors. How Freya and Lovisa went to great pains to ensure that the generations after them were protected. Some of what Birger had covered. Some of it new.

"They secretly put those guidelines on Freya's gravesite. At that time, this action put Lovisa at incredible risk. She could have been questioned and called out. She could have been murdered for witchcraft." He said the word witchcraft with a disdainful tone. The tone similar to one that Luna had heard as

a child and when others questioned their lineage as they terrorized her and her brother.

"You ain't a Chinaman," one stranger had said to her when
she was a child. "I ain't never seen a Chinaman with no blue
eyes. What the hell are you?"

But Chago's statement was said with the intent to get Luna
to understand the conflicts of the time period for Lovisa and
Freya. How horribly their kind had been treated throughout
history and how much they had suffered and risked to look
after one another.

"Their lycanthropic gifts had been accepted by their village
because of their protection of the town, but if they knew of
Lovisa's additional gifts of the seeress, then she may not have
been able to live a full and complete life," Chago continued.
"Instead, she most likely would have been burned at the stake."

"What do you want from me?" Luna said. This time she
forced her voice to be softer, gentler. She didn't know how else
to ask the question. She realized she was the one who had asked
for this meeting, but everything in Chago's tone and retelling
implied that the outcome of this conversation would result in a
request.

"You were meant for more than baking." He said "baking"
like others said, "typing".

"I know I asked for us to talk. But all I want to know is
how I can get Paul in jail?" She got up. A part of her knew
that her fury against Paul was extreme. She knew that she
should be focused on Javier but this was the only way she
could think of to make things right for him. "Paul deserves to
be punished."

"You could have killed that fool with a simple flick of the
wrist," Chago said. "You have powers you haven't even begun
to comprehend."

"I was going to do that and you stopped me," her frustration seeped through her tone. Her muscles tensed. "Besides, what does that have to do with anything? I simply want retribution."

The rest will have to wait, she thought. Secretly, she was intrigued with the idea of the powers he referenced. He had mentioned other powers before, but Luna was too distracted with her true purpose of meeting him to do anything about it. She made a mental note to look into this further, just not now.

"You don't need me to tell you how to punish that idiot. You have that ability within you."

"Then why did you stop me?" Her voice elevated. Her frustration and anger were evident.

"Because that was not the time nor the place to do so. You must be smart about it. You were meant to be among the gods. I can teach you how to use your abilities. How to control your powers."

Use them? Birger had given plenty of instructions, she thought. She did not need this guy to teach her anything. All she needed could be obtained from Birger or from her brother's damn laptop – once she got into it.

"I'm fine. Thanks for the offer." Luna turned. She didn't need this. She didn't need this kind of "help". She thought he would give her some way to get the cops on her side or something. One minute he's stopping her from taking out Paul and the next minute he's talking all secret-society-conspiracy-theory-like. She cupped her car keys in her hand. She did not look towards him. Instead she made her way down the hallway. She knew Chago had not followed her based on the singular sound of her footfalls as they echoed through the expansive space.

"He has other uses," Chago called after her. "You must be more strategic in your actions."

She returned to the front staircase and the main entrance. Her awe of the place was reduced with the realization that he had no intention of helping her. He never did. He only wanted to indoctrinate her into his group for a reason she hadn't figured out. Based on the cloak and dagger behavior, it couldn't be good.

"You will return," Chago said. "Like others before. You will return."

INTERLUDE 27 – CHAGO'S VISIT
WITH DANIEL – CONTINUED

I spoke to Daniel of his heritage, his bloodline. From all that had been done up to this date for our kind and to our kind. He became more agitated the more I shared. I tried to calm him.

"We can help you," I said with tranquil inflection. An intonation of a doctor visiting a dying patient's bedside.

Surprisingly, no one, literally no one, had prepared Daniel for this. Normally our kind is eased into the realities of our lives, which is why and how organizations like TRG and TLS were originally formed. Without an individual receiving preparation for this with an adequate support system, a being could go insane.

The most important guidance to be given is regarding the physical changing and the associated hunger. Back in the times even before my own birth, guidance and training had been passed down orally and then later documented for posterity.

No one had tried to guide Daniel on our path. At least not that I had seen. This truly surprised me considering how frequently he interacted with Birger on the community boards, but perhaps Birger assumed Daniel had already developed his own network in New Jersey. Knowing that we have one of the larger chapters in the tri-state area, he most probably assumed as much. Again, why no one from our area had interacted with him in a more standard manner to indoctrinate him truly perplexed me.

Due to both organizations' missteps, I had to perform damage control. I had not seen the indoctrination of one of our kind so badly botched in over two hundred years. I made a mental note to hunt down whoever had invited this young man to our gathering and have a reckoning. We must never have this happen again. We've spent too many centuries refining, training, teaching, creating a community of the lycanthrope so that we could reach our full potential and be the world leaders we were meant to become. And then this happens. Something so seemingly simple yet a mishap that could destroy us all.

No exaggeration.

"Daniel," I said. "I can help you. Please listen –"

I reached out to touch him and he recoiled.

"No. None of this can be true. This is some kind of bizarre fever dream. I've read about these things." He shoved his chair farther away from me. "This isn't real."

Daniel got up and made his way to the intimate kitchen, poured a glass of ice water and then tossed it at himself. He shook it off, his breathing accelerated.

"Daniel. Myself and those with me, The Righteous Group, we can help you learn to use your gifts."

It was time for me to take control.

"Gifts? Have you lost your mind? Bodies were torn to shreds! I've never seen anything like it. That was flat out murder!" He exclaimed.

I eased my way closer to him, my movements slow and careful. I changed my tone so it was that of a parent soothing a distraught child. "Listen to me. Please. I need you to calm down."

"Calm down!? What are you talking about!?"

"Please." I made eye contact with him. Deepened my gaze and guided him with more controlled breathing; brought him back to a more centered place. Through a guided trance, I enabled him to quiet the shaking and regain control of his emotions. He made his way back to the living room and settled in the chair across from me.

"That's better. Now, whenever you feel agitated or your emotions are heightened, then repeat what we just performed. It will help you stay focused and centered."

Daniel simply looked across at me without a word. This time I could see that he was grounded. Good, the conversation could continue.

"If you join us, then I can teach you more skills like this. You are at the beginning stages of your maturity. As you advance, I can train you on how to optimize yourself and your gifts."

"What do you mean, the beginning," Daniel asked. His voice elevated a bit, not dramatically, but more of a warning for me to be careful how I advanced the conversation.

I assessed my choice of words. "Those of us from the purest of bloodlines have many gifts. You are among gods, Daniel. Those gods you've read about in mythology and legends, they were actually of the Lycanthrope and they were of the purest heritage." Typically, when I brought forth these facts, the newly indoctrinated became engaged, often enthralled. Many immediately requested to be fully immersed in this world. They wanted every last detail of our history.

This was not quite Daniel's response.

His posture became one of defensiveness. "Okay. I'll go along with that. So what?" He crossed his arms against his chest. The shaking renewed a bit. Not enough for me to be overly concerned, but enough to note.

What had this young man read or been told? At this juncture I questioned even what Birger, who tended to be a bit conservative in what he shared with those via online and digital means, had told him. It's as if he was either completely ignorant, in shock, or in denial – or all three. Knowing Birger, however, my guess was this had to be denial.

"Like all aging, you become stronger the older you are. You will go through stages of growth. You are in the equivalent of puberty. In the next few years, you will mature through puberty and with that maturation you will find that you will be able to shift at will as well as establish other abilities. For each of us, the gifts are a bit different. You may even find that your aging slows with each passing year." I did not want to go into depth regarding this aspect. Due to the generosity of Hiwa, only Freya and Ulf's line naturally had this talent. Some of us had to borrow the knowledge to enable those skills from the seeress.

Immediately, I knew when I revealed the last bit of truth that it was too much for him. The energy in the room became agitated. The air around Daniel swirled. His emotions escalated, even though he tried to control them, to what had occurred at the TLS gathering. Thankfully we weren't in a room full of other shapeshifters, so his transformation and hunger weren't triggered. And even more thankfully, they weren't triggering others like a stack of dominoes.

I focused on my own centering. I needed to be sure that I did not lose control. I was a bit surprised at how much effort it took. At such a young age, he shouldn't have this much power, especially without training. I had never seen anything like this. I continued to focus on staying in control and recalling those methods that I had been taught, oh so long ago to assist in these situations. This exchange confirmed for me that I would need to renew our alliances among humans. If Daniel had this much power then I could only imagine what others of his line had as well. I would need to develop alliances among those within the police and medical communities who had a natural curiosity regarding our gifts. Daniel's natural powers confirmed our need for their allegiance.

He began to shift, his voice darkened.

"NO," he commanded. "I will not join you."

"You are among a superior race, Daniel. You are among gods." I reached out my hand to get him to follow me. I needed him to look at me so I could ground him again, bring him back to a place of center, but he refused. "Just for a moment, Daniel." I motioned towards me to encourage him to look at me, but his gaze remained in the opposite direction. "Daniel. You are among friends. We can help you. I can help you. Please. Join us. Join The Righteous Group."

Without control Daniel began to shift at a rate I had not seen before. It was clear that he was completely out of control. I fought the natural instant urge to shift with him. Thankfully, I had centuries of experience and training behind me.

This boy had so much power, so much ability. He could exceed even Lovisa, even me. If only he would listen. If only he would allow me to lead him through this time. The raw power available to him, I had never seen so much within a fledgling.

"NO," Daniel repeated, his voice barely that of a human. His eyes had changed to a muted yellow, his nose elongated, his body curved in preparation for the final stages of shifting. "YOU will do NOTHING for ME. YOU LIE." His hands turned to claws and he stretched as if he readied to strike.

Although this saddened me, I knew what I had to do. "If you will not join us in this life, then you will join us in the next."

CHAPTER THIRTY-FIVE

All the way home, Luna played back her conversation with Chago. Either the man was insane or there was a lot to this that she simply didn't understand.

She thought Birger had revealed all that there was to know about her gifts, but based on what Chago said and Bo implied, it seemed as though she was wrong. She knew Birger had wanted her to stay, but so what? She just figured he had exaggerated.

She honestly resented everyone's secrecy at each and every turn.

Why couldn't they just be upfront about it all with her and with Daniel. "You are a werewolf and here's how you manage it," or something like that. Waiting this late in the game didn't make sense to her.

Why did she have to go to Sweden to find out her lineage?

Why couldn't Birger have done all of this remotely? Heck, he could have FedEx'ed the stuff she needed to gain control of her transformation. This wasn't the stone age. She didn't have to be in the same room as another person for them to talk.

That's what phones and Zoom calls and web calls were for. She chuckled to herself.

Admittedly, if someone would have said any of this to her a month ago, she would have laughed out loud, called the person a fool and moved on without another thought. Now?

Holy shit.

Luna made her way into her apartment and stared at the piles of printouts and notes. Chago's repeated references of "gifts" and "powers" had intrigued her and secretly confirmed her suspicions. This wasn't just about being a shapeshifter. There was a lot more for her to learn, she just needed to find the tools to teach her.

She decided that she would return to her quest to make sure Paul was rightly punished, she didn't need Chago for any guidance or advice, but for now all she wanted...no...all she needed...was to better understand exactly what this guy had talked about. She knew he was right. She could kill Paul in a second. Based on the implications of what happened in the last few days, she could do it without anyone noticing it. Just the thought was *INSANE*. That said, she still didn't fully understand it so she needed to be careful. Very careful. And find out more.

She went through the papers again, this time with an eye for Chago's name or TRG. She flipped through the pages. *Nada.* Not a single mention. She did find references to Birger, the same discussions she had found before, but nothing new. If she wanted something new, she had to go someplace new, and that meant to stop behaving like the very definition of insanity – doing the same thing over and over while expecting a different outcome.

She made herself a pot of coffee, texted Margarite to let her know she'd be in extra early in the morning to get a jump on things, and then opened Daniel's laptop. She had tried the passwords she could think of, the ones that would have resonated with him, and none had worked. He must have anticipated someone would try to bust into it. She stared at it, sipped her bitter and full-tasting coffee with a touch of milk, and mentally went through what keywords and combinations might have caught his eye in the last few months.

What did he care about? What was his focus?

And that's when she figured it out.

What was the name of the group he had felt aligned to?

The one that brought him to Birger and their truth, their lineage? She typed in a few variations of it and bingo...she was in.

A folder on the desktop had her name on it and inside were letters, almost like personal diary entries. As she began reading, she realized many were written directly to her. He must not have had the chance to print these out before he killed himself. Or he figured they would be more secure on his laptop and he knew she'd find a way to get into it. Something like that.

Either way, she was in.

She started sifting through the documents when the exhaustion of the day hit her and she dozed with papers splayed around her, laptop wide open, coffee pot half-empty.

CHAPTER THIRTY-SIX

S he entered the hallway with light grey walls and before her loomed the quote:

"The UN was not created to take mankind to heaven, but to save humanity from hell." -- Dag Hammarskjold, Second UN Secretary General. UN Security Council chamber

Behind her a voice proclaimed, "Humans created their own hell and we are here to take back the earth and make it heaven again."

When she tried to turn to see who said these words, both ominous and promising, she could not. The area before her became blurry and she found herself at the tip of a room with deep red leather chairs in a semicircle, four rows, all facing a mural displaying images of people at war and humans with wings going toward the sky. At each deep mahogany desk, persons wearing clothes of varying origins, from tan suits to kimonos to dashikis, listened to a man in the center of the circle. He spoke into a microphone with many of the guests wearing earphones and listening to his speech as it was translated to their native languages.

Luna tried to see the man, but the more she tried, the blurrier he became.

"It is time for us to take over where humans have ruined our lands. Global warming, war, poverty, hatred. These indecencies that cause us all pain. It is time to end this." He made these proclamations to a standing ovation. The applause filled the room. "Let us begin."

The mural moved aside to reveal a screen that spanned the wall. The gentleman motioned and those in the room began to shift and change. Their forms became that of wolves and bears as well as animals she had never seen before. Animals of myth and legend.

The screen before them divided into four sections. Each section showed a different location, a different city. The likes of New York, Hong Kong, Singapore, London, and Havana. In each city, animals the size of buildings stormed forward ripping apart structures, trampling anything and anyone in their paths.

"We reclaim our rightful place as the world's leaders. Our rightful seats among the gods."

Luna looked on in horror as innocent people were torn apart in the ravenous bloodthirsty actions of the invading creatures. True innocents ran and screamed in fear, simply trying to get away from these terrorist acts.

Luna called out to them, trying to warn them. She approached the creatures in the room and begged them to stop, please stop. "This isn't how to change the world," she said. "You don't right the world's ills with equal if not greater wrongs. Please, stop the mass murder. Stop the destruction."

Her cries went unanswered.

She tried to shift so they could see that she was one of them. She looked down at her hands, but nothing happened. All that Birger had taught her, had shown her, simply didn't work.

How could this be happening?

The images on the screen shifted to other cities in other parts of the world.

"Please listen to me," Luna begged. "Please stop the killing, please."

She ran to the man in the center, the leader of this horror. She tried to grab him, shake him, force him to hear her but her hands moved through him like she was a ghost. All she could see was his wide grin. A smile that was all too familiar.

She screamed and awoke drenched in sweat. Still in her kitchen. The wee hour evident in the pitch black of the night outside.

CHAPTER THIRTY-SEVEN

"What's TRG?" Luna breathed into the phone; her heart still pounded from the nightmare.

"Wait, what?" Birger said. "TRG? They...how do you know about them?"

He sounded confused, which was atypical for Birger. Usually, he was the one who knew everything or at least almost everything.

"I met this guy, Chago. He talked to me about joining." Luna felt out of sorts explaining this to him. Was she not supposed to interact with the likes of Chago? What was wrong with TRG? Her instincts had already told her to be careful, but based on Birger's gut response maybe it was bigger than that.

"Why do they want you," he asked. He said this with a seriousness in his tone, like there was some secret she held hidden and this was her chance to own up. "Did you reach out to them? How do they know you? What did he say to you?"

"I don't know. They like my cooking?" Luna said with sarcasm. How the hell did she know what they wanted with her? She called Birger for answers, not the other way around. She played with the phone cord.

"That's not what I mean. They are...wait, are you on a landline?"

"Yeah. So?"

She heard shuffling and a hand covered the receiver. "I will call you back on your cell phone." He hung up before she could respond.

More cloak-and-dagger crap. This only got more and more interesting. Within moments, her phone rang.

"Hey. What's up with all this super-secret stuff?" she asked.

"Luna, don't start giving away information without being absolutely sure that you know who is on the other line," Birger said. He wasn't rude or angry, but his concern and sense of danger radiated through the phone.

She knew he was right and she almost apologized before he started talking again.

"Now back to TRG," he said. "They've been around for a long, long time. Longer than either one of us has been alive."

Luna shifted in her chair. The way he began this conversation made her uncomfortable.

"They are...they have a different belief system than anything you are familiar with."

"What does that mean?"

He paused. She figured he debated whether he should go into any details. She sure as hell wasn't going to travel all the way to Sweden again for him to do the grand reveal. "It means that they believe shapeshifters should usurp humans."

"Oh." Her mind flashed to the nightmare from only moments before. An extreme representation of one group taking over another. This couldn't be what Birger meant, *could it?*

He continued, "They equate shapeshifters to being gods. They think they should rule the world."

"Well, the god part is a bit over the top but the rest of it I get. I mean, humans have fucked up a lot of stuff." She made light of it, too fearful that what he talked about was a takeover, a revolution, the destruction of humankind. Possibly the destruction of the world.

"I'm not kidding, Luna. They are dangerous. I need you to promise me that you won't meet with Chago alone. Ever."

INTERLUDE 28 – CHAGO'S FAMILY HISTORY

I was born in 1898. My parents were peasants. They struggled for everything. Most of my early years were spent on the streets of a small town outside of Montesquieu-Avantès in France. I begged for much of what we had. It was simply our truth. Mind you, this was not uncommon during this time. My society was broken out as the wealthy and the peasantry. We did not have much in between.

My mother died in the middle of the night. I do not know how or why. I only know that my father woke us to say that she was gone and we had to move on.

On reflection, she had most likely been discovered for being one of us and condemned as a witch or unnatural. And my father did not want to tell me or my siblings for fear of terrorizing us. Instead, we grieved in silence as we moved in the middle of the night to a new location.

My father had a magical ability to talk soldiers out of their ration of pinard or wine. Again, another of our gifts that I would discover only later in life. He would combine the pinard with absinthe, when he could get it, and huddle in a corner of our meager shack without lights or electricity. He wallowed in the hallucinogenic intoxication. His misery solidified by his choices. Thus, he left me and my siblings on our own to make whatever life we wanted or could. This quickly taught me that I did not want this life. I wanted and needed more. And if I wanted more, I needed to get away from his toxicity. My siblings were not of the same opinion. I offered a chance for them to follow me, but they declined. Instead, they chose to stay with our father. I did not blame them, but I knew I had to move on.

I left my family and wandered to the next town. I needed to find someone or something to start my new life. I heard of three brothers who were preparing to investigate an infamous cave. They believed life-changing secrets waited to be revealed from within that cave. They had put out calls for servants and assistants. The work was difficult and potentially dangerous so few volunteered. I eagerly raised my hand to join their exploration.

I became the servant to Breuil who immediately dictated that I was to do whatever he said.

Seemed simple enough.

Upon the first day of my employment, we began our adventure and entered the cave. Within several meters of our entry, we found childish sketches on the walls. Breuil immediately saw the value in them and demanded that I gather pencils and chalk and paper so he could transcribe these sketches for posterity. I scrambled to obtain the tools he required, begging others for their wares. I raced back to him and he drew with a ferocity and passion I had never seen prior.

"These are miracles." He repeated as he painstakingly took down each image. I obediently sat next to him, awaiting his next command.

So eager to ensure he received all that he required, I did not think to proactively go forward and obtain what he would need to continue his work well into the night. So focused on his drawings, he did not realize the hour.

"Light!" he yelled. "Chago, where is my light?"

I ran from the cave and begged others for a simple candle or lantern. Something to bring back to my master, to the man who had saved me from poverty.

By the time I returned, he hunched in the darkness, fuming. "How dare you waste such precious time."

I begged him for forgiveness and brought forward the lantern I had absconded with from one of his brothers' servants. His fury was so deep, he could not hear my words. He swiped the lantern from me.

"For your punishment you must stay in the cave alone throughout the night."

I had never been afraid of the dark before this time, but with the mention of leaving me I felt fear like I had never felt before. I pleaded for him not to leave me. I knelt at his feet, bowing as if to a priest, thanking him for all that he had done and for allowing me in.

"Please, sir. I will not be so reckless again."

Without another word, he exited the space and left me in the pitch of night with only the drawings for company. I could not see them, but I could feel them. And they did not feel friendly. They felt like warnings. They felt like demon spirits had been trapped within the ink and clay and stone.

To this day, I do not know if what happened was a nightmare or real. If asked, I will say that the sketches came to life. The sketches that he had so diligently transposed, that he swore were of an unprecedented value, those images of shapeshifters transformed before me.

One had somehow removed himself from the wall and approached me. Only a few meters away, he called to me and proclaimed I was their future.

"You will do more than any shapeshifter before," he said.

Then he threatened me with unimaginable actions if I did not do as he commanded.

I told him that I did not understand. "I am not of your kind," I said. "I am but a simple servant. I am a lone boy."

I felt the chill of the night ooze through my skin and deep into my bones. His next words somehow solidified that coldness into a depth of my being that I had never reached prior.

"That is unacceptable," he began. "Soon you will become a man and when you do you will find your true form. With that true form you must fulfill all that we are meant to be."

"I do not understand. What does that mean?" I asked.

He must not have liked my response because he slashed at me in a flurry I had only seen done by rabid dogs.

Flustered, I awoke to the dawn breaking and light flowing into the cave. I found comfort in the thought that it had been a nightmare brought on by the events of the previous day.

And then I looked down at my arms and chest. Slash marks and open cuts gaped from my skin. The cuts seeped with blood.

CHAPTER THIRTY-EIGHT

She knew Birger warned her to stay away from Chago, but she wasn't always the best at listening to instructions. Too many unanswered questions had piled up, and the closest person who could give her any kind of answers, at least in terms of proximity, was Chago. She had tried to gather answers from Birger and although he was somewhat helpful, he didn't share enough.

In Luna's mind, it only made sense for her to find her way back to the mansion where she had last seen him and take it from there.

This said, her junior spy activities had to wait until after she put in a full day's work. She hung up with Birger and realized the time. Shit. She jumped into the shower and raced to the bakery.

Margarite had been so kind and forgiving to this point. When Luna arrived at the bakery, Margarite had made it clear that unless Luna had a fantastic reason then she couldn't miss another day of work.

Luna apologized, "I'm so sorry. It won't happen again."

Margarite nodded, acknowledging Luna's response. Luna hurried to put on her apron and focused on the awaiting orders.

For the first time ever, Luna had a hard time keeping her mind on her work. She kept replaying her interactions with Birger and Chago and trying to tie them back to the notes left by Daniel. That said, she had a job to do and expectations that she needed to fulfill. She forced herself to focus.

Even though she was exhausted at the end of the day, she found her way back to the mansion in the off-chance that Chago was there. She made sure to park her car off the main road which meant she had a bit of walking to do to get to the building. By the time she made it, the day had turned to twilight.

Chago's Mercedes was parked right in front. She snuck her way around the back to where they previously had the majority of their conversation.

She peered into the full-length windows and was surprised at the lack of furniture. She thought that the place had been fully furnished. She had assumed that this was his home, a natural assumption. Now that she thought about it, the furniture from the other day looked like staging furniture, the kind that real estate agents used when they were trying to sell a vacant home.

She had barely made her way to the side when he came barreling out of the front door, slid into his car, turned the engine over, and started down the gravel path. He made no acknowledgement of her. His fast exit was definitely a bad sign.

Taking his lead, she ran down the road on the farthest side of the trees, and got to her car and jumped into it. Out of breath, she did her best to regain her composure. She looked up to see his car at the end of the driveway. Either he drove incredibly slowly or she ran insanely fast. In the moment, she wasn't sure which was true. If it was the latter, she'd need to test that out again.

Luna waited a few moments, just long enough so she could be a few car lengths behind him.

INTERLUDE 29 – CHAGO'S LIFE

Not long after the cave incident, I began to experience shaking. Slight at first, barely noticeably. Meanwhile, the shamans of the cave continued to invade my dreams. The same shamans who had slashed me in the middle of the night. The ones who had told me of my shapeshifting abilities. At the time, I did not fully comprehend what was happening. I didn't understand the shaking and that it was the beginnings of the transformations. I simply knew that this trembling came at inopportune times.

Breuil kept me as his assistant. I learned to better anticipate his needs. I paid greater attention to his actions and his focus. He spent much of his time attempting to interpret the etchings and associating them back to known history. Adept at the subtle art of influence due to my time on the streets, I guided him toward the lessons the shaman and shapeshifters in my dreams provided. His receptivity was at first limited, but then, with time, he became more open to the concepts.

I began intentionally sleeping in the cave. It had become my sanctuary and the one place where I could go to obtain the clearest guidance from the shaman. I grew to understand that they used my dreams to materialize and speak directly to me. A rare and miraculous gift.

I awakened in the mornings and wrote down all that I remembered from the night before. Much of my notes were in my own shorthand, my schooling quite limited. In the future I would find those to educate me, but for this time I had to make do.

In one especially remarkable dream, the shamans spoke of a seeress and gave specific instructions of how to find her.

"You must seek her out," he said.

I awoke with the feeling of destiny upon me. I knew that Breuil would not allow me to leave freely, his reliance had become too great, so I swept off into the night. As he slept, I made my way forward with only a bag on my back and the limited coins I had saved during my time with the budding archeologists.

I traveled the countryside, obtained assistance through the kindness of fellow travelers until I reached the small village described by the shamans. There, I found shelter and waited for them to speak to me again. I hoped I had not made a mistake by leaving the vicinity of the cave. Even though this was as the shamans had directed, I had never received their direct messages outside of the archeological site.

Days passed, and I became convinced that I misunderstood them. Somehow, I had misinterpreted what I had been told. I readied to move on, unsure if I should try to return to Breuil and beg his forgiveness or find another town, another place to begin my life anew. And then I spotted a familiar face.

Just as described by the shamans, a woman of mid-size with long jet hair and hazel eyes with golden flecks wandered the market in this small town. She observed me watching her. A look of concern crossed her face. I nodded in acknowledgement so as not to seem like a man of ill-intent. At that juncture, she approached me with intrigue.

Her eyes locked on mine. Without a word, she touched my hand, the shaking initiated as if on cue. I had yet to find a means of managing the ailment.

Embarrassed, I pulled my hand away. She searched my face, for what, I do not know.

Later I would discover that she was a descendant of Hiwa just as I was a descendant of the first Chago. The Chago who had fought alongside Ulf for the king and later took down Freya due to her impetuousness.

"The spirits call to you," she said. She grabbed my hands and put them between hers. I felt an energy flow through her limbs and into mine. The tremors subsided. I sighed with relief.

"You will need help controlling your gifts," she said in a loving tone. "I can teach you."

CHAPTER THIRTY-NINE

C hago had nearly missed a board of directors call. He
thoroughly enjoyed the solitude of the empty house and
lost track of time. He found himself racing out of the luxurious
mansion and barreling down the highway to TRG's headquarters.

Although inconvenient, he had to take the call from TRG's
main headquarters in order to ensure he had a direct and secure
line. All board members had a similar mandate to make sure
their discussions remained confidential and unrecorded.

He knew that if an emergency occurred then he could
arrange for the connection to be reestablished elsewhere, but
this was not an emergency, simply the standard weekly call to
check in on status. The true urgency came from the fact that he
was the head of the board and as such, he could or should not
be late to a discussion.

On the drive, he noted a familiar car. He had observed a
similar one outside of the Camden County Hospital and he
knew, due to a variety of reasons, that this same car belonged to
Luna.

Based on her driving pattern, he also knew that she wasn't aware he had spotted her and that was good for now. He smiled to himself. As predicted, she returned. They always returned.

He drove into the underground parking and, with a remote, he closed the gate behind him. The building had been built specifically for the organization's use. An architect had been contracted to ensure the design was exactly what they wanted and then hired a specialty builder, under a non-disclosure agreement, to construct it to strict specifications which included a state of the art security system.

For purposes of enabling Luna to explore her untapped potential and gain a greater understanding of her true path, he conveniently *neglected* to turn on the alarm system while keeping the hidden security cameras on. He wasn't a fool. He needed to track her whereabouts the entire time she was present, but he also needed her to feel secure. The safer she felt in her exploits the better.

He made it to his office with barely a moment to spare and took his call, sure not to be too specific in his descriptions or in the discussion, just in case Luna wandered in. He made a mental note to have all of the buildings swept. If Luna was this far along in her exploits then there was a potential that Birger and TLS had other individuals acting as operatives, whether by request or not, in an effort to infiltrate their locations.

He continued the conversation, ensuring to use common keywords for specific topics, again, just in case there were unintended eyes or ears on this discussion.

Over the monitors, he watched Luna as she made her way through the building. He could feel her anxiousness and fear of being caught come through the screen. He marveled at her boldness. Yes, she was definitely of the Ulf and Freya line. He smirked. They would be proud of her investigative nature.

He observed her actions as she made her way into the

secret hall where all members were first introduced to the history of TRG and shapeshifting. She ogled the statues and paintings. Knowing that this was his cue to appear, he thanked the fellow board members for their participation and ended the call.

INTERLUDE 30 – CHAGO SHARES TRG'S HISTORY

You must understand that critical to our existence, to our history, is Mount Lykaion which is also called Wolf Mountain. It exists in the area that was the Ancient Greek kingdom of Arcadia. You may know it as the birthplace of Zeus. His followers and worshippers conducted games in his honor throughout the centuries.

The true believers performed ritual sacrifices to the gods on an altar atop the mountain. Some believed the sacrifices were of human form. Others believed humans offered other creatures, spilling blood in reverence to their gods of choice.

In 2016 archeologists found what they thought were human remains at the top of the mountain. They carbon dated the remains to over 3,000 years prior. We know that the full truth of what they found was not entirely present in the archeologists' discoveries. Our records show, and we have recorded proof, that humans had hunted our kind in order to sacrifice them to Zeus. The mountain's soil was drenched in the blood of our ancestors. Hence, Mount Lykaion earned its name. I do not say this in celebration.

I share this as a warning.

CHAPTER FORTY

C hago continued the tale, keeping Luna enthralled. The hall was filled with statues, artwork, and pieces that shared the history of the lycanthropes. The statue of Mount Lykaion with certified articles which detailed the anthropologists' findings were simply too hard to ignore. Had she been shocked at him finding her within the sacred walls? He was careful to approach her in a non-threatening way and imply that the building had been made open for members, which of course was the furthest from the truth. She seemed to believe his reasoning. He had quickly changed the subject to that of their shared history.

"At Mount Lykaion, after years of torture and abuse, the lycanthropes initiated a rebellion," Chago said. "We took over the mountain and reclaimed our place as the favorites of Zeus. With that came sacrifices of those who had imprisoned us, used us as cattle, treated us like lesser creatures meant to be enslaved. Their blood layered over our own."

"My god," Luna said.

Before this moment, everything that had been relayed to

her felt like heresy. Other than what Birger had shared, no one had shown her true evidence of the historical significance of shapeshifters. Even Daniel's notes heavily relied on personal stories shared on the community boards and articles on Wikipedia. And she never trusted Wikipedia.

"And this is the origins of The Lycanthrope Society which is the group Daniel interacted with on the community boards."

Chago led Luna towards a painting which displayed a group meeting in an open-air stadium, high atop a mountain. Their stances regal and their bodies half man and half beast.

"They are the ones who brought him to Birger and eventually directed me to you."

INTERLUDE 31 -- THE LYCANTHROPE
HISTORY CONTINUED - CHAGO

You must understand, Luna, that we are truly an ancient society with a history stained by torture, murder, enslavement, and abuse. Our banding is only a natural progression to becoming an organized and unified group. Our mistrust of humans was confirmed in the behavior of the king. Before we had overtaken the mountain, we were ruled and enslaved by King Lycaon.

The king had been visited by one who claimed to be Zeus. King Lycaon had questioned the individual's powers and divinity so he served his visitor human flesh. The king believed that this test would prove the visitor's limitations. He believed that only a true god could tell if he was served something so taboo as the flesh of his followers. Once this being had been proven to be an imposter, the king intended to jail him and use him as the next sacrifice to the true gods.

As expected, Zeus knew what Lycaon had done and in punishment, he had transformed the king into a wolf. The newly transformed king was then sent to stay with the shapeshifters who had been enslaved by him. This imprisonment had been done to demonstrate the exiled king's true place in the world, as a slave.

The former king began his days in mourning, questioning his own abilities. He swore at how stupid he had been by testing such a powerful god. Then he realized the gift that the god had given him and the real place of the shapeshifters in the grand scheme of the world.

In his human form, he had led with ignorance and bias. He had no idea the true force of those he had enslaved.

His eyes had been opened.

As a part of the transformation by Zeus, Lycaon had been gifted the power of Zeus to tell when flesh was of human or of animal. He too could identify with the mere shifting of the winds if someone was true or not. His senses heightened when in this bestial form.

Although not quite a god, what had originally been viewed by humans as the worst punishment that could have ever been given by Zeus, to be made into a beast, had clearly become the greatest gift.

At first, he thought he was forever a wolf until one of the fellow shapeshifters, feeling sorry for the dethroned and excommunicated king, showed him the secrets of transformation. With that bit of knowledge, Lycaon began plotting the takeover of the mountain.

He is the one who led the overthrow of the new king, a man who had been a weak second to the mighty Lycaon. The new king had been hand-selected by Zeus himself.

In many ways, this was Zeus's way of thanking Lycaon for the establishment of the mountain along with the continued sacrifices and ceremonies. Even though Zeus had to teach Lycaon a lesson, he also desired to thank him for his dedication. So he made the takeover a challenge.

The rebellion was bloody, but fast, due to Lycaon's in depth knowledge of the kingdom, he quickly reestablished his over-sight of the mountain. The humans were enslaved, the shapeshifters made the ruling class. Thus, the world had been righted.

The ruling class conducted annual ceremonies in honor of Zeus and to memorialize the day of King Lycaon's changing and the day the Lycanthrope gained their rightful place seated next to Zeus.

CHAPTER FORTY-ONE

L una stood agape before Chago. Amazed at the origins of the Lycanthrope, she had no idea of the history. She still wasn't sure she believed in Zeus, but she did believe that oftentimes legends were peppered with a blend of truth and myth. Before a few months ago, she would have thought all of it was mythology, but now, she had a lot to sink in.

She felt oddly comfortable with him. She had gotten into the building with unusual ease. Admittedly, she had entered through the front door, so she guessed she shouldn't be too surprised. That said, everything until this moment had felt so protected, so hush-hush, that the fact she got to this museum-like hallway as she had seemed a bit odd. She looked at Chago and noted his stance from formality to one of bodily aching. Like he was recovering from a huge physical test.

Chago felt the days of continued preparation weigh on his muscles. He leaned against a pillar and straightened his back. He had done all that he had promised with Luna and Daniel. All that he had agreed to with the board. He understood from the foretellings their importance and the necessity to have them both onboard.

He had also continued his work towards The Final Recalling. This moment, The Final Recalling, was what The Righteous Group had been waiting for since the days of Mount Lycaon. For Chago, The Final Recalling was his true reason for being. This was his true passion.

But the discussion with Luna had been disappointing. She had so much potential. She had shown the right amount of curiosity and spirit. She needed a bit more training on the art of spying, but that could come with time. They had plenty of TRG members who could easily train her. She had a surprising ability to control her shifting. A gift rarely seen. She took to it naturally, much more so than many others. He guessed this was true, in part, due to her purity of bloodline and closeness to the Originals. She would be easy to train.

But in this moment, her response to the family history saddened and disappointed him. She looked like a surprised child enthralled with a bedtime story. Before she could be fully engaged with TRG she needed to be much more. She needed to feel this in her being. She needed to be enraged by the historic treatment of shapeshifters. She needed to be horrified at their slaughter, enslavement, and mistreatment by humans. She needed to feel, believe, understand within her core that The Final Recalling was the only path forward. The only way that humans and shapeshifters could continue. In her soul she needed to believe in the shapeshifters' true place in the world. This had to be a part of her and not some fairytale.

She will get there, he thought, *just not today*.

"And with that," Chago said. "I must thank you for your visit."

"Wait, what do you mean?" Luna asked. "I thought you wanted me here."

He looked at his watch, a clear indicator that it was time for their conversation to end. "You have lessons you must go through. Teachings before you are ready to join us. Before you are ready to be taken further." He said this dismissively like he was speaking to someone who had failed her driver's exam by one point. He stood back up and motioned towards the main entry.

Luna was surprised at how hurt she felt at his refusal. When he first found her in the hall, she thought he would be furious, but instead he welcomed her and shared this history. In reflection, it shouldn't have surprised her that he welcomed her. She guessed he had wanted to bring her here all along so that she further understood who and what she was. But this, this discharge without a real explanation, this was infuriating. No, not infuriating. It was heartbreaking. Deeply heartbreaking.

"What is that supposed to mean?" she finally asked.

"Exactly what I said. Return to Sweden. Visit with Birger. Continue the teachings you were intended to have previously. Learn from him and his people. They will share with you and teach you. At some point, we will meet again. Just not today." His declaration was clear, his look decisive. He made sure the path to the front door was unencumbered. "Good night."

Luna stared at him, mouth slightly open. Then, resolutely, she shut it.

"Fine," she said. "I'll let myself out."

INTERLUDE 32 – THE TRUE LYCANTHROPIC HISTORY ACCORDING TO CHAGO

She was not ready to see the second part of the hall. Her childish response to the very origins of our kind, at least organized origins, betrayed her inability to absorb our further truths. Just beyond the door at the end of that hall was the second, truly secret, hall that only those accepted to TRG may see.

In that hall, the very first painting visible upon entry is of Mount Lycaon with King Lycaon overseeing a religious ceremony with his right-hand person. That person is my original self. I assisted in the procession. Only after I had been taught by Hiwa's descendant did I understand that I had been reincarnated from the original Lycanthropes thousands of years prior which is why she taught me how to elongate my years so that my soul did not go through the pains of reincarnation as frequently.

Enabling the body to stay in sync with the soul in its timelessness is a gift for which I can never repay her. A gift she chose to give up a hundred years ago. She had grown tired of this lifetime, tired of the progression of humans and their treatment of others. But that is for another story.

For Luna to see this painting, hear the accompanying story as well as the subsequent stories, each with their own validation of truth through anthropological finds, news articles, studies, and so on...she simply would not have been able to handle it.

CHAPTER FORTY-TWO

C hago had waited a moment and then followed her to the front door. Her lack of familiarity with the building proved to be a disadvantage since she began to get lost in the winding halls.

He came up from behind her. "Before you go, there is one final thing."

She turned out of frustration and confusion. "I thought you were done with me," she said.

He ignored her snarky comment. "There are many forces that will try to take advantage of you. They will try to use you for their own benefit. Many will try to destroy you." He guided her down the hallway, passed closed, and finally to the main door. As they neared it, he said, "You need to be prepared."

"What's that supposed to mean?" Luna asked.

Chago paused. He calmed his center and looked deep into Luna's eyes. He sensed her frustration, her disappointment, her anger. And from somewhere within her, he could see her need for a guide. "I can help you with that, but I must know that you'll remain true."

He knew from deep within his being that she was not ready for TRG. He had absolutely no doubt about it. That said, however, he also knew that he needed to keep her within his influence. It would be harder to bring her on board if she stayed aligned to Birger than if Chago had leveraged his own powers of influence to sway her to the beliefs of TRG. He also knew he had just directed her to return to Sweden and to be trained by Birger but in the few moments since he had made that statement, his instincts cried out that he couldn't have her return to Birger and be guided by him.

Officially, according to TRG's policy and the board's official agreements regarding how to handle Ulf and Freya's direct descendants, he was supposed to allow her to follow TLG (The Lycanthrope Group), but something about her made him uncomfortable.

Hiwa had taught him that all shapeshifters' instincts were heightened. Especially those of purer bloodlines. She had said that minimally their instincts were ten times greater than a human's instincts, and he believed that. In all of his years, this had been proven true over and over again.

Something within him knew that Luna could easily be as powerful, if not more so, than Daniel. With the limited training she had received from Birger, she had shown a mastery which exceeded that of those several years her senior.

That fact meant her power could be greater than anything he had ever seen.

Ever.

And he had seen a lot.

Luna stared at him for a moment. All she saw in his eyes was the darkness of night and complexity of time.

With that offer to act as her mentor and guide, Chago stepped aside, allowing her to walk out the door.

INTERLUDE 33 – THE ORIGINS OF THE LYCANTHROPE SOCIETY - CHAGO

I had helped King Lycaon form The Lycanthrope Society in the days of Zeus and Mount Lycaon because we needed to be organized. We needed to embrace our true selves. Ironic that the man who had once been destroying us, sacrificing us, was the one to organize us, but such is life.

With time, King Lycaon became more and more isolated. His teaching elevated us, but at the same time encouraged us to remain atop the mountain and, in his words, "among the gods." Down below, we could see humans hike trails on the mountainside as they sought a way to reach the top in an effort to gain Zeus' favor.

They neared our hidden entries and passed by unaware of the hidden paths. This was by the king's design. He told our people that we belonged with the gods and therefore he kept us from the inferior humans.

I did not believe that. Something in his telling betrayed a fear of us, even though he was one of us. Is that why he had subjugated us to such horrors? Because he feared that one day, we would overthrow him? One day we would take his place?

Others within our assembly heard similar uncertainty in the king's guidance, so we secretly met. A faction of the group decided to move on from Mount Lycaon and thereby become what we were meant to be.

Our objective had been to fulfill what we had spoken of since the king's first formation of The Lycanthrope Society. To actualize what he had spoken of when he lectured us on taking our rightful place next to the gods, ruling humans, taking over the world that was rightfully ours. When he spoke of these things each word rang true. And so we believed.

This assembly of true believers noted the official forming of The Righteous Group. The goal, to rule humans and fulfill our calling among the gods, easily and naturally emerged.

CHAPTER FORTY-THREE

Luna had been surprised by this entire interaction. First, Chago wanted her there, then he didn't want her there, then he did want her there. Then finally, at this point, he sounded like he wanted to train her in secret.

Why in secret? What the hell was all of this? Fully confused and dejected, she followed Chago's lead and decided she would go home, get a good night's sleep and then try to figure things out in the morning. Meanwhile, she'd check on Javier to see how he was healing.

"Thank you," she said. "I'll keep that in mind."

She made her way out of the door.

Without further explanation or acknowledgement, he lifted his arm, and with a bit of force, slammed his elbow into the back of her head, knocking her out.

CHAPTER FORTY-FOUR

Luna awoke on her couch, head throbbing. She immediately regretted moving when she tried to get up, the back of her head and shoulders screamed for her to lay back down. Which she did. What the hell had happened?

The last thing she remembered: she was in The Righteous Group's main office somewhere in, uhm...crap. She was talking to someone. Someone she had met before. Someone important.

Who was she talking to?

She tried to focus her thoughts on the last few hours, but the more she tried to remember, the less she could. She slowly sat upright, and held the back of her head. She sincerely pondered getting aspirin. Heck, maybe even CBD gummies.

She looked at her watch and hoped she didn't have to return to the bakery soon. She needed time to recuperate. Just as she had that thought, she realized she had not seen Javier in what felt like days. Her last memory was seeing him attached to a bunch of machines, unconscious, but thankfully, alive.

"Fuck," she said and checked her phone. On it a text from a friend at the hospital said that he was awake. And her gut said she needed to do something else as well. What, she wasn't quite sure.

She did her best attempt at racing to the bathroom, slid into the shower, because she wasn't sure when the last time she had bathed. If the ripe scent of her clothes was an indicator, then she definitely needed a good scrubbing.

The water hot and reinvigorating, she carefully washed, dressed, and downed some aspirin before she bolted out the door. She went to her typical parking spot and was surprised that her car wasn't there. She searched around the parking lot and found it several spots down. What the hell? She never parked there. With that thought, she refocused her attention on getting to the hospital.

Javier needed her. There wasn't time for any delays.

CHAPTER FORTY-FIVE

C hago had anticipated after he had met with Daniel that a day would come when he would need to move their base. This need had been triggered by his most recent actions.

He had knocked Luna out and performed a memory erasing spell he had used many times prior. Without him providing direction to her, he needed her to forget what he had shown her and what he had explained to her to begin her training. He planted the thought that she needed to reach back out to Birger and receive additional coaching. Another useful spell. In terms of his own interactions with her, he could always double-back and bring her under his mentorship at a later time. But for now, doing it all in stages was how it had to be.

She was clever and with that cleverness and intelligence came the ability to connect seemingly disparate topics. Under his tutelage, it would come back to her when the time was right, but for now he had made her forget. He had to control what she remembered...for now.

He could have used Uo126, a memory-erasing drug, to perform the function. He still had samples from the study that

TRG had financially backed, but he preferred natural means of erasing memories versus chemical means. Even though the natural method was questionable in terms of its sustainability, especially since she was not a willing recipient of the memory removal. Yet, he anticipated that if he had replaced her memories with new ones, it would have been worse. His instincts said she would ferret out the false memories and force forward the true ones. Yes, it had been a better choice to simply erase the details of the last twelve hours.

He knew he would see her again. To ensure that she would never return would require all her memories of the last few months to be removed and replaced. Considering the loss of her fraternal twin brother, trip to Sweden, and all related activities, that significant of a memory swipe was far too risky to even consider. Therefore, he had to stay focused on the last few hours, which was of his greatest concern.

In the meantime, considering the ease with which she followed him and her lack of understanding of the sensitive nature of TLS and TRG, he needed to uproot this central location. He made the required call and TCC (The Cleanup Crew) arrived within the hour.

CHAPTER FORTY-SIX

She entered the hospital room and immediately took the chair next to his bed. Javier was fast asleep, the monitor steadily beeped with the reassuring indicator of a heart-beat...the reassurance of life. Luna placed her hand on his cheek. At no point in the last twenty years did she ever believe she would be at his bedside in this situation.

They had always saved each other, been there for one another, but this was beyond anything she could have imagined.

"I love you," she whispered to him. As she looked at his peaceful face, she regretted never telling him this. She had more regrets than she had ever thought. Including not spending more time with her brother, not listening to him when he said they needed to be careful, not engaging with him more in all the activities - mundane and vital - of his life.

She leaned in and kissed Javier on the forehead and on his lips, then gently caressed his cheek and ran her fingers down the side of his face to his arm and rested her hand over his.

"I love you."

In the hospital doorway, a stranger appeared. The person, a woman with pale blonde hair and oversized clothes, looked familiar but not enough for Luna to put a name to the face.

"Can I help you?" Luna said.

The steady beeping of the heart monitor acted as the musical score to the moment.

"Are you Luna Auber?" said the stranger. She looked like she had lost an inordinate amount of weight in a brief period of time.

Her clothes hung off of her like someone who wasn't aware of how thin she had become so she wore clothing from two larger sizes ago. Her skin hung from her face reinforcing the assumption that she had lost weight at an unnatural pace.

"Yes. May I help you?" Luna said again. The stranger waved her into the hallway.

What is this with people and calling me into the hallway?

She kissed Javier again, and followed the woman just outside the hospital room entry.

The woman avoided eye contact. "You have been in talks with Chago, yes?" The woman seemed anxious, her eyes darted around the hallway and the room. Nervous energy emanated from her.

"Who's Chago?" Luna sincerely didn't recognize that name. Her concern, at that moment, was her future fiancé. Nothing more.

"The man you just spent the last several hours with." The woman said this with a huffiness that annoyed Luna. Who was this woman and how would she know anything about where Luna spent her time?

"I spent the last several hours at home and on Zoom calls with a librarian who I doubt you know. What is this about?"

The stranger looked at Luna at first in shock and then in confusion.

"Tall gentleman, slight of build, muscular, jet black hair. Incredibly handsome. Has the kind of voice that, for some women, makes them want to take their clothes off."

Luna's annoyance grew. She had no idea what this person was talking about and she needed to get back to Javier. As she talked to her, Paul passed and nodded at Luna, a quiet acknowledgement that simply increased her agitation. She wished he had never asked Javier to help with the overnight shift, but it was too late to have that wish fulfilled.

"Look, I need to go. I have to look after my fiancé." Luna began to head back into the hospital room when the woman took out her phone and pulled up an image.

"This man." She pointed at the phone. "This is Chago."

Luna's thoughts became fuzzy, her memory a blur. Her head began to pound.

"You need to stay away from this man." The woman emphatically pointed at the image. "He is the definition of danger. He is the reason Daniel is dead. He is the reason your boyfriend is in there." She pointed at the hospital room where Javier lay in bed, the lights low, the monitor steadily beeping.

"Who are you?" Luna finally asked. The photo brought back blurred images of the last day. The woman's claims heightened Luna's concern. If only she could focus. Behind her Javier shifted in the bed, his head lifted.

"No matter -"

"It does matter," Luna's voice raised. "You call me to talk to you outside of my fiancé's hospital room and tell me to stay away from someone I don't know and demand that I do so. Then you won't tell me your name? Why the fuck should I listen to you?" Luna rubbed her head from front to back and then stopped her hands on the back of her neck where she tried to caress away the pain of her headache. The more she tried to force herself to remember the greater her head throbbed.

CURE

"If Birger could, he would have come here to help you, but he cannot. So he sent me to look after you." The following words came out in a hiss. The stranger looked deeply into Luna's eyes. "You are fucking up everywhere. You need to listen to us from now on. Stop doing whatever the fuck you feel like. All you're doing is making things harder on all of us."

Luna locked gazes with the stranger. "Fuck. OFF."

The stranger grabbed Luna by the shoulder. "There are powers here that you don't understand. Your brother was a victim of them. You don't need to be one as well."

Before Luna could respond, several EMTs ran by. Emergency lights flashed as gurneys were wheeled into the emergency room. In the chaos and hecticness of the moment, the stranger slipped out of sight.

CHAPTER FORTY-SEVEN

The bare room had been vacated for this occasion. In prior years, a coven of members would have been present to welcome the newly indoctrinated. This being the last of the rituals, the final incantation that took mere mortals and made them lycanthropes, it tended to be considered of the utmost importance. The incantation epitomized the original transformation that Zeus performed thousands of years prior on the king. The ceremony adjusted through time to best represent the most historical moments of the lycanthropic heritage.

Chago placed his hands on the gentleman's short dark chestnut hair. The man's deeply sunken eyes were closed, his breathing steady and rhythmic as he had been directed. His build was solid, his stature shorter than the average man. His jawline squared itself with a sense of formidability.

Chago repeated the chant as the man sipped the elixir from the ceremonial cup. Made of silver and encrusted with rubies, diamonds, and opals, the cup had been a gift to the Group from a member several hundred years prior.

Once the final words were uttered and he motioned for the

gentleman to stand, Chago said, "This and only this will make you one of us."

The man bowed before Chago, thankful for the opportunity. With the downward motion of the bow, the man began to shake. He clutched his abdomen and then screamed in pain.

Chago waved off the man's begging for help. His cries of pain were all too familiar. Chago turned his attention towards the window facing the city below. In the distance, the United Nations building loomed. As the man's cries continued behind him, Chago said. "Thus we began your transformation. The final engagement to bring forward your true path."

CHAPTER FORTY-EIGHT

"Who the fuck was that?" Luna barked into the phone. She escaped the chaos of the emergency room as it was being overrun with patients and raced out to the farthest point of the parking lot.

"What or who are you talking about?" Birger asked. "I can barely hear you."

"Hold on a sec." The siren of an emergency vehicle screamed past as Luna pressed her hands against her ears. Once the sound had lessened to something manageable, she continued. "The crazy woman. The one who looked like she dropped a hundred pounds in a month. The one with stringy blonde hair."

"Oh," Birger said. The tone one of acknowledgement.

"Yeah. Oh." Her tone mocking. Luna paced the parking lot. "Give it up. Who was she and what the hell is going on?"

In a quiet voice, he said, "She's somewhat of an over-achiever. A little over eager." Luna imagined Birger shrugging his shoulders. "Some might say she's overly anxious."

"Don't play that bullshit with me," Luna said. Her headache had only increased with the emergency room's chaos.

"I had asked her to look out for you, and she took it a bit differently than I had intended."

"I'll say."

"I will talk to her," said Birger. "If it helps, her intentions were good."

Luna relayed the conversation with the still-unnamed woman. "You call that good?"

"Sometimes Rebecca gets overzealous. She always means well. I will politely mention that there's no need for her to be as aggressive."

Without another word to say, and acknowledging that there probably wasn't more that Birger could do, Luna hung up without a goodbye. She knew she would be talking to him again quite soon. Something inside of her said they had a lot more work to do together.

She watched as new patients were brought forth in ambulances and wheeled into the emergency room. She was glad that Javier had been moved into a standard patient's room but wished it was a bit farther away from the hectic emergency entry. She checked her pockets and found the police officer's card from when she had provided her detailed statement. He said she could call at any time. This was as good a time as any.

After being placed on hold for several moments, the officer picked up and informed Luna that the case was still open.

"And what about Paul? He must be considered an accessory or something, right?"

The officer sighed. "I need another witness. Something or someone to corroborate what you saw. Once we have that then I can do more."

"Then you won't do anything?" She knew the answer to

her question. Hell, she knew it long before she had even given her statement, but she had to try.

"I'm sorry," he said. "The good news is we have Ms. Samantha Lostgrove in custody. Her bail has been set quite high so it's unlikely she will be released anytime soon."

"You don't know that," said Luna.

"Seems as though she has few living family and even less friends."

"Considering her current physical and emotional states, that isn't really surprising," Luna smirked.

"We've been trying to reach the only remaining relative in the area, a sister, since we got her into custody. But we've had no success."

"A sister?" Luna asked. "What's the sister's name?"

Papers shuffled and then the clacking of a keyboard. "Rebecca. Rebecca Lostgrove."

In Luna's mind, she compared the woman who just verbally assaulted her and the drug addict. Same stringy hair, same facial features. "No shit."

CHAPTER FORTY-NINE

"I wasn't expecting to hear from you so quickly," said Birger. He had picked up the phone so fast it didn't have a chance to ring.

Luna had immediately called Birger as soon as she had been given the news of the Lostgroves. She figured he might be able to give her some insights into the sisters. She paced the hospital's parking lot. "Would you like to tell me what the fuck your little miss Rebecca has to do with the bitch who shot my boyfriend?"

The line fell silent. In the background, Luna heard someone ask Birger a question. It sounded like he placed his hand over the receiver followed by his muffled voice, a bit of indistinguishable dialogue, and then he returned.

"My apologies. We're nearing closing time and I have a few visitors who are checking out some items."

She held back the desire to scream. "The man I love. The man who I have known since I I first got to this fucking place, since I was eight years old is laying in a hospital bed after being shot by SOMEONE I thought was a random addict, but now

273

I'm finding out she has ties to YOU. Either fess up or I'll dig on my own and you won't like it if I do that." She growled the last words. She could feel her jaw clench with anger.

She knew this could be considered a useless threat, but if he didn't want her asking lots of questions and nosing around, especially of that guy, Chago, then he best start volunteering answers.

"I'll call you right back." He hung up without another word.

Luna found a spot in the farthest part of the parking lot. She made sure she was in the open air, away from other vehicles, with her back to the building. All in order to limit her risk of being seen or heard without her consent.

The second she saw a blocked number appear, she picked up. "Now talk."

Birger proceeded to share a story.

One that blew her mind.

"Rebecca and Samantha Lostgrove grew up among The Righteous Group. Considering your ongoing conversations with Chago, I am assuming you are aware of the organization," he said.

"Uh...okay." She couldn't help but let the sarcasm drip from her voice. "Continue."

"Their parents had been members of TRG as had been their grandparents and so on. They knew nothing other than the learnings and belief system of that community.

At some point, I don't know when, Rebecca had been deeply involved with Chago. He saw a lot of potential in her and what she thought would be a student-teacher relationship became...deeper.

Rebecca never told me exactly what had happened, but one day she appeared at my door, bloodied, exhausted, and distraught. I took her to the local doctor, one affiliated with The

Lycanthrope Society, in case her injuries were somehow related to shapeshifting.

Once healed, she swore that Chago was pure evil and that she never wanted to be a part of TRG again. She immediately swore allegiance to TLS. I informed her that wasn't how things worked. We didn't swear allegiance and, considering her long family history with TRG, I told her she had to prove her fealty to the greater good. Once she had proven her true intentions and rejected the ways and beliefs of TRG, then she could begin working more deeply with us."

Luna's head pounded. As he spoke, she searched the internet on her phone for the name Rebecca Lostgrove. After some scrolling, she found images of Rebecca and that guy Rebecca had pulled up on her phone. The fuzziness of her thoughts and mind returned. She did her best to fight it, the pains from her headache only increased.

"No," she said as if she could will the throbbing away. "I will not let you ..." She trailed off and focused on breaking through her mind's foggy barrier.

"Luna, are you okay?" Birger asked. "What's happening?" His voice gripped with concern.

"Goddamn it!" she wailed as she forced thoughts and images that tried to hide behind a black curtain to come forward. She dropped the phone and screamed from the exertion and pain.

She awoke lying on the cement, her phone tossed a few feet away with the distant sound of someone asking if she was okay, her body weak, her movements choppy, and her memory partially restored. She felt like she did after a long night that involved lots of tequila and too little sleep. She crawled across the black top to her phone.

An emergency room medic hovered over her. "Stay still. We'll get you checked out." She looked up to see a young man in a white uniform. He placed his hands on her shoulders and looked into her eyes. "Will you be okay if I leave you for a minute?" he said with concern.

She nodded.

"I'll be right back." He hurried inside and got a fellow medic and a stretcher.

Just beyond her she heard Birger's voice coming from her phone. She pulled it to her.

"Are you okay? Luna? Are you there?" Birger sounded panicked.

"I'm okay," she whispered. Her entire body ached from the effort. Her nerve endings tingled with tenderness. The two medics returned. She motioned for them to wait a moment. "Now I understand Rebecca's warning," she said into the phone and hung up.

CHAPTER FIFTY

Chago returned to the newly indoctrinated Mr. Bardales. His transformation was done; the newly-created Lycanthrope was physically exhausted. The elixir had been altered to force the person's first time changing to occur as quickly as possible, streamlining the potion into the bloodstream and through the initiate's body.

The transformation completed at hyper-speed; the indoctrinated had been changed and then returned to his original form within two hours. Chago had worked on this potion for centuries, realizing that he needed to be there for the first shifting so that if anything went wrong, he could perform damage control.

Mr. Bardales looked up to the man who had either given him gifts of heaven or catapulted him through hell. He had not fully decided which was true. In that moment, he felt like it was the latter. Mr. Bardales's clothing had been torn to shreds during the transformation, so Chago handed the vulnerable, naked, and sweat-soaked man a robe.

"I will teach you how to use your powers," Chago said to

the United Nations Security Council representative. One of many he had recruited and then turned. Chago leveraged the gifts of shapeshifting as a carrot for those he needed to manipulate. Sometimes he fulfilled his promise and other times it remained an enticement. Such was true with Paul, even though the ER doctor eagerly contacted Chago with the desire to be transformed. He kept reminding Chago that he had done what he had promised. Even so, Chago had yet to respond to the doctor's demands.

In the case of Mr. Bardales, Chago needed him to fully embrace his newly-acquired gifts. He had been one of the last new recruits that Chago needed to fulfill his destiny and the destiny of TRG. Chago wrapped the robe around the newly transformed's sweat-soaked body as he curled up on the ground like a frightened newborn. "You will learn how to control the shaking, the cravings, the need." Chago placed his hand on the man's back in support. "And I will guide you."

CHAPTER FIFTY-ONE

Luna pocketed her phone as the medics helped her onto the gurney and brought her into the hospital's waiting area. They checked her out, her pulse, her breathing, her blood pressure.

Only once they were convinced that she was fine did they allow her to get back up. She thanked them for their help and then quietly maneuvered her way to Javier's room. With everything that had gone on, she felt like she hadn't spent enough time with him. She needed to check on him and make sure he was okay. She entered his hospital room to find him unconcious, his eyes closed, the monitor beside him still beeped steadily.

She leaned over him and kissed him on the top of his head. She placed her hand on his forehead and gently caressed him. God, she missed him. She needed to talk to him, to tell him all that had happened, to have him by her side.

She placed his hand in hers and began whispering to him the events of the last few days. "You won't freaking believe this shit," she began. And then she continued to tell him of Chago and Birger and what she had found in Daniel's laptop, which wasn't much considering all of the running around she had done.

"I wish you were with me at The Righteous Group's headquarters. It was insane. You would have been amazing talking to Chago. And that mansion? Oh my god, Javier. It was off the chain. I thought it was THE headquarters, but I was SO wrong. I mean, totally wrong. I bet it isn't even where the guy lives."

She didn't tell him what she did to save him or how it would affect him. Even in this private setting, she wasn't ready. She hoped that one day when she was forced to tell him then he would understand why she did it. She knew her reasons were selfish. She knew that if he had been given the choice to either die naturally or live a life that some may consider unnatural then he would most likely choose death. But she truly needed him.

She couldn't allow him to die.

"I love you, so so much." She placed his hand between hers. "I'm sorry. I feel like I wasn't there for you. That somehow I could have prevented all of this." She smirked. "I don't know how but, somehow ..." her words trailed off and then she began again. "When you wake up, I'm going to ask you to marry me."

He shifted a bit and then turned his head towards her. "Marry me, huh?" he said. Slowly he opened his eyes and a grin came across his face.

"Oh my god!" she exclaimed. She covered her mouth in shock and then hugged him. "Holy shit!" She cupped his head in her hands and kissed him. "How much did you hear?" She asked a little bit afraid at what his response would be. He tried to sit up so she helped him prop himself up with pillows.

"I heard enough," he said coyly. "So when I had asked you to marry me, that wasn't enough? Now you have to do it?"

She laughed. "I figured I should reciprocate considering I never really gave you an answer."

He motioned to the water pitcher at his bedside and she poured him a cup, put a straw in it, and brought it to his mouth.

"Don't drink too quickly," she said, just like she had heard him instruct patients so many times before.

She knew the few times he had asked her to marry him previously she had said it was too soon or they were too young or they needed a house. She came up with something, anything to keep herself from fully giving her heart to this man. In this sterile environment, she realized that she had given her heart to him a long, long time ago. As she watched him carefully sip through the straw, all she felt was relief and joy that he was still alive. Her long standing fear of marriage had stemmed from the chance that she may lose him. Now that she had nearly lost him, she knew it was a bunch of crap. A silly fear since the true loss would be never to have fully given herself to him and not letting him know how much she loved him.

He stopped drinking and thanked her for her help.

"I love you too, Luna. I would be honored to marry you."

With that acceptance, she leaned in and they kissed. A soft, gentle, loving kiss. The kind of kiss that contained all of their love, their joy, their bonding in the embrace. The kind of kiss that she never wanted to end. She sat on his bedside and they kissed for a few moments more until he pulled away.

"I think you owe me an engagement ring," he said.

She laughed. "I do. I'll have to take care of that."

He smiled at her with an endearment filled with every ounce of love he had.

"I better let them know you're awake." She motioned to the monitor. "I'm sure they're going to want to check your vitals."

He sighed. "Yeah, that's true. It's about that time."

Luna checked her watch.

"Let me guess, you need to go?" he asked.

She hated to admit it, but she still had a lot of work to do at the bakery. And it dawned on her that she had no idea how long it had been since she had checked in with Margarite. Her boss was probably having a fit. At that moment, Luna was thankful that she had the weekend before her which bought her some time to get caught back up. Typically Margarite and Luna only worked the weekends if there was an urgent order. Thank god nothing like that waited for her so she could use the time for her standing orders.

"Not yet," she said.

She yawned and considered curling into the bed next to him so that they could fall asleep together and then wake up in each other's arms. She missed that. The desire for their bodies to be fully embraced throbbed between them undeniably, and yet she fought it. The aching need for him made her cry, a silent cry, but tears nonetheless. She took a better look at him and acknowledged his exhaustion. His voice filled with love and tiredness. His face and body showed signs of strain. He still had a lot of healing to do.

She kissed him and decided it was probably better to rest at home. "I love you, J. I'm going to get a nurse to check on you. Then I'll jet, okay?"

She could tell by the way he looked at her that although he didn't want her to go, he was almost too tired to stay awake. His body sagged back in the bed, his eyes barely open.

"I'll tell you what, I'll stick around until you fall asleep, okay?" she said.

He agreed and then shifted back so he was laying down again. Even though she knew she shouldn't, she curled up next to him in the bed. The warmth of their bodies was a comfort that she had missed. His scent was that of medicines and anti-septics while underneath the smell of his warmth, his centeredness, home, came through and made her bring him forward in a closer embrace.

She watched as he closed his eyes and then she thought of the work she had waiting for her on her brother's laptop. She was certain that it would result in multiple discussions with Birger. Of course, this assumed that Birger would answer the phone. Which was a completely different question. Hell, after their last few interactions, she was lucky if he picked up the phone at all. She hadn't given him many reasons to like her.

Javier's breathing slowed to that of a deep sleep. After a few moments, she navigated her way out of the bed and found an attending nurse to check on him.

She made her way out of the hospital, this time from the main entrance. The chaotic nature of the emergency room had become too much for her to handle. Plus, she didn't need to go through the heart of the ER. She wanted quiet.

She craved peace.

She realized that she had been going in and out of the hospital through the emergency room because of habit. She typically came to the hospital to visit Javier when he was working. In this instance, since he had been moved to a regular patient's room, her need to go through the ER didn't exist, so she gave herself the emotional break of leaving like any other hospital visitor.

She checked her phone for messages as she went through the sliding glass doors. When she looked up, she saw a familiar gait and a woman's profile. The walk wasn't as harried as before, but distinctive nonetheless.

"I thought the police officer said she was in custody," Luna said to herself.

Luna snuck around the side, just out of eyeshot of the person she followed. The woman turned to look both ways before crossing the street (at least she knew to do that much) and Luna's suspicions were confirmed. Crossing the two-lane road was none other than Samantha Lostgrove.

"That lying piece of shit," Luna hissed.

Samantha made her way across the street and down an alley.

"Oh no, you don't." Luna rushed across the street, nearly got hit by a car (She did not follow the "look both ways before crossing the street" rule), cursed herself for doing something so damn stupid, and then followed Samantha into the darkened alley to only-god-knew-where.

CHAPTER FIFTY-TWO

The man hurried into the back room with Chago several feet behind. This had been the same room where the transformation ceremony had been fulfilled a few hours prior. It had been scrubbed of all evidence of the previous inductee's presence and all had been prepared for the next candidate.

The previous inductee had been escorted to another room so he could rest and recuperate prior to returning to his responsibilities with the Security Council.

Chago showed the new inductee into TRG's ceremonial room and closed the door behind him. "Mr. Jun. Thank you for joining me at such short notice. The urgency behind our completion of The Transformation will become evident soon."

Chago brought forward the ceremonial cup and handed it to Mr. Jun and then directed him to the center of the room. The spot marked by ancient signs that only a spare few could read.

Clearly nervous, Mr. Jun, an Asian gentleman in his mid-thirties, had been easily convinced to be transformed and join TRG. He had been raised on the Chinese legends of huli jing, a fox spirit that shifted into a young woman. Through his relations with friends from other countries, he had heard of similar folklore.

Once Chago had demonstrated the truth behind shapeshifting and that not only was the legend of huli jing true, but that there were other shifters from the same region, then Mr. Jun's only concern had been whether he had to turn into a woman in order for this to work. Chago fought back a laugh and reinforced with the security council representative that he had nothing of that nature to fear. "The power you will gain far outweighs any pain."

Chago guided Mr. Jun to kneel in the center of the room, chalice in hand.

"We will need to move quickly. We must simply complete the final ceremony. Then you will fulfill your true destiny."

The inductee trembled in fear and anticipation as Chago poured the elixir into the chalice, which marked the beginning of the ceremony.

CHAPTER FIFTY-THREE

Tailing Samantha had been harder than when Luna followed Chago. Samantha didn't have a car, so Luna followed her down the alley and to the subway, doing her best to stay out of eyeshot. One train car behind Samantha, Luna was careful to exit when Samantha did while partially hiding herself behind other travelers.

Luna was sure to keep the tracker on her phone active so she knew exactly where they went. She just wished she had thought of this before. Surprised by where they went, Samantha went over the bridge into Center City Philadelphia and then hopped on another train. They made enough train switches that Luna worried that Samantha had figured out she had a tail.

They got off at the 30th Street Station in Philadelphia and made their way up the staircase. Every once in a while, the stringy blonde looked around as if she either tried to figure out where she was or she had figured out that someone was following her. Either way, Luna sensed it before Samantha turned and was able to hide in time to avoid being spotted. At least that was her assumption.

And that was when things got weird.

Luna would have bet that Samantha would have headed out of the iconic train station and to one of the major structures nearby like the Aramark building or Exelon Energy's corporate headquarters. Instead, Samantha made her way to the food court, said *hi* to the gentleman running the pizza stall, and then went to the back of the stall and snuck through what seemed to be a wall panel but turned out to be a hidden door.

What. The. Fuck.

The gentleman manning the stall cheerily greeted a customer who pointed out a slice of pepperoni and a deep dish slice of plain pizza. The pizza guy chatted with the customer while packaging the requested slices and rang him up. Luna waited at a nearby table and acted like she was reading something on her phone. She just needed to wait for the right moment when she could get past him unseen.

Just when she thought it would never happen, a delivery man with a flatbed full of supplies piled well above eye level came over and the pair began unloading everything from huge cans of tomato sauce to shredded mozzarella. Luna neared the stall and waited for both men to be distracted and then she slid through the same secret passage door.

She carefully closed the door behind her and found herself at the opening of a narrow hallway which quickly became incredibly dark with the closing of the door. Luna was surprised that she could make out the outlines of a staircase that curved the further it went downward. She guessed this was another benefit of her transformative powers. The questions became, "How deep did these steps go into the bowels underneath 30th Street Station?" and "What would she find once she got to where they were going?".

She passed doors that she only identified because of their outlines. This chilly passageway had clearly been made for fellow lycanthropes with similar abilities. No way a regular human could make her way without some type of light. She couldn't tell if Samantha had gone through one of these doors, but something about them told her that no one was behind them. As she passed, she sensed a coldness to them, an emptiness. Plus she did not smell the earthy, salty, musky scent of humans. She couldn't believe she actually thought that, but it was true. Unlike in the subway and the hospital where the scents were almost overwhelming at times, even before her transformation, these spots smelled empty. Her gifts must have been maturing.

She continued down the winding staircase. After a period of time that felt infinite, but must have truly only been a few moments, her senses heightened even more. At the risk of being caught based on what she might find, she reached a doorway that emanated warmth as the musky, earthy scent of humans rose from behind it. She put her ear to the door and listened for any movement or talking, anything. Once she had been certain that no one stood on the other side, she slowly opened it.

What she found.

Well.

As Luna would say, *holy shit.*

CHAPTER FIFTY-FOUR

The rooms glowed, softly lit with an aura of reds and golds. Luna felt like she had entered a sacred chamber. At the end of the hall, a door was rimmed with ancient symbols that had originated in an Asian country long, long ago. On the right side, a wall of ancient wooden cabinets with rustic metal pulls waited to be opened. Bigger than office cabinet drawers, Luna prayed they didn't contain bodies. She shook off the thought when she realized that if body parts were in this chamber then she would have sniffed them out before this moment. She carefully made her way down the hall and placed a hand on the face of a drawer just to see if she sensed anything from it.

Meanwhile, she listened intently for movement, still anticipating that Samantha might come barreling out at any moment. She slid a drawer open to find papers. They seemed to be lists of TRG members and their locations. She took a few snapshots with her phone and then continued.

She listened and felt the door, and then made her way

through it to another chamber. This one with a wall of monitors like she had seen security officers use in office buildings. On the top right screen, Chago hovered over someone. Luna moved in closer to see a man of light complexion, short sandy brown hair, eyes closed, kneeling before Chago.

The man drank from a seemingly familiar chalice. Luna held up her phone and recorded the moment and made a mental note to share it with Birger. She hated that she had such a heavy reliance on him, but at this point, he was the only person, other than Javier, she thought she could trust.

Just as she started to put her phone down, the man began to transform. She held her phone back up and watched in horror as he shifted so quickly and with such ferocity that Luna nearly threw up watching it. It looked like his bones were breaking and stitching themselves back together. An invisible force crushed his body into a bastardization of a shapeshifter and a human, then shifted him back into his original form. He lay unconscious before Chago whose smile reminded her of the Cheshire Cat in her dreams. Fuck, that's where she saw it before; that Cheshire Cat smile.

She hissed a curse under her breath when her phone told her she didn't have service. She needed to share this information with Birger sooner rather than later. Technology always seemed to be against her. The exponential increase in her natural instincts seemed to be having an impact on other diminishing aspects of what she had been conditioned to rely on.

She socked her phone back into her pants and started out of the room. Everything about what she witnessed screamed danger. Just as she reached to open the door, she sensed Samantha nearby.

And the woman was headed her way.

Luna figured she had enough time to hide before Samantha

would see her. With that intuition she entered the hall and immediately thought of as a hiding spot. She opened each cabinet door until she found a spot that was empty and then jumped inside. She used the force of propelling her bodyweight backwards to close it. The drawer slammed a bit louder than she had anticipated. She feared that Samantha or someone else nearby heard her. With that she cursed herself.

Fuck.

Immediately, she heard the echoes of Samantha's shoes running through a nearby chamber and back into the hall where Luna hid.

"Nothing," Samantha said.

"You need to ensure it's secure," said the voice of a man unknown to Luna.

"You don't worry about me. I know my shit."

"I've heard that before."

"You heard that from my sister, you jackass," Samantha said with a defensive huff. "And the last thing I am is my sister."

"I'll need you here before midnight. We only have one more council member to indoctrinate before we will have complete control of the council."

Luna heard Samantha lean against the wall. It felt like she was just on the other side of the drawer where Luna hid.

Of course, she is, Luna thought. She prayed Samantha didn't have the same gifts as she did. Based on how she acted so far, she didn't.

"These fucking humans have fucked up the world enough. It's time for us to take it back."

"We do this with peace as our final goal," said the male voice.

"Not all peacekeeping missions are nonviolent."

Luna swore she heard laughter as Samantha began down the hallway. Based on the echo pattern of her footsteps,

Samantha and the man returned to the exit which would take them to 30th Street Station's main food court. Even with the increasing distance between Luna and the pair, she could hear their continued conversation. *Interesting.*

"I got what we need," Samantha said. "I'll have it there before midnight."

CHAPTER FIFTY-FIVE

Chago finished the enchantment as the man before him completed The Transformation. Silently, Chago repeated the familial blessings to help this man on his new path among the Lycanthrope.

The ceremonies exhausted him. The heightened transformation elixir that had been developed specifically for this event triggered Chago as it would any lycanthrope nearby. Thankfully, he had years of training to prevent his change. Knowing how much it affected him, and considering his skill and experience, he couldn't risk other shapeshifters to be nearby when this new serum was used. Chago had to get mentally and emotionally lost in the enchantment and completely focus on it as the indoctrinated changed. If he did not, then he risked shifting and having the hunger become too great for him. Not a risk worth testing.

Even then, with all of his safety precautions he felt it affect him. He hated to think of what would happen if one of his assistants was nearby. Hence, why he insisted, no, demanded that they were not in the same building at the time of the

special Transformations. Highly unusual, the standard ceremony involved all of The Righteous Group's high council and
key members. But they simply couldn't risk it. There had been
too many tragedies already.

He went to the corner of the room and retrieved a blanket
that had been placed there for the end of the changing. One to
provide comfort to the newly indoctrinated. As the gentleman
awoke, he moved with a carefulness only found of those in
pain, his body severely bruised.

Chago could only imagine the pain he had felt in the
heightened change. He gently placed the blanket over the
man's shoulders.

"Thank you," the man whispered. Slowly he got up from
the floor and bowed before the leader of TRG. The new
member's fear and hesitation which had been present at the
beginning of the ceremony had disappeared. In his eyes, Chago
could see a sparkle, the rare sparkle of a true believer.

Chago placed a hand on the man's shoulder. "Our destiny
begins."

CHAPTER FIFTY-SIX

S he waited until she heard the door which led to the upper
floors close, and the footsteps had become distant and
then nonexistent. The darkness and enclosed nature of the
cabinet felt like a tomb, but an impromptu hiding place Luna
was thankful for. The last thing she needed was to have had
Samantha discover her.

She felt around the inside of the cabinet door and found
the latch to the lock, tripped it, and then used her weight to
force it a smidge open so her hands could slide it open wider
enabling her to climb out of the tomb. She hadn't sensed
anyone else in this sub-chamber so she hoped her instincts were
right.

So far, so good.

She climbed out and then returned to the cabinets where
she had found the paperwork, took several more images of maps
and documents that looked important, and then quietly made
her way back up the pitch-black narrow staircase and to the
back of the pizza stall. Unnoticed, she slipped into the crowd
and to help her become less conspicuous, she ordered a slice of

hand tossed plain with mushrooms, sat at a nearby table, and
sent a text to Birger.

She was pretty sure that one of the numbers he called her
on was a cell phone and she assumed it took messages. As she
devoured her slice, much hungrier than she had anticipated,
Birger responded and said he'd send her a secure video conference line and to contact him on it as soon as she was in a safe
place.

She sent a thumbs up emoji and made her way back to the
subway and went home.

Let the real party start.

CHAPTER FIFTY-SEVEN

They waited for him, as he knew they would. Chago had taken the last blanket-wrapped recruit to a quiet, enclosed chamber to rest. A nurse waited to check his vitals and to be sure that he had survived The Special Transformation without serious injuries. They would quickly need him to fulfill his duties and couldn't risk any unexpected issues.

Chago stood before the group of twelve - including himself, the TRG High Council made thirteen. Once upon a time, each member represented a key family of true bloods, the highest order. Now they were voted in by the membership. Even with the voting, no one questioned Chago's position. He had been a legend, an icon, for more years than he cared to acknowledge. Most of TRG couldn't remember a time when he wasn't in charge.

"Today, we completed the final indoctrination. The last piece of the first part of our plan," Chago said. He stood in the center of a circle formed by the council members, his hands crossed before him, his stance that of a professor addressing his students. "Our coffers are full due to our active investments.

Thank you to Member Johansen for the direction that ensured our success."

The council clapped in agreement. Member Johansen had been TRG's financial advisor for the last twenty years and multiplied what had been in the millions to trillions, ensuring TRG's continued ability to act independent of other organizations. To continue to work on the fringe.

"Our scholarships and teachings for true bloodline descendants have been put in place. We are fostering the next generation of leaders across industries and continents."

Again, the statement brought forward a round of applause to which Chago simply stood and nodded in acknowledgement.

"And thus our third area of focus has been fully enabled today. In the coming days, we will see our newest members begin a peaceful takeover of key countries throughout the globe. Initiating and enabling our formal takeover of the human world. Through this, we can end famine, global warming, hate, and bias while taking our rightful place as the world's high kings."

The council gave him an ovation. Some even cheered. In his mind, Chago completed his last sentence, "and I take my place as the true god and ruler of this world."

CHAPTER FIFTY-EIGHT

L una made sure no one had followed her home. Birger texted her instructions on where to send the information she had gathered and then on how to test her home for listening devices. At first, she felt silly and then, after she found a small circular metal device that looked like the inside of an earpiece, she took him - and her situation - more seriously.

He instructed her on how to get rid of the device without alarming those who were invading her privacy. She simply put it in an area of her apartment where she rarely went and changed her behavior so she only took calls in the farthest room from the device. He also had her double check that no air ducts were near the device so conversations couldn't be picked up and listened in on.

By the time she finally got on the phone with Birger, she had found four more devices. She couldn't believe it. How the hell did they get there? Once upon a time she wouldn't have believed it but considering all that had happened, she not only believed it, she expected it. And it pissed her off. How dare they invade her privacy? For a small one-bedroom apartment, all of these listening devices was definitely overkill.

Luna and Birger discussed the pictures she took, the video she recorded, and what she overheard.

She could have sworn he cursed but in a language she wasn't familiar. Even without being able to translate what he was saying, his tone informed her that this was some serious shit.

"This is bad, right," she asked. She did her best not to be sarcastic.

It didn't work.

"First, thank you for sharing this," he began. "Second, we are going to have a lot of work to do."

"Wait, I'm not doing anything until you start explaining what the hell is going on."

She waited through a long pause wondering what the hell he could be mentally debating. She needed to know. Her brother died, her fiancé nearly died, she'd been tailed like she's some super spy, she had been transformed by ancient bloodline powers, and she had subsequently witnessed another, freaky, ungodly transformations that just didn't seem natural even to her new nature. Not to mention the super-secret locations, people who were supposed to be arrested but weren't, and a half dozen other "Are you shitting me?" items. It was time for Birger to suck it up and start talking.

"Fine."

CHAPTER FIFTY-NINE

L una took a seat in front of her laptop, sure to have dialed in on a secured line, and waited for Birger to begin.

"We, The Lycanthropic Society, exist to keep the world in balance. The world is full of various species including lycanthropes. You have also heard us, including you, being called shapeshifters. And since the lycanthropes became organized, we have done our best to make sure that everything in the world is fair and balanced for the various species. Humans, shapeshifters, all."

Luna didn't necessarily like what Birger just implied, that there were many more species similar to humans and shapeshifters on the planet, but for now, she chose to ignore it, and allowed him to continue.

"The Righteous Group which is led by Chago, had originated as a part of The Lycanthrope Society. The primary difference is that TRG members believe that all other beings should be subservient to lycanthropes and that they are the true gods."

Luna leaned in towards her laptop screen. "Wait, what?

You had mentioned this before, but I need more explanation." She searched his face on the display and saw no signs of variance. "You are serious. They're all on some kind of hallucinogen, right?"

He laughed. "Maybe back in the days of Zeus, but not now. They truly believe this."

Her mouth slightly agape, Luna shifted back in her chair. This explained a lot, Luna thought. Realizing her look of shock, she shut her mouth and then nodded. "Now what? What does this all mean?"

Birger lifted a handheld device resembling an iPad, touched the screen a few times and then continued. "If I am piecing together everything you found then TRG is planning on taking over the UN and starting a world war." He said this like it was just another day in a library.

Unsure if she heard him correctly, Luna clarified. "You mean the United Nations?"

"Yes."

"Holy shit," she said instinctively. "But I thought the UN was all about peace."

"They are," he said. "But it's peace by any means, including force. Clearly this would put the world out of balance, which is why the TLS exists, and specifically why I am here to help you."

"Maybe we can get Javier's help too," Luna said without thinking. Her core desire was to have him with her as much as possible. He was truly the one person in the world she trusted. For a split second, she forgot that he wasn't quite mobile yet, even though she hoped the ad hoc ceremony she conducted while they were in the throes of being attacked by a maniacal drug addict had even bigger benefits than helping him get over the hump of being nearly fatally injured.

With the realization that she screwed up, she continued. "I

bet he'd help if I asked him to. I mean, I know he probably can't be there, physically but ... well ... we are going to need help." If she had to pick between Birger and Javier, then it'd be a no-brainer. She had had only two men in the world she trusted and one of them she lost only a few weeks prior.

Birger stared at her with a blank expression which only caused her to ramble on. "I mean, he can't go with me, but he could help, maybe do research, or be a lookout or something."

"A. Is he out of the hospital yet? B. We don't typically allow those not involved in the society to get engaged in our matters. C. What are you not telling me?" His tone had turned distrustful.

"What do you mean?" She tried to sound coy, but knew she had made a mistake and had missed the mark of covering up the fact that she technically inducted Javier into the society. Technically. Admittedly, what she did was rather *ol' skool* and in the heat of the "him being shot moment" but technically speaking Javier had every right to be at lycanthrope functions as she did. She was never very good at lying.

"This is more than you telling him about us. I can hear it in your voice and see it on your face," he said. "You bonded with him, didn't you?"

Luna did her best not to respond and fully realized it was too late. He had clearly figured it out.

On the video chat, she saw Birger run his hands through his hair in frustration. "I knew this had been a mistake. You shouldn't have left before having all of the information." He looked up at her, his eyes sad, his voice wistful. "I had hoped you would have been smarter. I didn't think you'd use the bonding on your boyfriend." His voice trailed off.

Luna flushed.

"Does he know what you've done?"

"Well, no. But I'm sure once I tell him what had happened, and why I did it, then he'll be completely fine with it."

Birger scoffed. "You made him into a creature that until a few months ago you thought existed in fairytales. And you think he's going to jump for joy to find out he's joined you? Oh, and you haven't told him about you either, right?"

She slouched and shook her head.

"Right." He paused, deep in consideration. "Give me a moment."

Birger left the screen and returned minutes later.

"I need you to listen to me," he said. He looked both grieved and serious. "I'm going to share with you something we haven't shared with someone of your junior stature in our organization since we've been in existence. That said, I have received special permission to do so."

Luna scoffed. "Oh yeah, what makes me so special?"

"Other than the fact that I have to tell you this because you already know far too much, you're of what's considered to be royal bloodline. So you'll be told everything, eventually. And, I need you to understand what we need to do next. Other than all of that, no reason at all." He threw on a faux smile which matched his dry sarcasm.

"Great. I'll follow up on the whole 'royal bloodline' thing and 'junior' thing later. For now, what do you want to tell me?" She fought her desire to get sidetracked with the other information he revealed.

Royalty?

Stuff she'd have to know anyway? Why?

The longer she was engaged in this crap, the weirder it got.

"Freya and Lovisa left us another gift. They had foreseen a time when we may need to reverse the gift of the lycanthrope."

"You can do that?" Luna asked.

"Not for just anyone. We can only reverse those who

became shapeshifters through the enchantment. For those who are of our type or rather lycanthropes by heritage, the reversal will not work. But for those who obtained our gifts through the enchantment and ritual, this should be quite effective." His voice quavered. He paused, deep in thought. His expression changed from being informative to expressing true concern.

"Why are you hesitating? What's wrong? " she asked.

Birger's gaze returned to the screen. "For everything, there is a price. And depending on how long ago the bonding was done, with whom, and how the ritual was completed, the price could be quite significant."

"What does that mean?" Luna was growing tired of the vague references, even though, this time, a part of her didn't want to know. She was pretty sure she had already figured it out. What could be the most significant price to pay for being made a shapeshifter?

He ignored her question and continued. "I will send you the recipe for the antidote and the necessary enchantment. We need to give the newly transformed world leaders the potion and then recite the incantation to force their bonding to be severed."

"Sounds easy enough." She studied the notes that he sent to her on her phone. What he sent her was written phonetically. She had no idea what these words formed. They were definitely from a foreign language. "What happens if someone has the potion and they aren't a shapeshifter?"

Birger shrugged. "Indigestion. Nothing more."

"And if they are? I mean, what if they are a lycanthrope through the spells and serum?"

Birger paused. "Truthfully, I do not know. I've never seen it used. I have only heard that it can be quite a dramatic change back to being only human."

The significance of this job finally hit her. She needed to

somehow get into the United Nations, identify the TRG-made shapeshifter members of the UN, somehow get them to ingest the potion while she recited the enchantment. *Holy crap.*

She needed help. She doubted she would be able to do this alone.

"You said before that I had other relatives who've come to see you. Why can't I get their help? And why can't I get the help of others in TLS? What about Rebecca?"

She wasn't thrilled with the idea of getting her help, but some help was better than nothing.

"Not all of your relatives who visited are alive and of those who are, many would rather remain in hiding."

"Are any of my relatives in TRG?"

Birger paused. His expression grew grave.

"Never mind. Based on your lack of answer, I understand."

CHAPTER SIXTY

C hago ended the council session. The newest members of the order rested in the center of the nearly bare chamber in the bowels of the building. The scents of molten wax from candles that rimmed the room blended with the beastial smells of sweat and the breathy hungers of the changing that had just occurred. Spent from the ceremonies, with a nod to acknowledge each individual present, Chago exited the building and retired to his own chambers near the New York Branch of TRG. His condo was on the top story of a twenty-story building near Penn Station. Only a few blocks from the secret TRG chambers, he loved the view of his condo, especially in the winter when snow coated the landscape. It reminded him of his early days in Sweden when the countryside had been blanketed by winter. The bright whiteness against the near-blinding rays of sunlight.

His modern, all-white apartment was sparse in decorations, though he rested in the thick cushions of a burgundy leather chair before his mahogany desk that faced the great expanse of New York City. He flipped open his laptop and began wandering through the community boards that had brought him to Daniel. The same boards had allowed him to find a family lineage that he had thought had ended long ago. These same boards, with some digging and discussions, enabled him to identify the true beings, the ones who belonged with him and his elected. Every once in a while, someone would appear online who did not deserve to share the same space as a lycan-thrope, and he took care of them as they were meant to be treated.

This is what he did every evening before he retired. This is how he rested and relaxed. This is how he rebuilt the core of his society - one precious Ancestry.com posting at a time.

CHAPTER SIXTY-ONE

"I have no idea how you landed us this." Margarite positioned the pastries on the special serving tray while Luna continued to prepare the delectable delights.

Luna had immediately called Margarite as soon as she and Birger had brainstormed the plan. He had gotten the broader board's permission to move forward. She had no idea who the "board" was, but she was familiar with this kind of thing through Javier. He had come home complaining about different things the "board" had discussed or turned down. In this case, all she cared about was that they agreed.

"I have a friend who has a friend. They heard about the special event, that's all." Luna piped icing on top of a coconut cupcake and sprinkled a combination of dark chocolate and coconut shreds on top. The scent made her swoon. This said, she knew better than to devour a cupcake on an empty stomach. The last thing she needed was a sugar rush followed by a sour stomach. She loved her confections, but not that much. "They were going to bring in some supermarket brand desserts for the party, but they prefer giving the work to a small business."

This wasn't a total lie. When TLG leveraged their contacts they found out that a break had been scheduled for the United Nations Security Council during their proceedings. The rest period was intended to encourage casual discussion. For the break, the UN's organizers had originally planned on bringing in snacks from Trader Joe's. When they were provided the option to have gourmet cupcakes, cookies, and pastries to be hand-catered by a small, woman-owned bakery, they jumped at the chance. And of course, Luna was right there with Margarite's phone number.

"But us? Not that I'm not thankful, but aren't there a dozen bakeries they could have ordered from the area that's closer to the UN?"

Before accepting the assignment from Birger, Luna had questioned why they needed her if they already had a big enough network and contacts to score this kind of setup. To that, Birger simply said, "We are not supposed to directly influence world events. Because you are so new to our organization, it is a fine line that we are gently walking along by allowing you to do this."

Interesting that he didn't reference the fact that she was untrained and risking her life for this, but she figured she would pick that fight with him another day.

"I guess they heard about us and thought we were pretty amazing." Luna said evasively. She thought back on her conversation with Birger and almost laughed out loud. If this wasn't directly affecting world events, then she didn't know what was. "Come on, Margarite. Your family bakery is legendary."

Secretly, Luna knew this opportunity to get their bakery in front of world leaders saved her skin with Margarite. When Luna had first called her boss, she thought Margarite was going to jump down her throat for all of the hours she'd missed and for basically avoiding more direct contact than emails and texts. But as soon as Luna mentioned a gig at the United Nations and the fact that this would give the bakery a shot at all new clientele, well, that was a game changer.

CHAPTER SIXTY-TWO

After Chago finished his evening wandering through the online community boards, he closed his laptop and gazed out over the evening skyline. The buildings dusted with snow blurred the city landscape. A purple-blue hue covered the night sky. When traveling, he often craved to be back in this spot, his favorite location in North America.

Another potential recruit had appeared on the boards. This one could possibly be as strong as Daniel and Luna. If so, and if he could get to her first, then all the better. He knew he could train her to be among the most gifted. Possibly even his second in command.

He remembered when his first incarnation had interacted with Ulf and Freya. In the subsequent reincarnation, he had retained or rather regained the memories of previous incarnations. Little did he know that Ulf and Freya would prove to be the strongest of the bloodlines and that their direct descendants would be the most powerful. They had demonstrated abilities even he had not discovered. Much of Chago's heightened gifts he had learned from the descendants of Hiwa. He later realized that some of what she had tried to teach him he was unable to do because of his own physical and spiritual limitations. That truth had always vexed him.

He pondered New York's skyline. So much in these lives was unfair. If he had those gifts, those of Freya and Ulf, then he could do so much with them. The key power that had been passed down to each member within that bloodline had been the ability to shift into multiple beings and tap into the natural instincts of those creatures. He knew Freya had never received this gift from Ulf, and Ulf had been careful to limit his changings to only that of a wolf when he was with his beloved. But Chago had seen at least some of the additional creatures when he had battled side-by-side with Ulf when they were both in service of the king. To this day, Chago felt awe at the thought of it. To have the gifts of the bear, the fox, the horse, and even mythical creatures like the phoenix. My god, it was unimaginable and such a waste on those who have the gifts naturally.

At least it was a waste on the likes of Luna...

For now.

CHAPTER SIXTY-THREE

L una pulled the van up to the rear of the United Nations Headquarters building along the edge of the East River and showed her security pass and her letter of confirmation to be of service to the Security Council on this day to the guard.

The guard, dressed in standard rent-a-cop grey polyester buttoned down gear, looked at the letter and eyed Luna. "Get out of the vehicle," he insisted.

Luna, playing the role of caterer in her white chef's jacket and matching pants, smiled and exited the van. Immediately, the guard, who stood only a few inches taller than her patted her down with a rigor she hadn't expected. Not in a sexual manner, but rather a forceful one.

Man, these people were serious.

He handed her a clipboard. "Read and sign." The guard's guidance was simple, as was the affidavit which basically stated that she was who she claimed to be and was there in peace. Luna went along without challenging the guard. Yet, silently she laughed to herself and wondered if they really thought that someone with evil intentions would say, "You know what? I'm actually here to start a war, so I can't sign this. Ciao" and then hand him back the clipboard and drive away.

Probably not.

Once she was done with the formalities, she popped open the van and transferred the trays of pastries onto rolling tables. The security officer directed her through the hallway. She realized that some of the security and staff looked familiar. Had they been at the hospital? If so then she doubted that they were here to represent TLS. If these additional officers weren't there to help her then ... She did her best to duck out of their purview.

"Shit," she exhaled. If she recognized them, then someone might recognize her. She knew she had to be even more cautious. The guard who had greeted her at the rear of the building proceeded to guide her into a side room with tables and chairs set up for dining. In the corner, a bartender prepared a moveable bar, and a waiter set up the tables for the delectables, plates, and utensils.

She acknowledged the waiter and began laying everything out. She placed all of the boxes on the tables and then excused herself to go to the ladies room. She slipped into the bathroom, and once she was sure no one else was present, she buzzed Birger on her phone.

"How do I know who has been recruited?" she whispered, sure to use language as vague as possible, just in case.

"Look for the telltale shaking. Based on the materials you found, they wouldn't have been changed long ago, so they probably don't know how to control their powers yet. If they even know that they have powers," Birger said.

Luna thanked him and before she hung up, she paused and said, "By the way," she sighed. "The guards. I'm almost positive I saw them at the hospital."

CHAPTER SIXTY-FOUR

Chago focused on his hand and made it switch from human form to wolf claw and then back again. He then put himself in a trance by whispering the incantation he had been taught so many hundreds of years ago. The words were now as familiar as his own name.

His eyes melded from a deep brown to a golden yellow. Next his face elongated, just enough so his teeth sharpened and protruded to become the fangs they were meant to be, their ferocity was unlimited. He stretched his arms outward as if he welcomed the moon and its vividness, and then held in a howl.

Only one as powerful as he could change in such a fashion. There was control and then there was the ultimate control of powers. And only Chago had this skill. At least to his knowledge. He switched back to his human form. "Now it's time to prepare for The Gathering."

CHAPTER SIXTY-FIVE

Luna came out of the bathroom and immediately regretted not being more careful. A guard with a distinctly familiar and very determined look walked toward her with a forthright-ness that let her know he was definitely up to no good. As he continued to approach her, she swiftly went down the hallway and followed signs to a reception room. She looked behind her to see that he was still there, still determined. She entered the reception room and then pretended like she had more work to do on the display. She could sense the guard nearing her. Even though she didn't know if he was a changeling or not, she figured she'd take the chance so she picked up a vanilla cupcake with lavender icing and divided it in half.

"Excuse me," she said to the security officer. "I wondered if you could taste this for me. I just need to be sure that it's of the best quality for such honored guests." She smiled, a faux meek smile.

He smirked and eyed her like he didn't trust her. She lifted the pastry towards his mouth and tilted her head in innocence.

He definitely didn't believe her act. He swiped the cupcake

from her hand. "Fine," he said. "then you will come with me." He chomped down on the cupcake.

Luna patiently watched as he chewed on the treat. She looked at her watch.

"It's okay. But that's enough of a delay. Time for you to come with me," he said and grabbed her by the arm. She had thought that he would take her to a secret lair or a hidden room, but instead, he shoved her into what she presumed was a cleaning closet with him right behind her. She guessed the TRG hadn't had secret lairs and hidden floors like they did at 30th Street Station in Philadelphia, which is why he opted to toss her into a cleaning closet. He slammed the door behind them. Thankfully the room was big enough to contain a vacuum, mop, sink, and a wall of cleaning supplies so it wasn't as cramped as she thought it would be.

He looked at her with a determination like he was ready to strike. He must have been given an order to keep her at bay while they completed their plans, otherwise she was pretty sure he would have already taken care of her in a not so gentle way.

She glanced at her watch again. "Now," Luna said, guessing that she had given the elixir enough time to get into his system.

He laughed as he struck a pose as if his hands were about to turn to claws and slash her to pieces "Yes, now."

She said the incantation once, struggling to remember the words, the guard looked at her quizzically. She started again and this time she said the full spell only to be perplexed as to why he remained whole. So she said it a third time and with the third repetition she picked up a broom and used it as a shield.

He allowed his hands to change into claws, his fangs drawn with a fierce roar.

She continued to recite the incantation, wary that she may have said it wrong or for whatever reason it wouldn't work.

Please god, let it work, she thought. She closed her eyes, anticipating the feeling of his sharp and deadly claws breaking her skin. After a few seconds of no impact, she opened her eyes to find him grabbing his throat.

He began to struggle and make choking sounds.

Shocked, Luna gaped in surprise. She wasn't sure what the elixir would do or how it would do it, especially since she didn't know if this guy was a blood relation or a creation through spells.

He bent over and curled up in agony, clutching his stomach, seemingly fighting the need to cry out in pain.

She lowered the broom and with determination, slammed it against the back of his head, over and over again until he was knocked out. She proceeded to smile. "You can call me Cuz.'"

CHAPTER SIXTY-SIX

"You have yet to learn how to control your gifts, let alone understand what they are." Chago spoke to an image of Luna he was holding. It was a photograph from an advertisement for a cooking class she had taught the year before. "Only I can teach you."

He put on his suit coat and prepared to go outside. If the timing was as he expected, the United Nations Security Council would go on their anticipated break and then shortly afterwards would vote on what had been loosely positioned as peace missions to China, India, Columbia, Saudi Arabia, and Ukraine, thus covering each continent. Therefore, initiating the next step of their plan.

He palmed her image. "We will need your gifts." He crushed the photo and tossed it into his fireplace. "I will teach you and you will join us. Or you will not exist."

CHAPTER SIXTY-SEVEN

With a handful of cupcakes balanced on her palm, Luna ducked into the main room for the Security Council. She had left the unconscious guard in the broom closet. She had used an old trick she saw on television and used the power cord of a vacuum to tie him up and gagged him with a rag like she had seen in an old *Alfred Hitchcock Presents* episode. Then, she pinged Birger to call in others to get him.

She made her way down the hallway to the main council chamber. She slid inside and reviewed the various council members. At first there was nobody of note. All were focused on the speaker at the front of the room. Most had headphones on, so she naturally assumed they were for translators.

And then she saw him. Mr. Jun, the representative from China. His hands began to shake. Lightly and then he seemed to get more agitated the more they trembled. Did he know what the shaking meant? Could he control it? That last one was a key question that she hadn't bothered to answer. Not that she could answer it.

She approached him and handed him a cupcake. He looked

surprised by her presence and more than a tad scared. Honestly, he looked quite afraid.

"This is a gift as a part of today's proceedings." She smiled. "Enjoy."

When she realized he may not understand what she said, she motioned for him to eat the cupcake, and then rubbed her tummy in pleasure and smiled. She bowed, and then became aware that she did not know if bowing was a sign of deferment for China or Japan or Korea or some other Asian country. She blamed her crappy Camden school system for the lack of knowledge and made a mental note to look it up. She quietly, deferentially, backed away from him, and prayed that his reaction wasn't quite as dramatic as the man she had told to call her "Cuz".

The speaker must have called for a break because the guests rustled and made their way out of their seats and into a side room. Luna smiled and nodded in acknowledgement of the other council members. She knew she had disrupted their meeting and hoped that it wasn't considered a negative disturbance. Based on the speaker's smile when he saw her, she assumed that her disruption was deemed a positive thing. She followed him, only a few steps behind the speaker, sure to keep her eye on the representative from China.

When it was clear that the speaker of the security council was about to bite into the cupcake, she began the incantation. He ate the treat like he had never seen food before. Faster than Luna had anticipated, his shaking became urgent and uncontrolled. She came up from behind him, whispering the foreign words. She searched the nearest side doors and opted to shove him into a small room with a couch and table, it must have been used as a greeting area.

"What are you doing to me?" he yelled, his voice transforming, his entire body shifting at a rate that shocked her. The security guard hadn't responded so dramatically. The speaker transformed from human to wolf to human so quickly that Luna shielded her eyes. The transformations were more horrific than she could have ever imagined. His bones crunched like they were being broken and put back together. His face changed as if it was made from puddy. He cried out as his body reformed itself over and over until he lay on the ground, spent. She wished that Birger had warned her a bit more effectively. What remained of the council member, the horror of it, was something Luna didn't want to ever see again.

CHAPTER SIXTY-EIGHT

The United Nations main security desk had been hidden to the far right of the main entrance. Originally, the United Nations had designed it that way so that it didn't spook visitors. It also enabled the security agents to quickly respond to an emergency, if one arose.

Chago had made his way through the main entrance, acting as a standard visitor. He had ducked into the security area and stood before the primary panel, a dashboard of monitors that oversaw each and every room, chamber, and hallway. Next to him, two security guards, both members of TRG and both working on a temporary basis at the UN, ensured that no one interrupted him.

He observed guided tours as they made their way from room to room. He saw smaller groups discussing world affairs. The one set of monitors he cared the most about, the ones that covered the security council's chambers, remained at the farther end of the dashboard.

On one screen, a guest speaker stood before the security council assembly. Members of the assembly were intently focused on his statements, some took notes, others nodded as they listened. The speaker made a general wave to those on the screen.

"These simpletons," Chago said. "They are toys." The guards snickered at the comment. They had taken this assignment so they could be closer to the man they had admired for ages. The one TRG leader who exceeded all others.

"Toys to be manipulated, controlled, ruled. And that is why we are here."

CHAPTER SIXTY-NINE

When the changing ended, Luna checked in with Birger. She sent him a snapshot of what had happened to the head of the council. His body became withered and crumpled like a ragdoll in the corner and had seemed to have aged fifty years.

"I know you said you've never seen it, but is that what was supposed to happen?" she asked Birger.

"I guess. It's the first time we've used it."

"Wait, what? You don't actually know that it won't do anything to non-shapeshifters nor to purebloods?"

She cursed herself for not figuring this out before. She could have guessed that this was true. They probably never had a reason to use such a thing before now.

"To date, everything that Freya and Lovisa left for us has been completely accurate. I had no reason to distrust it."

That's a fair point, Luna thought. Even so, she couldn't help but be resentful. "Now what do I do?"

"You leave him. He'll be fine in the closet by himself."

"Are you sure?" Luna felt like she should at least cover him with a blanket or give him something to provide comfort. She didn't know what TRG promised him to convince him to take the elixir. For all she knew it was completely innocent. This was not likely but she didn't want to assume the worst. Even though he had just tried to attack her with his claws, she felt bad leaving him there.

"In his current state, I doubt anyone would recognize him."

CHAPTER SEVENTY

C hago made his way with purpose through the United Nations' common halls toward the rear meeting areas. He had coached the security guards on what to look for and how to handle any situation that may arise as a result of their activities. He anticipated that TLS would interfere in some capacity. They always claimed that according to their objectives and beliefs, they could not interfere in world affairs. They claimed that they did not, because it would go against their *raison d'être*.

He nearly laughed; they always found a way to stick their fingers into everything. How hilarious that they pretended to be the innocents when they were the biggest meddlers. Always had been. If humans only knew the truth behind much of their most significant and truly remarkable events, they would be horrified. The Black Plague, World War I and II, the Holocaust. Heck, even Smallpox and the year 536 AD. But that mental meandering was for another time.

He turned the corner and entered the reception area where

all-too-familiar pastry boxes had been piled up next to the trash cans. He then went to the rear of the building to confirm what he believed he witnessed on the security cameras. There he found the bakery's van.

"Perfect." He smiled to himself. "Absolutely perfect."

CHAPTER SEVENTY-ONE

L una nudged her way out of the closet after shuffling through the rooms to find a blanket to cover the ambassador. She hated the thought of leaving him on the floor, curled in a ball, completely vulnerable. The blanket, however, would provide comfort and hide him, as Birger had suggested, and she still had a lot more work to do. The last thing they needed was to have someone find his still-alive but unconscious body in such a precarious location.

"You there." A security guard came up from behind her.

Damnit. What did they do, bring in quadruple the security for this one day? Had *anyone* heard of overkill?

"May I see your identification?" he said.

He looked like the real deal, Luna thought. Not a rent a cop or some minion of TRG.

She showed her identification with a flick of the wrist.

"I'm so sorry," she said, feigning embarrassment. "I just needed to finish putting these cupcakes and cookies out for the reception." She pointed to the already-empty boxes beside the table beneath the display of treats arranged for consumption.

He looked at her as if, among his list of priorities for the day, she was on a different list.

"The reception already started, so I'm a bit behind. If you don't mind." She motioned past him and smiled, then brushed herself off, as if she had gone into the side room to put some equipment back. She politely prodded her way past the guard and towards where the ambassadors had begun assembling.

He looked at her with eyes blurred by disbelief. Thankfully, he didn't take it any further. Instead he watched her for a few moments and then continued on his routine.

They must have officially announced the break, meaning Luna only had so much more time to find her other newly-created cousins.

Standing behind the tables along the wall farthest from the entry, she adjusted cakes here and cookies there, anything to allow herself to stay within the reception area and observe the guests. Based on the paperwork and what she had overheard, she was pretty sure who had been indoctrinated into TRG.

She handed a guest dressed in a grey suit with a starched white shirt, who she guessed was a member of the Malaysian representation , a special cookie and thanked him for the chance to be there. "It's an honor." She slightly bowed and the slight of build man with jet black hair bowed in return. Luna smiled, a small quiet smile and observed as he bit into the treat.

Good, she thought. She continued reviewing the guests as they entered the reception space. Some dressed in clothing indicative of their native countries like Dashikis from West Africa, Saris and Dhotis from India, Ghos and Kiras from Bhutan and Mosuo and Hmong from China.

While others were more modernly dressed in suits of subdued colors like might more commonly be found in a corporate environment.

Luna looked for some tell-tale sign of their recent transformation like light hand shaking. The more she observed them, the more she realized that she could sense them, even in their relatively new states. Something about the difference in their bodies triggered a sixth sense within her so that she gravitated towards them.

When she closed her eyes the feeling intensified. Like a mental compass that pointed her to where they were in the room. She sensed at least four. Just as she readied to open her eyes, she sensed a stronger power in the room. One that nearly overpowered her senses. One that gave her pause. She opened her eyes and looked in the direction of the greater power. There she saw Chago speaking to the French Ambassador, a man who evoked mental images of Salvador Dali.

"Fuck," she said. "This just got extra complicated."

CHAPTER SEVENTY-TWO

C hago placed his hand on the French Ambassador's shoulder. They had been friends for years, having first met when Chago had visited the Hague in the Netherlands. They chuckled and reminisced. The luminary and the ancient one had been friendly co-conspirators for ages. Chago had first gotten the idea for this little event from the esteemed dignitary.

"It's almost time," Chago said. "I need you to go along with that young woman." he nodded towards Luna. "She has some lessons to learn. Only we can educate her."

The ambassador smirked. "Of course."

CHAPTER SEVENTY-THREE

L una hoped he hadn't seen her. After the work they had done to get her there, the last thing she needed was for it to be ruined because of a slip-up. She messaged Birger to let him know of Chago's presence.

Birger had mentioned she could expect backup. They wouldn't leave her alone in such a dangerous situation. Luna and Birger had already discussed several escape options, if the need arose to quickly vacate the building. At that moment, she stood in the open area across from Chago, the one man who had already caused her harm she couldn't fully articulate. At this exact moment, she didn't feel like she had the backing of a global underground organization. She couldn't help but feel very much alone.

Instead of remaining behind the tables filled with treats which seemed to be far too much in the open air, she decided to move behind the bar to provide a little more coverage. With that shift, she greeted the bartender.

"You look like you could use some help." She picked up an empty ice bucket.

"I'd really appreciate that," the bartender, who looked like a mild-mannered Keanu Reeves, said to her. *He must have been picked for his non-threatening demeanor*, Luna thought. He leaned into her and whispered, "I never knew dignitaries drank so much."

She politely laughed as she took the bucket out of the room and made her way through the crowd into the hallway. She found the kitchen and texted Birger letting him know now would be a great time to get her some assistance. She still hadn't seen anyone clean up the mess with the security guard or the official from China or the head of the council.

He texted back, *Working on it.*

She reentered the room and checked the space for Chago. She no longer sensed him, which was good, she hoped, although she wondered where he had gone. She returned the ice bucket to the bartender and then excused herself.

She had seen where the dignitary, the gentleman with a thick French accent who had been speaking to Chago earlier, had gone and knew that she needed to get to him while she had the chance. Based on his energy he was a critical piece of the takeover puzzle not to mention that, according to Birger, France was one of the permanent members of the UN which meant he had a lot of decision-making power. The fact that he was in deep conversation with Chago earlier couldn't have been an accident. The sooner she put together all of the pieces, the faster she could get out of there.

She found the French dignitary across the room as he finished a conversation with an official from Russia, another permanent member of the UN Security Council. She pulled the French ambassador aside.

"Excuse me," she said. "I have this special ability. A kind of gift. I can tell by looking at people exactly the kind of desserts they love."

"Really?" the French dignitary replied.

"And you, sir. You are a canelé." A classic French dessert filled with custard and coated in a caramel crust. At that moment, Luna was quite thankful for her studies in culinary school which is where she first learned of the dessert.

He laughed. "Very good. It's been my favorite since I was a child."

"In lieu of a canelé, we have a custard-filled cupcake with a caramel infused topping." She handed him the decadent item.

"Why, thank you, young lady. I will enjoy this." He took the dessert and then made his way across the room and ducked through a side door into the corridor. Based on a map of the first floor that Luna had reviewed earlier, he had exited the Delegate's Lobby and must have been heading to another space.

She did her best to nonchalantly follow the dignitary. She was sure to wait until it seemed as though no one was paying attention and made her way into the hallway. Before her was the tour desk, to her right was a wall, and to her left was a hallway that led to a gallery of artwork from around the world. She headed towards the gallery and silently greeted others as she continued. Just beyond the gallery, she found a staircase leading to the basement. She saw the ambassador begin his descent. *Where in the world is he going?* she thought.

She knew from talking to Birger that she needed to confirm that each of the permanent members of the Security Council weren't associated with Chago -- whatever that may mean.

She made her way across the hall and followed the ambassador downward. Just beyond the stairwell, she saw him pass the UN Gift Shop, Coffee Shop, and then head down the corridor and into a conference room.

She readied herself to initiate the incantation. Based on the little bit that she knew, she had to be within earshot of the individual in order for it to work. That meant she had to at least be in the same room as the ambassador. With that in mind, she slowly opened the door to the conference room.

Just as Luna slid into the room, the ambassador stepped up to her. He had been waiting. His presence seemed to fill the room. Even though he was only a few inches taller than her, his distinct overconfidence made him seem bigger, more powerful than even moments prior. His excessive confidence was evident in an arrogant smile and stance. He viciously shoved her across the room and away from the door, then immediately lunged for her.

"This will be easier than I thought," he said with a lusty grin.

Taken by surprise, Luna wanted to run, but there was no time, no avenue of easy escape.

And so as he grabbed her, she could not fight against itit. His large hands caught fistfuls of her chef's white coat and he shoved her back against the wall. In that moment she knew she needed to regain her composure. She couldn't allow the fact that he had taken her by surprise be the reason that after all of this effort, all of this work, she would fail. No, she would now allow herself to fail. Not after losing Daniel. Not after nearly losing Javier. Not after all that Chago had done to her and her family. There was nothing that Chago and his cohorts had planned that could possibly be good.

Her memory flashed to the street fighting classes she had taken after she and Daniel had first been bullied and beaten when they were kids. With that experience refortifying her confidence, she tucked her chin down on her chest to minimize the impact of the back of her skull rapping against the brick wall. The ambassador's smile became a leer as he leaned in, using his upper body mass to pin her.

Luna reached over and between his arms and grabbed his shirtfront. Then all at once she dropped down into a nearly boneless squat while raising both arms up and over her head. The effect was immediate and shocking. Because the ambassador had leaned on her, as she slid suddenly down gravity pulled him forward. Her raised hands steered his leaning mass. Her arms prevented him from either letting go or using his hands to stop his fall. His head hit the wall inches above hers.

And hit it hard.

Still squatting, Luna released her grip, knotted her hands into tight fists and punched him in the balls. Not once, not twice. Again and again.

The ambassador let out a high, whistling shriek and collapsed down, bleeding from a gash on his swelling forehead. Luna tumbled sideways, scrambling up before his mass dropped on her. She got to her fingers and toes and launched herself like a runner coming off the blocks. Just as she thrust herself up and across the room she repeated the foreign words that Birger had taught her. Without looking back she said them over and over as she made her way through the conference room entry. The shrill screams behind her let her know that his violent shifting had begun.

CHAPTER SEVENTY-FOUR

Watching and understanding what was taking place, Chago had warned the French ambassador to eat whatever Luna offered him, and then to pretend to be a human initiate with artificially-induced powers of transformation.

He had not authorized the ambassador to attack her. Annoyed, he knew that he now had to clean up what his old friend had made a bit more messy. As he made his way out of the security guard's station and down the hallway, he cursed that his old friend hadn't used his natural lycanthropic powers to overtake the girl. He was to subdue her until Chago could arrive, that was the agreement, since Chago needed to gain a greater understanding of what exactly the girl could do. Considering her lineage there was a distinct possibility that she was much more powerful than even she understood.

As he passed the Gift Shop and UN Coffee Shop, he greeted other guests. Just as he approached the conference room, Luna bolted past him and into a neighboring room. He was fairly certain she did not realize who he was considering her speed.

He entered the conference room to find the Ambassador partially changed, his shirt hanging in tatters from his frame, his thighs burst through his pant legs. His face partially changed so that if someone knew the man then they would recognize the beast.

Chago checked his watch. "That's enough," Chago said to the ambassador. His voice rimmed with annoyance.

CHAPTER SEVENTY-FIVE

L una slammed the door behind her and pressed her body against the wall. She closed her eyes and focused on catching her breath. She hadn't anticipated the French Ambassador coming after her like that. In her mind it should have been a simple interaction. He would bite into the laced cupcake, she would say a few magical words that she didn't understand, he'd transform - or not - and that would be that.

But she did not figure he'd attack her. She consciously slowed her breathing by taking one deep breath in and then releasing a deep breath out and repeated that pattern until she felt her heartbeat return to normal. She texted Birger to tell him what had happened. Even as she sent the note, she realized what this really implied - Chago and the TRG knew of her intentions. They knew she was there and they had figured out that she was aligned withTLS.

Fuck.

Her cell phone rang. Birger.

Without a greeting, he began, "I researched the French Ambassador and I'm pretty sure he's a member of the TRG."

"I can certainly confirm *that*," she interrupted.

"No," Birger began. "I mean he's been a member of the TRG for at least a decade, maybe longer."

"So he's powerful."

"You could put it that way," Birger said.

"He just attacked me," Luna said, shocking herself with the way that sounded.

"What?" Birger started. "Luna, I know there's more to do, but I want you to leave. It's too dangerous."

"What happened to us stopping a world-wide catastrophe?"

"That was when I didn't think that they knew you were there or that we were aware of their plans --"

"Which are?" Luna thought she had figured it out but she wanted Birger to confirm it.

"To cause a world war by pitting the Security Council members against one another."

"And then taking over once the major superpowers had basically been destroyed."

"Correct," Birger replied. "I need you to understand that they are much more powerful than I had originally thought. If the ambassador knew who you were and was trying to take you out, then that means that their network of intelligence is much bigger and stronger than I had thought."

"Great. It would have been even better if you could have figured this out earlier," Luna said, her voice laced with sarcasm. In the back of her mind, she felt her sixth sense engage.

"Take the first chance you get to leave. Your safety is more important. I'll have my other agents take care of this."

"What happened to not influencing world events?" Luna asked. Slightly annoyed, she felt like Birger picked his battles at weird times. At first he didn't want to be involved, and then because Chago was going to affect the current world order, he was okay with her reversing whatever the TRG did, and now, only now, he was going to send in agents who were more experienced? She needed to talk to him about his choices. Luna's sixth sense fired up again. She focused on that feeling, as if she could sense another dimension and sniffed the air. The distinct scent of a shapeshifter grew stronger. Was it the ambassador? If so, then shouldn't he be knocked out like what had happened with the Ambassador of China? It couldn't be Chago, *right*?

"I may have a problem --" Luna began. Before she could finish her thought, the conference room door flew open.

CHAPTER SEVENTY-SIX

Chago did not need any explanation of what had happened when he found the body of the China Ambassador. The man had been curled up in a ball on the bottom of the broom closet. Unconscious and somehow smaller than he had been before. The second he saw the ambassador, Chago knew who had been the culprit. It was just an event Luna and he shared knowledge of without needing to mention it.

Prior to making his way down the corridor to intervene in the French Ambassador's attack of Luna, he had beaconed guards the few guards that he had brought with him.

Chago had little faith that they would be able to do much more than stand watch over someone, because of their limited abilities. They had only been with TRG for a few years, not enough time to truly mature their gifts. With that, he commanded them to take the ambassador to a safe place to rest.

"What about the hospital?" A guard in the standard starched grey uniform asked. He looked on at the ambassador with a horrified look. Chago doubted the recruit had ever seen anything like this before.

The China Ambassador was not moving, the only evidence of his still being alive was his chest lifting and falling with each shallow breath.

"No," Chago replied. "No hospitals, not yet." He knew there had to be a spell that could reverse the effects of the elixir, but for now that would need to wait.

"Take him to the Meditation Room down the hall and ensure he's comfortable. Then wait for me." Chago pointed at the two other guards. "You and you - I need you to grab at least two others and guard the ambassadors for the United Kingdom, United States, and Russia."

CHAPTER SEVENTY-SEVEN

Luna dropped her phone as the still partially changed French ambassador burst into the room. His features were still human enough for Luna to recognize him. *What the hell?* He should have been totally unconscious after the elixir and the spell. He should have barely been able to move, let alone attack. She reached for the nearest light switch and slammed it off. She needed whatever advantage she could create.

He turned into the room and roared at her, his claws extended, his back arched so that his chest burst forth. She could make out his outline even in the darkened room. He came at her, eyes blazing, nostrils twitching as he smelled her flesh, her blood.

Luna knew that she could not outrun this thing. This half man, half wolf. It was already into its transformation, and when it was paused between human and monster it possessed the strengths of both – instinct and knowledge, heightened senses and the ability to reason and strategize. Luna knew this because of the readings Birger had given her. Thank god for that homework. Because of this, she knew that in this moment it was at its most dangerous.

And also its most vulnerable.

If it wanted her dead, she would have died right there. She had figured that much out. Considering that the TRG must have known about her before she had even walked into the United Nations building, they had to have wanted her alive for a reason.

In the moment, it felt like the creature wanted to dominate her. Defeat her. Force pack dominance on her. If he wanted her to be a part of her pack, then that meant that TRG wanted her alive and to join their forces. Luna noted the inadvertent advantage of this truth.

It leaned in, sniffing the air to confirm her location, its eyes glowed as if with real heat. Luna slowly backed away. Just enough so she would have a better stance, to help increase her advantage. Even in the dark, she saw its black lips curl back from razor-sharp fangs. Fangs that nearly glowed in the dim murkiness of the room. Drool hung in fat treads from its jaws. Luna winced while she forced herself not to panic, not to react.

It began to growl. Instinctively, she raised her hands defensively, palms out. She knew he sensed her, he felt her movement, and it grinned at her apparent surrender.

That's when she struck.

The half man-half beast did not even try to stop her. Luna had no time for the transformation that would have helped this to be a fair fight. It must have known it as well, considering it didn't burst forward in an attack. In that moment, it must have considered her to be prey, or, at best, someone to be forced into a submissive role within his pack.

She used the advantage of her own heightened night vision and shot her right hand forward between the werewolf's reaching hands and struck – not in the chest or ribs; and not to deflect his grab. The heel of her palm crunched into the monster's black nose. Hard. The blow backed by all of her desperate strength, her need, her terror.

Within the structure of the half-snout the nerve endings exploded as cartilage compressed and collapsed. She hit with her left, this time with the side of a bunched fist. Same target, but a harder and more precise blow.

Two hits in less than a second.

The snout collapsed into red ruin.

Luna snapped out with a flat-footed kick to the werewolf's right knee and its leg buckled. As the monster dropped down, she boxed his ears, which sent a shockwave of compressed air into its ear cavity.

It fell, screaming.

And she ran like hell.

CHAPTER SEVENTY-EIGHT

Luna raced down the hallway and towards the nearest exit taking her to the Conference Building which contained the United Nations National Security Council Assembly room. The Conference Building connected the Secretariat Building and the General Assembly Building. She frantically made her way across the lawn and to the nearest entrance. At this juncture, she didn't care how she got in, just that she did. She kicked open a side door and flew through the entry and down the hallway breaking through the double doors and into the empty Security Council Assembly room. The round room was dominated by a horseshoe shaped table with chairs for each council member. The back of the room had been occupied by a screen that was used for floor to ceiling projections.

Her senses screamed that she wasn't alone. That more waited for her. Something more powerful than the French Ambassador. Much more powerful.

She took the chance to fully transform into her wolf-self. She had learned to simply focus within and allow the beast to come out. She felt her bones reshape, her muscles lengthen, her facial features elongate to what she would one day believe to be her true-self. Her native self. Her natural self. The transformation completed, she refocused her senses. She could sense the colors of another's energy nearing. She could see his own color emanate through the entry to the assembly.

She watched as a bright yellow energy leaked through the edges of the doorway. She felt the creature's power grow more and more distinct.

She needed to get away.

She searched the room for an exit or else to find something that she could use to her advantage. She ducked under the center of the horseshoe shaped table in the hopes that this would buy her some time.

She heard the main door open and felt his presence grow. The creature murmured something in a language Luna didn't recognize. She peeked up from her hiding spot to see a fully changed beast, one that she had recognized by his energy, his presence.

Chago.

"It's time," he said in English.

And let out a roar.

CHAPTER SEVENTY-NINE

U nable to understand Chago's incantation and unfamiliar with the language that defined it, Luna stared at her paws as they uncontrollably shook. Not like someone with Huntington's Disease or with a nervous tic, but rather like someone shedding her skin. She began transforming but not into her human self. No. She began transforming into a different beast.

This wasn't possible, she thought. What else could this be? "What's happening?" She said with panic rising in her voice. Her legs shook along with her hands. She felt like she was in the pangs of a violent seizure.

"No!" She cried out in pain.

CHAPTER EIGHTY

C hago continued with the spell and guided energy towards Luna. He needed to see what forms were readily available to her, to confirm that his suspicions were true. Knowing her bloodline, that of Ulf and Freya, he had assumed that she wasn't simply a werewolf.

No.

With her bloodline she should be able to shift into multiple species, just as her ancestors had been able to do. A very rare gift indeed. He focused on her, murmuring the enchantment to ensure that she was hit with the full force of the spell and observed as Luna's body morphed.

Bear.

Wild cat.

Deer.

"What are you doing to me?" Luna cried in terror.

CHAPTER EIGHTY-ONE

Her body in mid-transformation, Luna couldn't control it. Her entire body screamed in pain, her mind filled with a fog she didn't understand. She felt as if her mind had separated from her body as she observed her limbs change from that of a bear to a wild cat to a deer to what she thought was some type of bird.

Terrified and unsure how to change back to her human form, Luna tried desperately to regain control. She knew this couldn't simply be a physical fight. This was a mental battle, a spiritual battle. In her mind she envisioned herself changing back to that of her human self. She ignored everything before her and instead focused on her internal self. She could feel the morphing slow down, but it didn't stop. The shifting continued as the curious nerd in her focused on all of the different shapes she took. By keeping her focus on what was happening it also helped her keep the pain at bay. She had no idea that she could do this. If she made it out of here, she definitely needed to regroup with Birger. She needed to get training.

She never wanted to be stuck in this predicament again.

Chago continued his spell as she continued to fight the effects, but that quickly exhausted her. The more she tried to control her transformations, the more she felt beaten. Her spirit dwindled.

She had lost control of her own body.

Then she realized that if fighting it was ineffective then she should just let it happen. Maybe there would be something in the shifting that would strengthen her. Maybe by some miracle Chago would stop.

Quietly she prayed for help and that she would live through this predicament. She prayed for Javier and her adopted parents. She prayed for Margarite and her family. She prayed for the bakery. She prayed for her customers and those who she knew were going through hard times.

She closed her eyes and simply allowed the pain of the shifts to take hold, the pain so great that at times she wanted to scream out loud. She used that pain to be her center of focus. Unlike before, when she used her thoughts and emotions to force her to ignore the pain, this time she envisioned it as a ball before her that she held in her hands. Within the ball, she envisioned those she loved and wanted to protect. She heard a loud piercing scream just beyond her and realized it was her own voice.

Within the ball she saw herself in her wolf form and absorbed it into her body. She could feel the shift, the change.

And that's when it began.

CHAPTER EIGHTY-TWO

Chago's smile waned as he saw Luna shift to her werewolf self. This wasn't what he had anticipated. When he had used this spell on others of similar bloodline, they simply continued to cycle through their beast-selves until they were exhausted, spent. He had never seen one cycle back to its werewolf self and seemingly stabilize. With that switch back to being a werewolf, her eyes brightened with a vigorous ferocity.

Her look bored into him and then she leapt at Chago and released a howl. The impact was far more savage and powerful than Chago expected and it drove him backward for dozens of steps until he finally slammed against the wall of the assembly.

Luna grabbed his throat and pressed forward with her thumbs to crush his windpipe, but he staved her off by unnaturally and unexpectedly thickening his tendons which forced her fingers apart. With a growl Chago shoved her back, renewing his own bloodlust, his own passion for power. He snarled with sharp teeth revealed through his animalistic lips.

"You will not win," he rumbled.

Luna ignored his warning and slashed at him with her wolf-like claws. Each curved and pointed deadly sharp claw wrenched through Chago's clothes and slashed into his body where blood burst through rippling down the fabric.

Luna paused for a second, aghast at her own ferocity. This didn't surprise Chago. He was almost confident that she had never caused harm like this to another being; at least not in her wolf form. He smirked knowing that he had been a beast for far, far longer than she could ever anticipate. This truth made his own beast self a hundred times stronger.

With that knowledge, Chago reinforced his own transformation by swelling his chest and shoulders with even more fierce and bestial muscles, his mouth elongated as his crooked fangs lengthened to vicious sharpened points. Now he was fully his werewolf self.

He roared with a deep and angry hunger and struck a shocked Luna with a blow so hard, fierce, and fast that she couldn't have anticipated it. The attack forced her backwards, toppling over the horseshoe-shaped table and into the room's center.

Right behind her, Chago in wolf form, leapt onto the table and then crashed down with only several feet between them. His eyes ablaze with the fierceness and fire of the fight. Luna sniffed the air, smelling the intoxicating blood that spewed from Chago's wounds saturating his matted fur. He saw her pause with a wooziness that could only be caused by her own bloodlust; her own hunger. He had seen this hundreds of times before, the move distinct; the hunger evident.

CHAPTER EIGHTY-THREE

Luna sniffed again, excited by the metallic and ancient scent of blood, but also surprised. She watched as her opponent wavered, her attack had clearly weakened him. With that weakness she expected there to be fear, but instead she sensed his renewed vigor; a reinforced challenge. The fierceness she felt in the midst of battle, she sensed emanating from him.

Chago in werewolf form began circling her. Instinctively, she matched his moves. Both beasts with deadly arms, fangs, and claws meant to kill. Neither's human self was in control. Both were driven by their beasts.

Chago pretended to charge Luna only to pull back. Causing her to at first be confused and then to simply be angry. She didn't have time for this. She needed to take care of this.

To take care of him.

She attacked him with a murderous speed, causing him to respond in kind. They collided with an intense impact, slashing together in a tangle of needle-sharp fangs and razor-edged claws. Each bursting through skin and muscle and tendon;

insanely close to bone. The pain and scent of blood only increased their ferocity and their inherent need to dominate, to win, to kill.

Each repeatedly attacked with an intent to cause the other one injury that would end this battle: to slash and destroy the throat. And with each attempt the other instinctively avoided the deadly move.

They continued their fight. Luna knew that she wouldn't be able to get out of this unless Chago was either critically wounded or dead. With that knowledge she braced herself as he darted for her and clamped his ferocious jaws onto her arm. The werewolf form of Chago flailed its head back and forth as he deepened his hold. She could feel her arm being wrenched from its socket. She howled in anguish feeling the bone snap and tissue tear apart. She threw her weight so that they toppled backwards and rolled across the floor. The werewolf clamped his jaw even tighter, holding on, unwilling to be forced from his prey. She could see within his eyes a ferocity, a determination, a blood-lust. And with that blood-lust and her own exhaustion, she felt her body crumble underneath her. Like a puppet, she no longer could control her arm, her chest. Her legs crumbled, causing her to fall underneath her opponent.

With a shriek of pain and anger, the werewolf, formally Chago, got its legs under it and rose to its feet, attempting to drag Luna with it. The pain nearly unbearable, Luna readied for the final blow, the kill-strike.

She looked up, anticipating to see his deadly teeth or claws going for the final kill, yet saw him jarred backwards instead. His eyes widened in confusion, in surprise. She turned to look where his sight had been to see three warriors dressed in full black gear break into the room with their weapons aimed at Chago.

CHAPTER EIGHTY-FOUR

L una's rescuers had been quite powerful and long-standing members of TLS. Based on their energies, Chago quickly knew who they were and that he had encountered them before. For TLS to have sent them meant they desperately wanted to protect her. This was no surprise to him and only confirmed his concept of her great powers. It also implied that although their battle had been relatively short, he had lost control of the United Nations Building. He had no idea what had happened to his covert operators, but if these TLS warriors had made their way in to protect Luna, that could have only meant Chago's men had been forced to retreat.

Leaving him to be taken.

CHAPTER EIGHTY-FIVE

"Are you okay?" asked one of the TLS guardians. Luna, in her human form, nodded. One of the guards handed her a change of clothes, her own tattered, and she swiftly put them on. She moved with care, every once of her body felt like it had been beaten down. She was exhausted and more than ready to go home, but she knew more had to happen and that she had a limited time to get things done.

"We've got at least one more to take care of," Luna said. She guided the guardians out of the bathroom and into the main reception area. As they searched for the French Ambassador, Luna knew this was the one chance she had to capture him and get intel on TRG.

A guardian nudged her. "You have to give them credit, they focused on the key leaders," he said. "No point in wasting time on others."

Luna knew this was true, but, in the moment, she didn't want to have small talk. She wanted to get this done.

They entered the hallway to continue their search. Luna closed her eyes to help heighten her other senses.

"Yesss," she whispered. "That way." She pointed toward the loading dock and ran. The TLS guardians followed a step behind on her swift-moving flanks.

She stopped for a moment to refocus her senses and closed her eyes. "There," she pointed, the word a whisper. She led them to a curtained area. Luna swiped the curtain away to find the ambassador in the midst of shifting.

"Oh my god." Luna gasped.

The ambassador's face was contorted in pain, his body twisted in indescribable and excruciating ways. She could do nothing but watch him self-destruct.

A cupcake wrapper had fluttered to the floor beside him.

EPILOGUE

Luna rolled Javier down the hallway. Tired after making her way home from Sweden and then the UN only a few days prior, her body ached from the battles with Chago and his men. Chago and the French Ambassador had been taken away by TLS's men to some undefined location. She figured it was probably better that she didn't know where they had gone.

The Chinese Ambassador had been taken to the hospital and treated for some unknown ailment. From the little Birger had told her, all of those who had been present for the escapades at the United Nations had had their minds wiped due to the TLS's mandate not to influence human's world events (she still wanted to talk to him about what that actually meant considering all that had happened). And Luna, well she had been taken away in an ambulance and treated at a secret TLS location.

As she wheeled her fiance along the path to the parking lot, she was thankful to be home and to be bringing him home as well. Javier patiently sat in the wheelchair and allowed Luna to push him towards their compact car.

"I'm glad the doctor finally gave you the clearance to go home." She kissed his cheek and continued pushing him. She had every intention of keeping her promises from before. The promise to tell him she loves him every day, to marry him, to do all of these things that she had simply never done.

Before she had lost her brother, Daniel, and all that had transpired since his death, she didn't realize how lucky she was to have such wonderful men in her life. She smiled to herself as she remembered the pizza and home video nights that she, Javier, and Daniel had enjoyed every Friday night. Javier looked up at her and smiled. She knew that smile. It was the, "shut up and take me home because I want to cuddle" smile.

"I have surprises for you at home," she said. "I think you'll like them."

"Surprises, huh," Javier mumbled.

She pulled them up to the curb where she had parked their car.

"You don't have to do anything," Javier said. "I'm just happy to get home."

She moved around to the front of her fiancé, put the wheelchair's stopper down so it wouldn't go flying as she helped lift him up from the chair. He kept his hands on her shoulders for stability as she helped him into the front seat of the car.

A few days prior, she had been carried off from the United Nations in the back of an emergency medical vehicle to be treated for the wounds she had gotten during her bestial battle with Chago.

Of course, TLS members who had broken into the building, shot Chago with tranquilizers just when he was about to strike her down, knew better than to take her to a hospital. Instead they used the emergency medical vehicle as an excuse to get her the hell out of there as fast as possible and to the nearest TLS member-owned safehouse they could find. That's

CURE

where her wounds were treated and her own rapid healing powers were given a chance to take hold.

`By the time she left, barely 24 hours ago, all that was left as evidence of her fights were fresh pink scars and incredibly sore muscles. Of course, her arm that had nearly been torn off felt like it had been through a war, because it had, but now that she was with Javier, it felt more heavily bruised than anything else.

"I think you'll like what I have," she said to Javier.

That is when she noticed Javier's light tremor in his hands. Just as she noticed it, so did he.

"That should go away soon," he said. "It's a side effect of the medication."

In the moment she wondered if she should tell him about the incantation, about the lycanthropes, the societies, the underground war, the life that awaited him. She glanced at him and the content look on his face. The same face that had declared when they were still in junior high school that he wanted to save lives. That he wanted to be a nurse because it would allow him to do it faster than if he went through the years and years of medical school. And that's when she wondered if she should simply do the reverse spell and never tell him a thing.

It hadn't been that long ago when she had done the incantation on him, so his reaction to being switched back to a pure human would probably be the equivalent to heartburn.

At least she hoped it would be that mild.

Luna shifted his legs into the car and then closed the door. She didn't know what to say. This didn't feel like it was the right time to tell him about his newly acquired abilities. Plus, maybe he was right. Maybe it was the medication. Wouldn't it be weird if he had already started the beginning stages of transforming? It didn't start for her until she was in her mid-twenties.

"I love you," she said to him.

Javier looked surprised. He had never heard her declaration before. Even if he had told her the same hundreds of times. "I love you, too," he said with a slightly confused tone.

Luna leaned down and kissed him before she got into the driver's side.

"What's going on?" Javier asked her in a questioning voice. "You don't usually say 'I love you'."

Luna slammed the door and started the engine.

"I'm good," she said and then leaned in and kissed him with the gentleness of a thousand kisses. When she leaned back from their embrace, reveling in the feeling of him, she said. "Just wanted to say it. That's all."

AUTHOR BIO

Kali Metis is the pen name for Lisa Diane Kastner. Lisa was born in Camden, NJ which was one of the most dangerous cities in America. In high school, she was a dancer and co-host on *Dance Party USA*. At the age of 20 she came home to find her house had burned down and she was suddenly homeless. She spent the next several years rebuilding and obtained her Bachelors, MBA, and MFA. While fulfilling an amazing corporate career, she began Running Wild, LLC which consists of Running Wild Press where they publish great stories that don't fit neatly in a box and RIZE Press where they publish great genre stories written by people of color and other underrepresented groups. Running Wild has been honored with two best of 2019 and two best of 2020 books according to Kirkus Reviews as well as several starred reviews and additional acclaim. Lisa was named to Yahoo Finance's Top 10 Entrepreneurs to Watch in 2021 and nominated to FORBES NEXT 1000, a list of American self-funded entrepreneurs who continue to strive during the challenging times of COVID. She was named to New York Weekly's Top Ten Females to Watch in 2021, LA Wire's Top 10 Businesses to Watch in 2021, and was featured in the August/September 2021 edition of FORBES magazine. She resides in Los Angeles, California with her husband and their two felines, The Master and Margarita.

ACKNOWLEDGMENTS

To everyone who supported us throughout the making of this book, we thank you.

To the wondrous people at Horror Writers Association, Pennwriters, San Diego Writers Association, Sewanee Writers Conference, Squaw Valley Writers Conference, Writers Coffeehouse, Yale Writers Workshop, Breadloaf Writers Conference, thank you for creating homes for the writing souls that come to you for nourishment.

To my husband for always listening to my wild tales, crazy stories, and next-level ideas.

To my amazing friends, Barbara, Peter, Ben, Mona, Nicole, Tori, Jeff, Jonathan, David, Inez, Martina, Josefa, Alex, Lee, Sona, Shahzad, Doug, Eric, Andre, Alexis, Tihi, Alicia, Derrick, Lisa, Christopher.

And to you for taking a chance on this little known author. I hope you enjoyed the ride.

Running Wild Press publishes stories that cross genres with great stories and writing. RIZE publishes great genre stories written by people of color and by authors who identify with other marginalized groups. Our team consists of:

Lisa Diane Kastner, Founder and Executive Editor
Mona Bethke, Acquisitions Editor, Editor, RIZE
Benjamin White, Acquisitions Editor, Editor, Running Wild Press
Peter A. Wright, Acquisitions Editor, Editor, Running Wild Press
Rebecca Dimyan, Editor
Andrew DiPrinzio, Editor
Cecilia Kennedy, Editor
Barbara Lockwood, Editor
Cody Sisco, Editor
Chih Wang, Editor
Pulp Art Studios, Cover Design
Standout Books, Interior Design
Polgarus Studios, Interior Design
Nicole Tiskus, Production Manager
Alex Riklin, Production Manager
Alexis August, Production Manager

Learn more about us and our stories at www.runningwild-press.com

Loved these stories and want more? Follow us at www.running-wildpress.com, www.facebook.com/runningwildpress, on Twitter @lisadkastner @RunWildBooks @RwpRIZE